# NURSERY
# CRIMES

Also by Karen Mauck

*Scraps*
*Pomp and Circumstantial Evidence*
*Last to Know*

# NURSERY

# CRIMES

## BY KAREN MAUCK

iUniverse, Inc.
Bloomington

# Nursery Crimes

*iUniverse books may be ordered through booksellers or by contacting:*

*iUniverse*
*1663 Liberty Drive*
*Bloomington, IN 47403*
*www.iuniverse.com*
*1-800-Authors (1-800-288-4677)*

*ISBN: 978-1-4620-2393-6 (sc)*
*ISBN: 978-1-4620-2394-3 (ebook)*

*Printed in the United States of America*

*iUniverse rev. date: 6/3/2011*

To the CherryBombs, without whose support and encouragement this probably never would have happened.

# CHAPTER ONE

## MONDAY, SEPTEMBER 18

THE AFTERNOON WAS DARK WITH ITS end of summer thunderstorm, and Jillian juggled an umbrella while unloading bags from a shopping cart into her trunk, trying to keep her groceries dry, unaware she was being followed.

Her off-key rendition of *Rain, Rain, Go Away*, a silly rhyme she sang with the students in her kindergarten class that afternoon, was interrupted by a shout.

"Miss Hobart!" She turned from her well-worn Grand Am toward the voice calling her name. The grocery store's teenage bagger and cart collector, Billy, clad in a yellow rain slicker to ward off the elements, waved his arms wildly at her as he exited the Shop'n'Fresh Market. She waved back absently in greeting. "Miss H.! Look out!"

Jillian turned in the direction he was pointing. She gasped when a bolt of lightning in the storm-darkened sky illuminated a tall figure rummaging through her purse. In her haste to get her purchases into the car and keep them dry, she had left her purse in the shopping cart. Angry with the thief, and with herself for being so careless, she shouted to get his attention. "Hey!"

The man, camouflaged in a baseball cap, a hooded sweatshirt, and sunglasses despite the dreary Michigan skies, stuck her purse under his arm and turned to run.

"No!" Without thinking, Jillian dropped her umbrella, regretting it when she instantly became drenched. Her shoulder-length brown hair plastered to her head, her gray silk blouse and black skirt clung to her body. This jerk was trying to steal her favorite purse, a Coach bag she'd received as a gift from her mother and could not afford to replace on her meager teacher's salary. She lunged forward and grabbed the dangling end of the purse strap, planted her feet on the wet pavement, and pulled.

"Give that back!" she ordered, her voice dropping low with anger. Despite their similar heights, he was stronger than she, and her flat sandals offered no traction on the smooth, wet asphalt. She wasn't afraid, not yet, as she felt herself being dragged along the slick pavement. "Stop! Help!"

Out of the corner of her eye she saw Billy running across the parking lot. How could the gangly high school student possibly stand up to this brute? Her shout to him to go back inside and call the police was drowned out by a resonating thunderclap.

Then her vision of Billy, and the thief, was blocked by another tall figure looming before her. Suddenly she felt very small. Now she felt afraid and a scream strangled in her throat. If this man, with shoulders like a linebacker, was an accomplice of the purse-snatcher, then even at two against two she was still outnumbered.

"What the hell are you doing?" The newcomer shouted, his voice angry and deep. He grabbed the would-be criminal by his shirt, all but lifting him off the ground. The thief instantly released Jillian's purse, sending her flying backward, arms reeling in an attempt to regain her balance. She slammed into the side of her car and bounced off to the ground next to her purse, landing heavily on her hands and knees in a pothole filled with cold rainwater, bare skin digging into the hard surface. She cried out as jolts of pain shot through her limbs.

Dazed, she blinked rainwater out of her eyes to see Billy staring, slack-jawed, as the man held the thief's soaked shirt in his fists, keeping him nearly eye level with himself, glaring into his disguised face. "Why don't you pick on someone your own size, asshole, and not defenseless women," he growled.

The purse snatcher's fist shot out and caught the man hard in the right temple, causing him to loosen his grip and stagger back against a parked Escalade, setting off its howling security alarm. The thief took the opportunity to wriggle free and run empty-handed across the parking lot, roughly shoving Billy aside as he fled into the trees behind the store.

"He's getting away!" Jillian said.

The man appeared surprised by the attack, wincing and shaking his head. "Son of a—." He took a few steps after him, but the thief was already out of sight and he stopped short. "He's just a stupid kid. I don't think he could grow a beard if he wanted to. But I'll call the Sheriff just the same." His squared features softened, the anger fading into a gentle concern as he leaned over Jillian, still huddled on all fours on the wet ground. He held out a hand to help her up. "Are you hurt?"

She took inventory of herself. The initial shock of hitting the pavement was over, but her skin stung where it had scraped against the ground. She hesitated before taking his hand, strong and wide with large palms and thick fingers and completely covering hers. His hand was warm despite the weather.

Even when she stood, the man seemed larger than life. He was well over six feet tall; she had always considered herself tall at five-feet-ten, but she found herself only at eye-level with his broad shoulders. With a gentleness that belied his size, he held her hand palm up, then took her other and did the same. "Scratched them up pretty good." He glanced down at her legs, bare under her wet, bunched-up skirt. "Knees, too."

"I'm okay," she said, hoping her voice sounded stronger than she felt. Her legs were wobbly with nervous energy, and adrenaline still coursed through her body. She was trembling but couldn't say whether that was caused by the mugging or the dark-haired stranger holding her hand in the rain. "Thank you."

He smiled, a wide, warm, sincere smile that left deep dimples in his cheeks. "My pleasure. I'm Peter."

She fidgeted, feeling awkward. She never had been comfortable talking to adults she didn't know, men in particular. She felt more at ease with school-aged children, which was why she became a teacher. It didn't help matters now that he still held her hands, hands that seemed so tiny and delicate compared to his. Defenseless, he'd said.

Billy scrambled up to them, his face flushed with excitement.

"Miss H.! Are you alright? Do you want me to go get you some Band-Aids or something? I get a store discount."

She stifled a laugh, not wanting to hurt the boy's feelings. Pulling away from the man, she looked down at her legs to see why the boy had offered her bandages. Her wool skirt ended just above her knees, where rainwater stained pink with blood trickled down to her shins from the scrapes inflicted by the hard pavement. "Beautiful," she mumbled, but offered Billy a tired smile, relieved that he distracted the man's attention away from her. "No, thank you, Billy. I think I'll be fine."

Peter bent to retrieve her lost umbrella, slapping against the side of her car as it rolled back and forth in the wind. Snapping it shut, he handed it to her. "I don't think this is gonna be very useful anymore." Water beaded and rolled off his brown nylon jacket, but it offered little protection in the driving rain. His slacks were sopping wet, and his black hair plastered down across his forehead over piercing blue eyes as water ran rivulets down his angular jaw. "Your bread is wet."

Jillian blinked, confused. "What?"

He nodded toward her shopping cart. "Your loaf of bread. I'd say it's toast, but it's more like mush."

Forcing herself to focus, she tore her gaze from his face and looked to her basket. A loaf of French bread in a traditional open-ended paper bag indeed was a ruined, soggy mess. She sighed and reached for it, holding it up with two fingers. "Oh well," she said to herself as she examined the remains. "I suppose I can start that no-carb diet now." She jumped, startled, when Peter laughed; she didn't realize he had overheard and blushed.

"I can get rid of that for you, Miss H.," Billy said eagerly, taking the bag from her. As she nodded her thanks to the boy, he ginned and ran off to dispose of the no-longer edible bread.

Peter picked up the remaining bag from the shopping cart and dropped it in her car, slamming the trunk lid shut. "Let's go make that report." She picked up her purse and followed him back to the store.

Once out of the rain, he made a brief phone call on his cell phone, and in moments the grocery store parking lot became crowded with deputies from the Malcolm County Sheriff's Department, more than Jillian thought necessary for a simple attempted purse snatching. Peter seemed to be garnering the most attention from the deputies, which seemed odd, since she was the one with the purse. *Better him than me.* She stood in the background, quiet, shifting her balance from foot to foot with nervous energy while she waited. Finally, a young deputy asked her a few perfunctory questions before casually dismissing her.

She was free to leave and nothing sounded better, but knew she should probably thank her rescuer. Turning to Peter, she flinched and stumbled backward when his hand raised toward her face. Quick but gentle, he reached over to push limp, wet hair that stuck to her cheek away and behind her ear.

"Shop here often?" he asked, smiling again.

*He did not just hit on me,* she thought. *Did he? Not with a cheesy line like that, and not when I look like a drowned rat with skinned knees.* Flustered, Jillian only stared at him and nodded.

"I'll have to come back, then. Maybe I'll run into you again sometime, under better circumstances." His gaze ran down the length of her body in a manner that made her wish she'd worn pants before his eyes met hers again. "You'd better get home and out of those wet clothes." With a jaunty salute, he turned on his heel and jogged across the parking lot. She stood in the rain, clutching her purse to her chest and watching as he picked up the plastic shopping bag he had dropped next to his vehicle to come to her aid, climbed into an oversized black pickup, and drove away.

\*\*\*

When she drove up to the curb in front of the tiny bungalow she rented on a sleepy, tree-lined street and unloaded her groceries, she didn't bother with the umbrella; she was already too wet for it to matter. She made a mad dash for the front door and found it unlocked. *Oh just great.* She was late because of the police questioning, and her dinner date had apparently made herself at home. Pushing the door open with a sigh, she plastered on a smile and announced, "I'm home."

Her mother, graying blonde hair neatly in place with enough hairspray to withstand a hurricane and dressed in a pale, crisp, designer pantsuit, stepped out of the small kitchen into the narrow foyer, a smile of greeting disappearing from her lips. "Dear God, Jillian, you're absolutely drenched. Don't you have an umbrella? I'll have to get you one for your birthday."

Jillian rolled her eyes, as her birthday wasn't for another two months, and wished not for the first time she hadn't given a spare house key to her mother. "You're late," her mother continued as she took the plastic bags containing the evening's supper from Jillian's hands and peered into them. "And you forgot the French bread again."

Jillian took a clean dishtowel from a kitchen cupboard and rubbed it through her wet hair. "I didn't forget it. It got ruined in the rain."

"That's because you didn't use your umbrella," her mother said, a note of accusation in her voice that always put Jillian on the defensive.

"It's not like I killed somebody," Jillian muttered out of her mother's earshot. She dreaded explaining what happened to her mother, who would surely over-dramatize the incident. She tried to speak in an upbeat tone to lighten the news. "I did use my umbrella, Ma. But I accidentally dropped it when I was busy getting mugged."

Jillian knew her mother well. With a loud gasp, Mary Hobart gripped her daughter's damp shoulders. "Mugged! Are you all right? What was stolen? Did you call the police? Did they catch the man? Oh my God, look at your knees! You're bleeding! Why didn't you call me?"

She pushed her mother away gently. "Nothing was stolen. He tried to take my purse, but someone stopped him. He got away. I just have a few scrapes is all."

"He got away?" She pouted. "Well, if the township residents had voted to pass the millage for a police force instead of depending on the county sheriff to come all the way out here, he would have been caught. You live in the sticks, dear, and I'm not happy about it."

The rural community of Cray Township, 30 miles north of Detroit, was just beginning to see the evidence of urban sprawl. Land once designated for corn, cows, or simply vast expanses of nothing was slowly being taken over by shopping centers and large homes. She had defended her adopted hometown so many times, she didn't bother doing so again now, knowing it was useless to argue. "I like it here."

"Here?" Mary scoffed. "There's no reason for you to stay here in the middle of nowhere. You could get a full-time job closer to home. Closer to civilization. You could get a real job anywhere you wanted if you just applied yourself!"

She knew her mother only wanted what was best for her, but she was sick of her constantly insinuating—or in this case, telling her outright—that she was somehow inferior. Jillian learned long ago that the best way to avoid a confrontation was to keep quiet. In response, people called her shy. She preferred the term prudent, even if that was denial.

Her mother was on a roll tonight. "It isn't safe here. You could have been killed."

Jillian shook her head, dismissing her mother's melodramatics. "Peter said he's just a kid."

Mary's eyes took on a new glow. "Who's Peter?"

*Oh crap. Here we go again.* Jillian started unloading the bags as a distraction, pulling out chicken breasts, fat red tomatoes, and a bottle of Australian shiraz. "The guy who helped me."

Her mother smiled brightly. "A Good Samaritan. How wonderful. Peter who?"

"Um … I don't know."

Mary clucked her tongue. "You didn't ask? How can you properly thank him for saving your life now?" When Jillian rolled her eyes, Mary pouted again, then brightened. "Did you at least ask if he's single?"

"Mother!" Jillian exclaimed, surprised by the new level to which her mother had sunk.

"Well, I'm only thinking of you. If you had a boyfriend or a husband—"

"Mother…" Jillian sighed, but the other woman didn't acknowledge the interruption.

"— you wouldn't have to go out shopping alone and this never would have happened. Even your sister, Jacqueline, is married and already has two babies. Whatever happened to that teacher you were seeing?"

Jillian closed her eyes and wondered if there was a polite way to ask for her house key back. The telephone on the wall next to the fridge rang, saving her from finding out. Almost gleefully, she picked up the receiver and sang out a cheerful greeting, then paused, wrinkled her brow, and repeated herself in a more doubtful tone. Receiving no answer, she shrugged and returned the phone to its hook.

"Well?" her mother asked impatiently.

Jillian shrugged again. "Wrong number."

"Not the phone. I was asking about your date."

Jillian sighed and sat in a chair at the dinner table, defeated. There was no escaping now. "Mike and I aren't seeing each other. It wasn't even a date."

"Why not? Didn't he like you?"

Jillian rubbed her temples. She should be used to her mother haranguing her over this subject after thirty-one years. "It's not like that. We were just talking about work most of the time."

Her mother interrupted to continue with her unsolicited dating advice. "Well, you have to give him a chance, dear. How can you tell after just one date? Love has to grow on you, you know. I didn't love your father right away."

"Ma…" Exasperated, she stood and walked away, not wanting yet another rehash of her parents' first date.

"Where are you going?"

She remembered Peter's final words to her. "To get out of these wet clothes."

# CHAPTER TWO

WEDNESDAY, SEPTEMBER 20

JILLIAN PREFERRED SKIRTS IN WARM WEATHER, but she had worn pants the last couple days while the scabs on her knees healed. She didn't want to be seen in public with bandages sticking out from under her skirt, looking like a little girl who tripped on the playground. But there was nothing she could do about her hands.

She smiled as she walked through the tiny Cray Township Charter Elementary School toward her corner classroom, listening to sounds of older children laughing, reciting, or asking questions in the rooms she passed. The familiar sounds pleased her, and she felt at peace here. She had come to work early and didn't expect her students to arrive for another two hours. She wanted to prepare the classroom for the upcoming parent-teacher conferences by hanging the children's artwork on the walls, partly to impress their proud parents, but mainly to draw attention away from herself. One-on-one discussions during parent-teacher conferences always made her nervous and she dreaded the event.

The community had a low population, and not enough students enrolled in kindergarten for the prestigious private school to offer both the usual morning and afternoon classes. As a result Jillian only taught a single class, with the children arriving after lunch. The slight commensurate cut in pay as a result hurt, although she didn't mind the shorter hours; they allowed her to run errands or do research on her proposal for a new educational program. She hoped the decline in enrollment would be the impetus she needed to convince the principal to switch to an all-day kindergarten program that was popular in schools around the country and, in her opinion, offered students a better education.

Child-size desks sporting die-cut apple nametags were lined neatly before her adult-size desk. Behind that stood a large metal cabinet covered in children's paintings held up with apple magnets. Her cabinet door hung wide open; she thought that odd because she remembered closing it the night before. Glancing idly at a stack of colorful, messy finger paintings on the desk, she went to close the door when it suddenly slammed shut, pushed from behind with such force the old cabinet rocked. With a shriek, she fell against her desk, scattering paintings and a cup of pencils, as a figure dressed in black leapt from behind the cabinet. The ancient cabinet swayed wildly again before it tipped forward and landed on the linoleum floor with a deafening clatter. The figure charged past her, shoving her aside, and she fell against the toppled cabinet, tumbling backward over it onto the hard, cold floor. When she managed to look up, she saw the dark blur speed out the classroom door.

A moment later Mike Georginidis, the fifth-grade teacher from down the hall with whom she had shared an unsuccessful non-date before the school year started, ran into the room. "What was that noise? I heard it from the library!"

Jillian struggled to speak, the breath knocked out of her. "Intruder! Call the police!"

Mike's pale brown eyes widened in surprise, but he scurried toward the principal's office. She felt better when she heard the announcement over the pubic address system calling for an immediate building lockdown.

By the time Mike returned with the school principal, Antoinette Jones, a short, round woman with ebony skin and a multi-colored blazer, Jillian picked herself off the floor and sat on the edge of her desk. Her breathing had returned to normal, but adrenaline caused by the surprise and fear still made her tremble. When did her life get so much excitement?

Mike ran up to her, eyes wide. "Are you okay?"

Jillian considered that for a moment. "Yeah, thanks, Mike. Just surprised, more than anything, I guess."

"I called 911. The Sheriff is sending someone out," Antoinette said, her high-pitched, slightly nasal voice going even higher with concern. Jillian could already hear sirens in the distance. Within minutes, the building filled with Sheriff's deputies doing a room-to-room search for anything suspicious. She was glad for the quiet support Antoinette showed, standing steadfast beside her, but she wished Mike would stop pacing in front of the blackboard, his black tassel loafers squeaking on the linoleum floor with every step as he tugged at his blond goatee, making her even more anxious.

Two deputies entered the classroom, dressed in their standard crisp brown County Sheriff uniforms with meticulously knotted ties and thick black belts holding their tools of the trade. She heard one of them speak to the principal. "I'm Deputy Anderson. Is this the teacher who was attacked?"

Antoinette patted a still-shaken Jillian on the shoulder. "Yes. Jillian, these deputies would like to speak with you now."

She didn't respond, but continued to stare dully at the glaring black scuff marks left behind when the cabinet slammed into the beige floor.

"It's Sergeant Dack, ma'am," a deep, slightly gravelly but pleasant voice corrected the principal.

Jillian's head snapped up to attention. The voice sounded familiar. Then she noticed the broad, strong shoulders that filled out the Sheriff uniform so well and recognized him as her Good Samaritan. *So that's why he garnered most of the attention after her mugging. Of course, assaulting an officer is a more serious offense than an attempted purse snatching.*

"Nice to meet you again, Miss Hobart. " He stepped forward, a serious but friendly smile on his face, one of his large, capable hands extended in greeting.

She stood quickly, knocking more pencils onto the floor in her haste. She took his hand, her body on automatic pilot, stunned because he was standing here, in her classroom. And holding her hand. Again. "Peter?"

His smile widened. "You remembered."

His hair wasn't black after all. Water and darkness had combined to make it appear much darker than its true shade of chocolate brown; unruly waves of it fanned out over his high forehead and short sideburns accented carved cheekbones. His eyes were even more striking and blue than she remembered, and the dimples more pronounced in daylight. She fidgeted and averted her gaze, mumbling her reply. "How could I forget?"

She felt eyes boring into her, and looked up to see Mike and the deputy staring at her, agape. She didn't know which was worse, the electrically charged scrutiny from the sergeant, or the surprised stares from the other two men. She looked back at her feet.

Peter turned her hand over in his, regarding her scabbed palm. "These seem to be healing pretty well," he said, tracing a finger lightly along one dark, jagged line.

Jillian felt the familiar heat of a blush and chewed her bottom lip. She had hoped no one would notice those. She told herself he was just doing his official duty by asking after her injuries, but the gentle way his fingers brushed against her skin made her spine tingle.

A gentle cough from Deputy Anderson startled her, and she yanked her hand back while sending him a sheepish glance. He was shorter than she and had a cherubic-cheeked, freckled baby face under short strawberry-blond hair, an amusing contrast to his brawny physique and wide, athletic shoulders.

Sergeant Dack straightened, his smile fading into seriousness, and pulled a small notepad from his breast pocket. "What did you see?"

Jillian clasped her hands behind her back, safe from the sergeant's scrutiny. "Not much. Someone just jumped out at me, but it was too fast."

He grunted and turned his attention to Mike. "What about you, Mr. Georginidis?"

Mike resumed pacing, his thin shoulders hunched, his hands shoved into the pockets of his black corduroy pants. "I didn't see anything. I heard the cabinet fall, so I came to check on Jillian. It was over by the time I got here."

Sergeant Dack wrote in his notebook and addressed his next question back to Jillian. "Anything taken?"

Jillian glanced around the chaos of her classroom, now looking smaller than usual filled with adults instead of children. She shrugged and muttered, "Not much to take, unless he has a thing for crayons."

Out of the corner of her eye, she saw the sergeant's lips twitch into a quick smile and she felt a warm rush of embarrassment. She hadn't meant to be funny, especially not at a time like this. "You're sure though? You looked?" he asked.

Her gaze stopped on the overturned cabinet. "Well, I haven't looked in there yet. It's too heavy for me to lift."

"We can fix that." Peter strode over and slid his fingers under the top edge of the cabinet. In one swift movement that seemed to require little effort, he had it standing upright again. "How about now?"

Jillian reminded herself it was impolite to stare at his muscular arms as she carefully stepped over the spilled contents of the cabinet to take inventory. Broken crayons, scattered construction paper, a copy of Mother Goose nursery rhymes, a crushed box of graham crackers for snack time, her spiral-bound lesson plan. Almost everything was accounted for.

"I don't see my day planner," she said.

Peter again wrote in his pad of paper. "Anything important in it?"

She pressed a hand to her forehead and nodded. "Yeah. I use it for things like students' addresses, allergies, birthdays ... Oh no!"

"What?" Peter leaned closer, his brow knitted over his eyes.

"My research! I'm making a report for Principal Jones on the benefits of switching to full-day kindergarten. All my notes from interviews with some teachers who do that in Florida and Washington, D.C., are in that planner." She closed her eyes, feeling nauseous. Those interviews had been stressful to conduct, even if they were over the phone, providing a buffer to her shyness. Now she would have to find the courage to talk to these people all over again.

Antoinette hurried to her side. "Now don't you be worrying about that. You can tell me what they said from memory. I trust you." She patted her on the shoulder. "And we have duplicate information on all the students so you can make new files. See? No harm done."

"I wouldn't be so sure about that." Peter said. "Principal Jones, I think you should send out a letter alerting parents to what happened here today. They should know their personal information might be compromised."

"Yes, of course." She nodded tersely, dangly gold earrings swaying.

He turned back to Jillian. "I'll have my deputies dust your cabinet here for fingerprints, though I'd bet it won't matter. Your students have access to this, don't they?" He continued speaking after she nodded her head in crestfallen agreement. "In the meantime, I'll need your address and phone number, in case we have any further questions."

Jillian recited her phone number and was halfway through her address when a commotion from the hallway cut off her words. Sergeant Dack and Deputy Anderson stepped in front of Antoinette and Jillian as the classroom door flew open and a middle-aged man in an expensive black Italian suit and an obvious toupee that didn't quite match what remained of his own white-blond hair burst into the room. "What's going on here? Will my son be able to attend class this afternoon?"

Jillian sighed in resignation as she recognized the illustrious township supervisor and father of Jonathon, one of her students. Simon Brothers was not only overbearing; Jillian worried he harbored feelings for her that went beyond a traditional parent-teacher relationship, which she did not desire on many levels, only one of which being that he was married, and for the third time at that.

Peter held up a hand to hold Mr. Brothers back and spoke over his head, an easy feat as he was several inches taller. "Who let him in here?"

Another young deputy motioned toward the round window in the classroom's back door. It lead to the playground and parking lot, where concerned parents were milling about, desperate to see their children after news of the intruder spread. "He got past security, sir," the deputy said.

"Then security is not doing its job," Peter said in a low, even voice. The deputy winced and nodded.

"Miss Hobart! I'm so glad you're okay. I heard something

happened and rushed right over." Mr. Brothers reached for Jillian, offering her a smile that was more like a leer.

Jillian was too tired to try to hide her distaste for the man. The sergeant glanced from her to Mr. Brothers and back again, then smoothly moved between them, blocking the older man's path.

"This is a police situation, sir," he explained in a tone that could not be confused for pleasant. "I'll have to ask you to leave."

Mr. Brothers kept his eyes fixed on Jillian as he dismissed Peter. "Thank you for your concern, Sergeant. But my son attends school here this afternoon and I want to make sure everything is in order."

Antoinette stepped up before Peter could to speak again. "Not today, I'm afraid, Mr. Brothers. Class has been cancelled due to circumstances beyond our control. I'm sure you understand."

"Of course, Principal Jones." He sidestepped her and laid a hand on Jillian's arm, and she tried not to visibly cringe. "Miss Hobart, I'm glad you weren't hurt. Is there anything I can do to help you?"

"Oh no you don't," Antoinette said under her breath, loud enough for only a grateful Jillian to hear. But when she addressed Mr. Brothers, a charming smile graced her dark features. "Mr. Brothers, let's leave this horrible event to those who can handle it best. We'll talk about it further in my office, where we can have some privacy." She took his arm and led him away, sputtering and unsure how he had lost control of the situation.

"Pompous jackass," Peter muttered under his breath. "She's good though." Jillian tried not to smile as she silently agreed with him on both counts.

The classroom, and the entire school building, slowly emptied. Parents who heard of the situation came to take their children home, and just as Antoinette said, Jillian's kindergarten class was cancelled. She was getting a headache and her backside hurt from the fall. Wanting nothing more than to go home, take some aspirin, and lie down, she put a hand to her throbbing head and leaned against the corner of her desk. Instantly Mike stepped to her side.

"Can I do anything for you, Jillian? Maybe I can drive you home. You look tired, too tired to drive yourself. This must have been horrible for you. Here, let me help you." He put an arm around her waist, hugging her close.

Her body tensed under his touch. She hated being thought of as helpless and resented the implication. But making her even more uncomfortable was the fact that strangers were watching — Peter was watching — while Mike was touching her in a way that felt far too intimate for the relationship they had. She tried to keep her voice soft but direct. "I can drive myself, thank you, Mr. Georginidis."

The other teacher looked hurt at her withdrawal and use of formal names. He took a step back. "Yes, of course, Miss Hobart. Sorry to bother you." With a curt nod to Peter, he stalked out of the room.

The crushed look he sent her tormented Jillian. She couldn't stand knowing she was responsible for making someone feel bad. "Wait. Mike…" She called after him, but he was gone. She sighed and slumped back against the edge of her desk. She'd have to apologize to him in the morning.

Peter's eyebrows lifted. "What was that all about?"

Jillian hunched her shoulders, unable to look at the sergeant. *He must think I'm a bitch*, she thought, then heard herself trying to explain. "Oh, well … We both taught fifth grade before I started teaching kindergarten." She fidgeted under his intense scrutiny, nervously twisting a gold and yellow topaz ring on her right hand. "Sometimes Mike thinks that just because I'm shy, you know, I must be helpless, too. He's been playing up on that, acting the knight in shining armor to my damsel in distress since…" Feeling foolish, she shut up and shrugged offhandedly. "It gets annoying."

"I bet."

Jillian heard the amusement in Peter's voice, and looked up to see the corresponding emotion etched in his features. She stuck out her chin in defiance. "I don't need a man to take care of me. I can take care of myself just fine."

"Like the other day with the purse snatcher?" His one cocked eyebrow conveyed both doubt and mirth.

Crossing her arms over her chest, she said, "I was handling that!"

His humor disappearing, he said, "Actually, you were holding your own pretty good, but I wouldn't recommend you trying that again. What if he had a gun?"

A protest died on her lips as she realized the danger she had put herself in. She bit her bottom lip and lowered her head in chagrin.

Gently, he reached toward her and with a single finger, lifted her chin until she was forced to look at him, then quickly removed his hand. "I'm sure you *can* take care of yourself just fine. But if you ever do need anything, help with purse snatchers, crayon thieves, whathaveyou —" he retrieved a business card from his back pocket and scribbled something on it with a pen from her desk — "I'd like you to call me, even if I am only a man."

She took the card and read it: Sergeant Peter Dack, Detective Bureau, Malcolm County Sheriff Department. Turning it over, she discovered he had written his personal cell phone number in bold, square handwriting across the back.

"You can call me any time," he suggested with a devastatingly handsome smile.

*What the hell just happened?* She could only nod as she shoved the card into her pocket. She could still feel the electricity of his touch, unnerving her. She couldn't think of a thing to say to him, and wasn't sure she could speak anyway, even if she had been able to think of something clever.

"Uh, boss?" Deputy Anderson sent Peter an odd look. "Suppose we should get back, write up this report," he said from his position in the corner of the classroom.

"Right," Peter said, suddenly authoritative again. "I'll be in touch, Miss Hobart." He tipped his hand to his head, reminiscent of the way he had left her in the grocery store parking lot, then took his leave, the deputy trailing after him, their footsteps echoing in the wide hallway.

*** 

Walking away from the crime scene, Peter let his mind wander. He remembered the way Jillian caught the corner of her lip under her eyetooth, the flush of her cheeks, how her holly-green eyes that darted shyly around the room to avoid his scrutiny matched her dark blouse. He quashed the fleeting thought that if he weren't so busy with his job, she might be fun to get to know better.

The last thing in the world this woman was, was helpless. That impressed him. Her eyes flashed fire at him as anger cracked through the shell she hid behind, and damned if he didn't enjoy every minute of it. He especially liked the way her husky voice went an octave lower when she let her emotions boil over. He found he missed that temper when she hid herself away again, but he couldn't resist the bashful way she fidgeted, either. He was still surprised by the heat he felt when he touched her, just that one brief touch.

His pleasant thoughts were interrupted by Deputy Aaron Anderson. "So, I suppose I can ask you the same question you asked her." Aaron didn't take his baby-blue eyes from his notepad as he spoke.

Looking over his shoulder at him, he asked, "What would that be?"

"What was that all about?" Aaron's voice light and casual.

Peter feigned ignorance. "What was what? If you're going to be on the detective bureau, you have to learn how to interrogate and ask a direct question."

"Come on." Aaron looked up at his friend and boss with a knowing smile. "You always take your job way too serious, everything straight and by the book, but if I didn't know any better, I'd have sworn you were flirting with the robbery victim back there."

*Like hell I was.* Peter stopped mid-stride and frowned. "It was nothing."

"I didn't even know you knew how to flirt." His grin grew wider.

In contrast, Peter's scowl deepened. "Drop it."

Aaron paused as if contemplating, running a hand through his short brush cut. Finally, he said, "She sure is cute."

Peter started walking away. "I'm not telling you anything, Aaron."

"All I'm saying is, if you're finally gonna lay off the workaholic-martyr routine and find a girl, well, she's cute." His look of innocence didn't fool Peter.

Peter stopped again, turned, and stared. "What are you, my mother now?"

"Might as well be, since you're becoming your father." Catching the full brunt of Peter's angry glare, Aaron spread his hands in a conciliatory manner. "Forget I said that. But, hey, if *you're* not gonna date her, maybe I'll –"

"No," Peter snapped, interrupting him with a vehemence that surprised both of them. "I'll think about it, okay? Now will you get back to work, Opie?" he said in a gentler voice, using the nickname he liked to use to taunt his younger friend.

"Sure, boss." Offering him a mischievous grin and a friendly punch on the arm, Aaron left the building. Peter followed, grumbling, but not before one last contemplative look back over his shoulder toward Jillian's classroom.

# CHAPTER THREE

## THURSDAY, SEPTEMBER 21

THE STAFF WAS ABUZZ OVER THEIR lunches about the previous eventful day when Jillian entered the teachers' lounge. Unable to avoid them, she answered everyone's eager questions but hated the attention she received. She wished she could go back to being the resident wallflower, but for the time being she had to deal with being a celebrity in a town where very little happened and the slightest incident was cause for gossip.

She made her way to where Mike sat with the janitor, Wally Barczyk, an amiable, gray-haired gentleman. They were discussing the Little League team Mike coached over the summer. Mike didn't look up at her as she stood next to the small table. She felt like she was being ignored on purpose, and waited in uncomfortable silence until Wally noticed her. "Jillian! Please, sit down. How are you feeling? Any news from the Sheriff about yesterday?"

Jillian shook her head. "Not yet. Actually, Wally, I was wondering if, um, I could speak with Mike? Alone?"

Wally smiled. "Of course! I wouldn't want to get in the way of a lover's spat." With a wink to Mike, he stood to let Jillian take his place in the metal folding chair. The chair scraped the floor with a screech so grating Jillian shuddered.

Looking over her shoulder to make sure Wally was gone, she swallowed hard and said to Mike, "Lover's spat? Where would he get that idea?"

Mike shrugged but his smirk was sly. "He asked about our date, so I told him."

"It wasn't a date," she mumbled, too soft for him to hear. The entire school was going to think they were an item, because Wally, although he was a dear man, could gossip with the best of them. Now she would have to field unwanted questions about her love life, or lack thereof, as well as about the prowler. She sat and covered her eyes with her hand, but she couldn't call Mike out on his indiscretion, not in front of the entire staff. To save face, she changed the subject. "I'm sorry if I was rude yesterday. I was under a lot of stress and I didn't mean it."

Mike reached under the table, and under her brown plaid skirt, and placed his hand on her bare knee, giving it a firm squeeze. It reminded her of how he had acted on their so-called date. She was too shocked to object but scooted her chair back, moving her legs from his reach.

"I know, that's alright," he said. "I suppose if I were you, I'd be upset too. I mean, there's so much stress with teaching to begin with, and now a burglar, too? Hey, to show there's no hard feelings, how about I take you to a movie tomorrow night? We could continue our little discussion." He smiled at her, hope in his eyes.

*You can't discuss anything in a movie theater,* she thought. He was patronizing her, and she bit her lip to hold her anger back. She didn't need to bring any more attention to herself right now, even if he was being forward in front of their colleagues. She figured she owed him for the way she treated him the day before, even if he was a little too boring and a lot too touchy-feely for her liking, and outright rejecting him in front of all her co-workers was out of the question. Taking a deep breath, she made her reply as polite as her nerves would allow, forcing a smile to her lips.

"What do you want, Mike?"

"I want to spend time with you." His smile widened. "And I'd love to hear more about your ideas for an expanded kindergarten program. So what do you say? Is it a date?"

"I'll think about it." She didn't mean to be coy; she only hoped that by being evasive, she could get out of it without making anyone

He tilted his head down to look into her eyes. "Isn't that what you're supposed to give a teacher when you're trying to impress her?"

"Oh. I guess it is." She accepted the apple, turning it over in her hands nervously. *He wants to impress me*, she thought, giddy, and felt a blush heat her cheeks. Outside, some of the children were laughing and singing a nursery rhyme, "Do you know the Muffin Man."

Peter tilted his head in the direction of the singing. "You've got some cute kids out there."

This was a topic she felt comfortable talking about to anyone. "Yeah. All the kids this year can already count past twenty, and some can even read. Little words of course, like their names, or cat and dog, but it's wonderful. They're so bright."

"They've got a good teacher to help them."

Jillian bit her lip. Not used to accepting praise, nor feeling a man's intense, appreciative gaze, she looked down at her shuffling feet.

Peter cleared his throat and stepped back. "So, back to yesterday. Have you found anything else missing? Has anyone else seen the assailant or possibly recognized him?"

He took notes while Jillian nervously twisted the woody stem of the apple in her hands and answered all his questions in the negative.

"Okay." Peter flipped his notebook closed. "So. I've got some time off this weekend, so I was wondering—." His words were drowned out by screaming outside on the playground. The children's sounds were no longer playful and happy, but instead held notes of terror. Jillian's head snapped up to attention, her eyes wide, and she shoved the apple into Peter's chest as she ran past him out of the room toward the noise. Peter bobbled the apple a moment before he set it on her desk and followed close on her heels.

Jillian's heart stuck in her throat when she stepped onto the playground and saw a child sprawled face down on the grass, a few other children around him crying and pointing. She ran up and knelt next to him, turning him over to see his face. The boy moaned, a miserable sound that made Jillian want to cry.

"Isn't that Joey?" Peter asked, kneeling beside her and reaching to take his pulse.

"Yes." Jillian was shaking. She tried to keep her voice calm so she wouldn't frighten the other children when she asked, "What happened?"

The youngsters started replying all at once.

"I don't know!"

"He just fell down!"

"Is he dead?"

Jillian paled. "I'm sure he's fine," she said quickly, starting to panic when she saw the seriousness on Peter's face. "What was he doing when he fell?"

Tyler Watson, another of her students, piped up. "He was just eating a cookie. Then he started coughing and fell down."

Spying a half-eaten cookie on the ground beside the boy, she picked it up and her fear turned icy cold. "Where did you kids get these?" she asked, unable to keep the hysteria from rising in her voice.

"The Muffin Man gave them to us," Tyler said.

"Who?"

"That man. He said he was the Muffin Man and taught us how to sing his song." Tyler pointed to the fence on the other side of the playground. No one was there.

"Child predators," Peter said under his breath.

Jillian refused to believe, naively she supposed, that someone so twisted could be lurking around her students. "No, it can't be. It was just an accident." She gripped his arm. "Peter, this is a peanut butter cookie. Joey's allergic to peanuts."

Peter tilted his head and leaned down to Joey's mouth listen to for breathing. "He's going into anaphylactic shock," he said in a low voice. "Get the other kids out of here."

Jillian jumped up and corralled the kids, hoping her voice didn't reveal just how scared she was. "It's time to go home now, everyone. I'll make sure Joey gets home all right. Everything's okay." *Please let it be okay.* She pushed them toward a short yellow school bus waiting to take them home. She looked back over her shoulder and was terrified to see Peter crouched over the boy, performing rescue breathing. Forgetting the children, she ran back to him. "I'll call an ambulance."

"No time," Peter said, grabbing her wrist as she ran by. "We have to take him to the hospital now." He dug into his pants pocket and retrieved his car keys, shoving them into her hand. "You have to drive."

"What? I can't drive a police car."

Peter scooped the boy's limp body into his arms. "You have to. I need to breathe for him." He yanked open the vehicle's back door and spread the boy along the vinyl bench seat, then climbed in and positioned himself over him, one knee braced on the seat and one foot on the floor. Tilting the boy's head back, he pinched his nose shut and blew a short, quick breath into his mouth.

"Oh God," she squeaked, her hands flying to her mouth. If it was anaphylactic shock, the child's throat would completely close before any emergency help arrived. Trying to ignore the cold terror gripping her insides, she ran around the vehicle and climbed in, started the engine.

"Flip that switch right there," Peter commanded, pointing to a spot on the overhead console above the rearview mirror. She did and the sirens and lights roared to life. The sound galvanized her, and she stomped on the gas pedal, sending the vehicle racing forward.

The car shot west on the lonely country road away from the school. For a few precious moments, there was no traffic, allowing Jillian to feel more confident about driving a car as big as a whale at ninety miles an hour past the sod farms and dilapidated barns that would soon be razed to make way for the inevitable urban sprawl and its McMansions. She needed to keep her eyes on the road at that speed, but she was desperate to know what was happening in the backseat. A quick glance in the rearview mirror showed Peter still silently hunched over the boy. She shouldn't have looked. She focused her energy back on the road and concentrated on not freaking out.

As they came nearer to civilization, she saw other vehicles in her peripheral vision. To her horror, when she reached busy Van Dyke Road that headed into town, several cars were converging upon the main intersection.

"The light's turning red!" Jillian cried, automatically pressing on the brake pedal and laying on the horn. "What do I do?"

"They'll stop. Trust me. Drive. Go, go, go!" Peter demanded, emphatically banging on the Plexiglas partition designed to keep criminals in the back seat separated from the driver.

She hoped he was right as she leaned on the accelerator again. Miraculously, the other cars on the roadway heeded the siren and moved to the shoulder, creating a narrow path for the hurtling sheriff's vehicle to squeeze through. She took the next corner on two squealing wheels, praying the car would stay upright and that she wouldn't kill them or any innocent bystanders. She heard Peter swear under his breath as he braced a hand on the window and another on the limp boy to keep them both from flying off the backseat.

After what seemed an eternity but was really only a few minutes, Jillian screeched the car to a halt with just the barest hint of a fishtail in front of the emergency trauma center. Blue-clothed doctors, alerted by the squad car's siren, came running to meet them. By that time she felt certain the boy was dead. She watched, helpless, as a female doctor yanked open the car door and pulled the child's lifeless body from Peter's arms. He quickly informed the woman of the boy's allergy before she rushed him back into the hospital.

Jillian couldn't move. *He's dead.* She was still clutching the steering wheel with both hands, her knuckles white with the force of her grip, and breathing so hard and fast she was close to hyperventilating. *Joey's dead. I wasn't fast enough. He's dead because of me.*

Peter opened her door and reached over her to move the shifter knob on the steering column into Park, then switched off the police cruiser's siren. Gently he pried her fingers away from the steering wheel, speaking soothingly as he pulled her out of the car. "Come on, sweetie. Let go of the wheel. It's over. You did good. It's okay. Everything is going to be alright."

*No, it's not,* she thought in despair. When she was standing, she closed her eyes and took a long, steadying breath to quell the hysteria rising inside her. Peter pulled her toward him, stroking her hair. It wasn't shyness but nervous energy that had her pushing him away, pacing and running her trembling hands through her hair where his hands had been only seconds before.

"He's dead, isn't he?" she asked dully, knowing he was but wanting Peter, needing Peter to tell her otherwise.

Peter reached for her, but she moved away again. "He's in good hands now. They'll take care of him."

"But he's dead." Now her voice bordered on hysterical.

Peter licked his top lip and shook his head almost imperceptibly. "I don't know." He sounded so helpless that Jillian stopped pacing and looked up at him. He was pale and his shoulders were slack with fatigue. But it was his eyes that caught her attention. They were ocean-blue and full of sorrow and focused intently on her, studying her. She swallowed hard and turned away again.

Another car skidded to a stop beside the Ford, and a couple Jillian recognized as Joey's divorced parents jumped out and ran inside. "I told you he needed an Epi-pen when he stays with you!" the woman shouted.

"Shut up!" the man replied. Both rushed past Jillian without acknowledging her.

Jillian covered her face with her hands. "At least they're blaming each other and not me."

"Let me take you home," Peter said softly.

She let her hands fall to her sides. She wasn't going to fall apart. She wasn't going to let him see her cry. "No."

"You're not in any shape—"

She snapped at him, taking her fear out on him because he was there. "I said no. I'm fine."

"I know it sounds like I'm trying to be the knight in shining armor here," he said, his voice gentle. "And I know you hate that. But right now you don't have a car."

"Or my purse," she said. They were both back at the school. She sagged against the vehicle as the last of the adrenaline drained from her body and reality took its place. "Alright," she relented. "But don't take me home. I need a drink."

# CHAPTER FOUR

THE BAR WAS DIMLY LIT AND smoky, just as Jillian remembered it. She spotted her friends sitting on tattered vinyl stools at the bar near the door, but hesitated. Peter had followed her inside, apparently not believing her when she said her friends were waiting. He still wore his sheriff's uniform and several of the bar patrons stopped to stare at him, looking uncomfortable in his presence. The added scrutiny made her all the more nervous.

"Where are they?" he demanded, scanning the room over her shoulder. "I'm not leaving you here alone. I've been here before, and it wasn't for the atmosphere." She watched as two men playing pool stopped to move out of his way, avoiding all eye contact.

"I'm looking," Jillian lied. She didn't want Donovan and Tina to see him, knowing they would make a fuss. The last thing she wanted right now was more fuss. Hoping Peter would get bored and leave, she backed into a dark corner and listened to her friends talk instead.

She overheard Donovan Parker and Tina Fernandez lamenting her absence. "I know I told Jillian to be here at six," Tina griped. "I swear, that girl needs to start wearing a watch. She is never on time." Jillian winced.

Donovan, tall and almost painfully thin, wearing rectangular black-rimmed glasses and bright clothes more appropriate for a New York City disco than semi-rural Michigan, waved his hand dismissively at her. "Then why are you surprised she's late now?"

Tina took a sip from her bottle of Dos Equis beer. "Because she's

never been *this* late before. It's after seven. And she's not answering
her cell phone." She took a drag on the cigarette clamped between the
first and middle fingers of her other hand. The petite woman had café
au lait skin and looked as if she had poured herself into the jeans and
low-cut gold-colored shirt that accentuated her voluptuous curves.

"Those cigarettes are going to kill you one day," Donovan scolded,
taking a sip from his own glass.

"So you keep telling me." Tina rolled her eyes. "Well, then she
had better hurry up and get here before I die." She tossed her head,
sending her waist-length, wavy black hair whipping through the air,
and batted her eyes at a man sitting on a stool at the other side of
the bar.

Donovan shook his head. "Don't waste your time, honey. He is
so not your type."

"Whose type is he then?"

His grin was salacious as he wiggled his eyebrows. "Mine."

"I saw him first." Tina stuck out her plump bottom lip in a sexy
pout.

Donovan turned his attention to the front door, and Jillian knew
she'd been spotted. There was no avoiding them now. He stood and
waved to her. "Oh look, Jillian's here," he told Tina, then winked.
"And she brought dessert."

Jillian glanced anxiously at Peter and hoped he hadn't overheard
her friend's taunting comment. She knew Donovan wasn't talking
about food. Under normal circumstances, she would have blushed
and jokingly chided her best friend for uttering such innuendo. But
this was not a normal circumstance. When she opened her mouth to
scold him, the emotions she kept bottled up the last few hours poured
out in a torrent. A sob escaped as she fell into Donovan's arms.

"Well," he said, clearly baffled, "this was not the response I
was expecting." He patted her back uncertainly as she cried on his
shoulder.

"What the hell happened?" Tina demanded, jumping in front of
Peter, a commanding presence despite the fact she was only as high
as his elbow. "My God, you're the Sheriff. Is she under arrest? Why
is she crying? What did you do to her?"

"She's not under arrest." After scrutinizing her friends, he said, "I'm just giving her a ride back from the hospital."

"Hospital!" Donovan and Tina exclaimed simultaneously, sending each other worried glances. Jillian felt Donovan shudder at the thought and lifted her head from his shoulder. "I'm okay," she told him, patting his cheek, comforting him despite her own tears. She didn't need them both hysterical.

Peter's cell phone rang and he excused himself to answer it while Tina and Donovan tried to pry information out of Jillian. Between sobbing breaths, she managed to tell them the basics. By the time she finished her story, her tears had subsided into pathetic hiccups.

"Oh my God. Here, drink this, you need it more than I do," Tina said, pushing her half-empty beer bottle into Jillian's hand. Trembling, Jillian drank deeply and tried not to cringe. She didn't particularly care for Tina's brand of beer — she would have preferred a simple Coors Light, or better yet an amaretto sour — but she desperately wanted to be drunk right now. She held out her hand for Donovan's glass, but he shook his head sadly. "Water on the rocks, darling. Doctor's orders," he said. In resignation, she continued to drink the heavy beer because it was the most readily available.

"So you got to drive a police car with the sirens and everything?" Donovan sounded so impressed with that fact rather than being concerned about the reason behind it that Tina smacked his arm for being insensitive.

"I just know he's dead," Jillian said, her voice wavering. She lifted the beer to her lips and took another much-needed drink as Peter approached them.

"No, he's not," he said, giving her shoulder a gentle, reassuring squeeze. "That was Aaron — Deputy Anderson. They've stabilized the boy. They had to give him an emergency tracheotomy and he's on a ventilator, and being transported to the ICU at Children's Hospital in Detroit, but he's alive."

On impulse fueled by an overwhelming sense of relief, Jillian hugged Peter. "Oh, thank you!"

He wrapped his arms around her, and rubbing a hand along her spine, he whispered into her hair, "I told you everything was going to be alright."

Jillian carried her empty plate to the sink to wash it. Tina joined her to wash the frying pan. They discussed the previous night's events while they did the dishes.

"Quit worrying," Tina advised her. "I'm sure everything will work out fine. The kid's alive, and no one is going to blame you because somebody baked cookies."

Jillian sighed and leaned into Tina's side. "You do know me well."

"Can't be your friend since tenth grade and not know you."

The telephone by the refrigerator rang. By the time Jillian dried her hands and answered it, no one was on the other end of the line. "Stupid telemarketer computers," Jillian muttered and hung up.

No sooner had she hung up than it rang again. "Let me," Tina said. "I love chewing out telemarketers." She picked up the receiver and barked an angry, "Hello!" Her face instantly cringed into amused chagrin. "Oh, yeah, sure Sergeant, she's right here." She passed the phone to Jillian, silently mouthing the words, "Sergeant Dack."

Unsure what to expect, Jillian cautiously said, "Hello?"

"Hey, Jillian. Peter. Feeling better? Did you sleep well?"

She felt her insides turn to jelly. "Hi, Peter. Yes, I did," she lied. She has tossed and turned so much her bed looked like she'd had way more fun in it than she actually did. "You're calling early."

"I've been on duty since six-thirty."

*So this is a work-related call,* she thought with a tinge of regret that surprised her. "How's Joey?"

Peter sounded cheerful. "He's doing great. They took him off the respirator and he might even go home in a couple of days."

Jillian sagged against the counter when overwhelming relief made her weak. "Oh, that's great! I've been so worried."

"You're a hero, you know," Peter said. "Everyone's talking about the teacher who drove a cop car to save one of her children. Ever think about driving an ambulance? You'd have a spot here waiting for you."

Jillian shuddered, remembering the drive and the terror. "I never want to do that again."

"I didn't think so." Peter deftly changed the subject. "Listen, I had another reason for calling. I started to ask you last night, but things got a little hairy."

"More questions about the burglar?"

"Nope. Do you like sushi?"

"Uh…" Her stomach went from jelly to butterflies. "Yeah. Why?"

"I get off tonight at seven and was wondering if I could take you to dinner and a movie."

She froze. "Oh! Um. Okay."

"You don't sound too eager," Peter said. Was that disappointment she heard in his voice?

*Quit being a wimp*, Jillian chided herself. "No, I am! Really. Seven o'clock. Sounds great."

Peter chuckled, a low throaty sound. "Great. I'll pick you up." Jillian started to recite her address, but he cut her off. "I know that already. You gave it to me during questioning at the school."

"Oh. Right." Jillian was glad he couldn't see her blush. After parting pleasantries, she hung up the phone and turned to a giddy Tina.

"A date! You have a date with the cop!" She was dancing in circles in the tiny kitchen.

Jillian slumped into a kitchen chair. "How did that happen?"

"You underestimate yourself, girl. You have guys drooling over you all the time, you're just to shy to notice."

"I do not." Jillian laughed at her friend. "Look at me. I wear a size twelve. It's not like I'm going to win any Miss America pageants."

"True," Tina agreed with a nod, and Jillian frowned at her. "But you've got that whole sweet, innocent, helpless thing going on. Guys lap that up. Makes them feel needed and manly."

Jillian's scowl deepened, and she stood and forcefully shoved clean dishes into the cupboard, slamming the door shut in a huff. "I am not helpless."

"Nor innocent," Tina said, making Jillian giggle. "What I'm saying is, you lucked out his time. He's got the whole tall, dark, and gorgeous thing going for him. Unless you want to go back to the other guy, you know, short, pale and average. Whatever happened to him, anyway?"

"Mike? Nothing happened."

Tina nodded in sympathy. "Too boring?"

"Yeah. But it wasn't a date! Why does everyone think it was a date? He just wanted to talk about work. That's all he ever wants to talk about. And it's gotten worse since I got the kindergarten position." Jillian shrugged.

"You sure he just doesn't want to get into your pants?" Tina laughed out loud when Jillian's cheeks turned crimson.

"No! God, I hope not. Look. He applied for the kindergarten position same time I did, and ever since I got it, he's always right there, eager to offer his opinion."

Tina rung out the dishrag and draped it over the faucet. "Face it, he likes you."

Jillian shook her head. "Doesn't matter. He was a bad kisser anyway."

Tina's eyed widened. "You kissed him?"

"No way. He kissed me."

"Isn't that the same thing?" Tina teased her with a grin.

"No." Jillian stuck out her tongue in a grimace. She remembered considering using some moves she'd learned in that self-defense class Donovan talked her into taking with him to get Mike to back off. She might have done it, too, if she hadn't been worried about how that would affect their working relationship the following Monday.

Tina shook her head with a laugh. "Well, either way, you can always find something to talk about, but there's no way around a lousy kiss. Not worth the time if you have to teach them. Nope, at our age, we need someone who already knows what he's doing."

Giggling, Jillian agreed, but only with half of Tina's statement. "We're not that old."

"Girl, thirty-one is old enough." Tina checked her watch. "I've got to get going, or Pop will skin me alive and not let me leave in time for *my* date if I'm not there for the lunch rush."

"Who's the lucky guy this week?"

"Denny. He's hot. Dumb, but hot," Tina replied with a lecherous grin and wiggling eyebrows. "Have a good day at school. And a good date." She winked and ran out the door.

\*\*\*

Silver bells hung above the door tinkled merrily when Peter walked in to the crowded pizza parlor. The hostess greeted him by name. He met Aaron at Papa's Pizza for lunch every Friday unless they were bogged down with a case. Aaron, in full uniform like Peter, was already sitting at their regular table, the one on which some kid had carved, "Tom loves Nikki," after which someone else, presumably Nikki, had scratched, "Tom is a lying bastard." Ambience. But the pizza couldn't be beat.

"Stats?" He said as she slid into the seat across from Aaron.

Aaron shrugged. "Slow. Two motor vehicle accidents and a domestic so far today. You?"

"Worse. One drive-off from a gas station. Filled the tank of a Beemer with premium and left without paying. Wasn't too hard to track down a BMW out here, though. Case closed." He shook his head. "You'd think, if he can afford a car like that, he can afford the gas to put in it."

"I've been tempted myself, with these gas prices." Aaron grinned.

"Not something to be telling your Sergeant." Peter raised an eyebrow, but returned the grin.

Aaron laughed and folded the menu. "Ran into your old man at the station this morning. Did you see him?"

"Not since yesterday's reelection campaign pancake breakfast at the VFW hall. It never ends." Peter hoped he sounded aloof. His father was very serious about his campaigning, and little else.

Aaron looked sympathetic. "He still trying to get you to take his place as Sheriff?"

Peter nodded. "He just happened to mention that it's good practice for my own inevitable run for office." It was assumed by all that Peter would one day become Sheriff, just like his dad. There was little debate in the matter as Sheriff Patrick Dack groomed his son for what he considered bigger and better things. Peter loved his job, helping people and catching criminals. It was the sitting around eating pancakes and listening to old men gripe about dogs trespassing on lawns that made him insane. But he sucked it up because he figured he would have to get used to it.

"Hope you like pancakes." Aaron's smile was wicked now. "So, do I get a promotion once you're Sheriff?"

Peter's impassive face crumpled into a scowl, and Aaron quickly retreated. "Hey, I got an extra ticket for the Red Wings hockey home opener tonight against the Avalanche. Tracey cancelled at the last minute. You in?"

His father and his campaign easily forgotten, Peter relaxed. "Tracey, huh? I thought her name was Melanie."

"Melanie was last weekend." Aaron shrugged. "So, are you in?"

Peter shook his head. Must be nice to have women falling at your feet and not care about it. "Nah. I'll have to pass this time."

"Dude, you always pass. You gotta quit working so hard. Haven't you heard, all work and no play makes Pete a dull boy?"

"Jack."

"Huh?"

"Makes *Jack* a dull boy."

"Whatever. Those seventy-plus-hour weeks you're always pulling just can't be healthy. Take a night off, have some fun for once, before you turn into your father after all."

*No.* Peter pushed the comparison from his mind. He may have inherited the workaholic gene from his father, and he may one day carry the same title as his father, but that's where the similarity ended. Peter cared about people and believed in justice. Unlike his father, who cared about nothing more than to see himself on TV. He was torn between telling Aaron off or telling him his reason for declining the offer; he knew if he chose the latter, Aaron would make a big deal out of nothing. He was interrupted before he could decide on a course of action. Their regular waitress, Missy, brought out a large Pepsi for each man without having to be asked. "The usual, boys? Pepperoni, onion, and green pepper?"

"Better not today," Peter said. "Make it ham, mushroom, and extra cheese. Got a date tonight and don't want to scare her off."

"No way." Aaron's eyes widened with disbelief when Missy left to place the order. "You're actually taking time off work for fun?"

*Here we go.* "Had to." Peter sipped his pop through a straw. "You threatened to take her out if I didn't." *Aaron would eat that girl alive.* He had no idea why that bothered him.

"When's the last time *you* went out on a date?"

Peter had to think about that one, and didn't have an answer. It didn't really bother him. Work always came first, and fun was a distant second. Very distant. He'd always denied himself the luxury of getting too close, too emotionally involved, with a woman. Previous girlfriends may have called him commitment-phobic, but in reality the opposite was true. He was very committed — to his work, which made him realize he could never be committed to a relationship, not in the way a woman would want and deserve.

"Do you even know what to do with a woman?" Aaron continued. "If you need any pointers, I'd be glad to help." Aaron's eyes twinkled as he teased.

Peter knew Aaron wouldn't deny his a rep as a lady-killer, with the ladies constantly falling for his boyish good looks and charm, a fact he took advantage of every opportunity that came around, which was often. He raised an eyebrow in a glance that was made less stern by a grin. "I think I'll figure it out."

"So, the teacher, huh." Aaron nodded his approval. "She's something. Did she really drive your squad car near to 90 miles an hour?"

"Yeah, but don't remind her. She took that kinda hard." He pushed the memory of Jillian crying, and of how good she felt in his arms, out of his mind.

"Speaking of which, find anything about the Cookie Monster?"

"Muffin Man," Peter corrected him, even though the name was apt. "No. Jillian thinks it was just a well-meaning stranger or maybe one of the parents, trying to be nice to the kids. The only witnesses we have are a bunch of five-year-olds who were more interested in the cookies than in the man who delivered them. The only thing we can say for sure is it's a white male."

Aaron snorted. "That's about, oh, forty percent of the population in Malcolm County. But what guy walks around a playground coaxing kids with cookies and is just being nice?"

Peter drummed his fingers on the table. "Not many. But I'm not sure there's a case anyway. Even if we do find him, what do I charge him with, unlawful possession of baked goods?" Their conversation stopped when Missy delivered their food, setting the large pizza between them. Both men attacked the pizza and ate in contented silence, gooey mozzarella strings stretching from their mouths to the pie. After devouring three slices in quick succession, Peter spoke again. "The school sent out letters to alert the parents, and we'll send another patrol car around there more often, so everyone's got an eye out for anything suspicious. I don't expect we'll hear from him again."

# CHAPTER SIX

THE DAY SEEMED TO DRAG INTERMINABLY. The children had already forgotten about the excitement, but the adults hadn't. Jillian was forced to address the questions and admiration of her coworkers and parents for her action in saving Joey. Mike Georginidis seemed particularly attentive, even more than usual, much to her annoyance. He remained glued to her side during recess, and whenever he overheard her speaking with another teacher in the hall, he inserted his tacit agreement to whatever compliments were being paid to her, wearing a goofy smile the whole time. She felt uncomfortable accepting their praise, knowing things would have turned out much different if Peter had not been present. But whenever she tried to explain, no one would hear of it; they just wrote off her protests to her natural shyness and modesty. She resorted to accepting their comments with a nod and bashful smile, just to make them stop. She was glad when the school day ended and she could escape to home to fret about her upcoming date.

Mike flagged her down in the parking lot before she could leave. "So, what time is good for you?"

Jillian cocked her head and squinted at him. "For what?"

"The movie. There's that new George Clooney movie I want to take you to. Then I thought we could talk over dinner." His smile fell just a little. "Don't tell me you forgot."

She didn't forget; she never accepted his invitation to begin with. "Yes, I forgot. I'm sorry," she lied, her gaze shifting to avoid his scrutiny. "Yesterday was just so crazy."

"Oh. I see." His smile was completely gone now, his pale eyes narrowed as he regarded her.

She couldn't bear the accusing way Mike stared at her. "Maybe some other time," she blurted insincerely, knowing as soon as the words were out of her mouth she was not making matters any better in her poor attempt to let him down easy and avoid a confrontation.

Mike's smile returned, but didn't reach his eyes. "Sure. When you're feeling better. See you at school Monday." He turned on his heel and walked across the parking lot to his ancient Honda.

Jillian didn't have time to dwell on Mike's hurt feelings. She rushed home to get ready for her date. When she opened the door to her house, the phone was ringing. Dropping her canvas tote bag of school papers, she rushed across the kitchen to answer it, breathless from the exertion. "Hello?"

"Sorry, wrong number," a man mumbled and hung up with a slam.

Jillian flinched at the loud clatter in her ear. "Jerk." But she forgot about it as she riffled through her closet to dress for her date. She finally settled on the third outfit she tried on when the phone rang again. Perturbed, she answered the phone on her nightstand with a less than friendly greeting.

"Oh my baby, going out on a date! She's so grown up now!"

"Hi, Donovan." She grinned, her good humor restored. "I guess you talked to Tina."

"You know she could not let something this juicy stay secret for very long. Now honey, I've just got to say something, and you know I only say this because I love you. You're not wearing those shoes tonight, are you?"

She looked down at her inexpensive brown leather mules. "These shoes? Yeah, why — wait. You can't see what shoes I'm wearing over the phone."

"They're still wrong."

"Want to go shopping, Donovan?"

"Yes, please!" he answered cheerily. "We can go after my next oncologist appointment. It can be either celebratory shopping, or retail therapy. Either way, I'll need it."

Jillian remembered that a few weeks earlier, Donovan had

completed his last round of chemotherapy for testicular cancer, and she immediately felt guilty. "Oh. When's your appointment? Do you want me to go with you?"

"October six, and stop that. We're talking about you tonight. So, what else are you wearing?"

"Um ... My favorite denim skirt."

"The indigo one? Well, it's a bit dark, but it flips up a bit above the knee and shows off your gams. So I'll let it pass. And are you wearing the scarlet boob shirt?"

"Donovan!" She had to laugh at her friend. Surely he wasn't serious. She had briefly considered the bright, low-cut shirt, a gift from Donovan, but quickly rejected it because it showed more cleavage than she was comfortable in revealing.

His laugh was light but smug. "Oh, stop blushing. You know you look hot in it. Put it on. Now."

"Alright..." Reluctantly, she changed out of her brown cardigan while balancing the telephone to listen to her friend's incessant chatter. But he was right: she did look good in it. She admired herself in the bathroom mirror, spinning to make the skirt flare.

"Now, I want you to behave yourself tonight, young lady," Donovan advised. "Don't do anything I wouldn't do."

"You'd do a lot."

Donovan laughed heartily, a sign that he agreed and was not the least bit insulted. "Then you're going to have a very good time. If, of course, you would ever break out of that little shell of yours and just live a little."

Jillian rolled her eyes. "Should I start calling you Mom now?"

"I thought you already did. Well, good night. Call me tomorrow. I'll want the full scoop, you know."

"You'll be the first to know."

When Peter arrived at half past seven, Jillian's nerves ratcheted up several notches. He was not wearing his uniform, instead looking surprisingly approachable — and disconcertingly sexy — in jeans and a well-worn brown leather bomber jacket over a pale green oxford shirt. The top two buttons were undone to reveal broad collar bones and wisps of dark chest hair. She stood frozen in the doorway, staring up at him. She could almost feel his eyes on her as his gaze roved over her long legs and hourglass hips, lingered on Donovan's shirt, and moved up until he finally met her eyes. He blinked and swallowed hard. "Hi. You look nice."

"It's chilly out tonight, isn't it?" Jillian said in a rush as his voice spurred her into action. Pulling a well-worn, oversized gray sweater that used to belong to her grandfather from the hall closet, she wrapped it around herself, completely negating the effects of her sexy shirt. "Donovan made me wear it," she mumbled, knowing a self-conscious flush was creeping across her cheeks.

"Remind me to thank him." Peter offered his arm. She tentatively linked her arm with his, and they walked together to his truck.

***

Men always seemed to know just the right kind of movie to see on a first date. During some of the more intense moments, Jillian had clutched Peter's arm in fright, burying her face into his shoulder without any shame. It happened so often that halfway through the film, he put his arm around her shoulders and left it there, and she did not protest. In fact, she liked it. He kept his arm around her waist as they walked toward his truck after the show. Smiling up at him, Jillian felt herself leaning into his body, solid and warm, surprised at how easy it was to do.

He was laughing at her. "I thought you didn't need a man to protect you." He grinned devilishly.

She bit her lip to hide her smile. "You took me to a scary movie on purpose."

He looked thoughtful for a moment, then smiled. "Maybe."

"You're mean," she said with a deep, infectious laugh to prove she didn't really believe it.

They approached Peter's chrome-trimmed heavy-duty pickup, his cell phone rang. He used his free hand to answer it, but after a few brief words, he backed away from her, holding up a finger indicating for her to wait.

"Damn it. You've got to be kidding me," he kept his voice low, but she could still hear him. "Yeah, alright. Crap. I have to drop Jillian off. Never mind who she is. I'll call you when I'm close." He clicked his phone shut and walked back to Jillian with long, fast strides.

"Change of plans. I've got to take you home."

"Uh, okay." She looked up at him, confused, but his face was unreadable.

"There's been a break-out over at the county jail, and they're calling in all available bodies." He grabbed her elbow and helped her into his truck before she could speak.

They rode in silence. She wouldn't know what to say to him even if she had felt so inclined. She had to assume he was telling her the truth; he did work for the sheriff's department, after all. But Tina's dating advice echoed in her head: if a date is going badly, use the cell phone as a scapegoat to make up an emergency to escape. There's been an accident, someone's sick, so-and-so has a flat tire ... there's an escaped convict on the loose. And here she thought the date was going well. She tried to keep her disillusionment hidden and stared out the window.

They made it back to her house in record time. Certain the date was a complete disaster, Jillian walked ahead of him to the front porch, her back straight with as much dignity as she could muster, and focused on retrieving her house keys from her purse before gathering the courage to turn and face him. Surely a good-night kiss was out of the question. Then why was he still standing here on her porch? She couldn't just keep standing there like an idiot. Too shy to initiate a kiss herself, and too unsure of the situation to know if he even wanted one, she took a deep breath and stuck out her hand, hoping Peter would shake it, hoping the action didn't seem cold and formal, hoping he would hurry so she could go hide under her bedcovers.

"I had a nice time tonight," she said, then chewed her bottom lip while she waited for his reaction.

He did take her hand, but did not shake it. Instead, intently holding her gaze, he brought it to his lips and planted a warm, lingering kiss on her knuckles. Jillian's eyes glazed over and her jaw went slack. It was so simple and yet ... sexy as hell.

"So did I," he whispered against her hand.

Jillian's stared up at him through her lowered lashes, speechless and confused.

"I'm sorry." Straightening, he said in a louder voice, "I want to call you again, when things get straightened out." It came out sounding like a question rather than a bold statement.

She tried to make her smile more believable. Maybe it was his vague way of letting her off easy, just as she had done with Mike. Faced with her own avoidance tactics, she resolved to be more truthful with him, and she replied hopefully to Peter. "I'd like that."

His smile brightened for a moment, and he touched his fingers lightly to her cheek. Then he turned and sprinted back to his truck, tires squealing in his rush to leave.

Jillian never knew she could feel both dejected and turned on at the same time. She went into the house and changed out of her date clothes and into more comfortable attire of an oversized jersey tee-shirt and blue fuzzy slippers. Curling up on the couch with an ancient yellow hand-crocheted afghan and a bag of microwave popcorn that was now serving as dinner, she idly flipped television channels while she dialed Donovan's phone number. He answered on the third ring.

"It is far too early for you to be calling me!" He must have read her name on the Caller ID. "What happened?"

She confessed her doubts to Donovan. He sounded as perplexed as she but tried to reassure her, repeating all the reasons she had already told herself.

"He said he'd call you again, right?"

Jillian sighed. "That's the ultimate male blow-off line and you know it, Donovan."

"Right. Okay. Well, he kissed your hand! That's something. No one's ever kissed my hand before."

She was about to offer another cynical retort when the television station interrupted its programming with a breaking news report. She rattled his eardrum with a shriek.

"What happened?" Donovan shouted.

She spilled the popcorn in her excitement. "Channel seven! Turn on channel seven!"

A reporter was broadcasting from the county jail. Jillian felt only a little guilty for being so happy to hear about a jailbreak in progress.

Her glee turned sour in an instant as her heart fell into her stomach. "Oh, God."

"It's not Peter, I'm sure," she heard Donovan say as the reporter announced the escapee had been captured, but not before wounding a Sheriff's sergeant in a shootout.

# CHAPTER SEVEN

SUNDAY, SEPTEMBER 24

R EPORTS SAID THE INJURED SERGEANT WAS shot in the leg and would recover, but the Sheriff's Department wasn't releasing any names. Jillian couldn't eat and barely slept, even as she told herself she was being stupid. They'd only been out on one date; half a date, even. His life was none of her business. And, going back to her original theory, which was starting to sound more realistic the more she thought about it, who's to say what he said was even true? Maybe the jailbreak was a convenient coincidence and he it took it as a quick way out. She'd been unceremoniously dumped and she'd just have to deal with it. It wouldn't be the first time, nor the last, probably. Then the phone rang.

Peter called, just like he promised. Jillian sank onto the couch as she heard his voice, relieved and surprised at how tired she was.

Peter apologized profusely leaving in the middle of the date, but she cut him off.

"It's not your fault, but when I turned on the television and heard about the sergeant who was shot, and they wouldn't say who he was, well, I didn't know what to do, and..." She was babbling, sounding foolish, and her voice trailed off.

"You were worried about me?" Peter asked.

She heard amusement in his voice, and took offense to that. "No, I was not. We were only on half a date. Why should I be worried about you?"

"Yes, you were." Now his voice held a tinge of surprise. Before she could protest or worry any more, he continued on in a more confident voice. "I owe you a real date. How about next Friday?"

"Oh." It took her a moment to find her voice. "Okay … Sure. Yes."

Peter laughed. They spent almost an hour talking, ending with an agreement on another date, after he rearranged his busy schedule. She got the impression he worked more hours than normal, even for a sergeant.

After the phone call, she felt fidgety from being cooped up in the house and had to get out. She drove to the grocery store a few miles away for Doritos and butter pecan ice cream, her favorite comfort junk foods, to calm her frayed nerves. While there, she loaded her cart with a few others things she might need for the rest of the week.

It was late in the afternoon so not many shoppers were left in the store. She picked the shortest checkout line and started stacking her purchases on the conveyor belt when she heard her name. Looking up, she smiled and nodded when she spotted Billy at the end of the checkout line, bagging customers' groceries. He looked out of place, with his six silver hoop earrings, a stud in his nose, a thin bar pierced through his left eyebrow, and spiky hair died black as pitch. A glaring black eye completed the sinister look. He would have been more at home at a Marilyn Manson concert than in a grocery store. But then he grinned back at her, his sincere smile lighting up his young face. His smile disappeared as he picked up the first of Jillian's items to bag: feminine maxi pads. He dropped them into a paper bag, mortified.

She heard her name again, and realized it wasn't Billy who had addressed her. To her dismay, Township Supervisor Simon Brothers was pushing his cart, and his young trophy wife, to catch up to her in line.

"Miss Hobart! I didn't know you shopped here. You must live in the area. Glad to know you're a constituent as well as my Jonathon's teacher. So, where is it you live, then?"

Jillian felt a distinct discomfort at the supervisor's overly friendly tone, so she made her answer polite but evasive. "Just a few miles from here, sir."

He laughed. "Oh, no need for formalities. Call me Mr. Brothers. Better yet, call me Simon." Jillian heard a cough behind him, and he flinched before turning to introduce his wife. "Tiffany, dear, this is Jonathon's teacher, Jillian Hobart. We have a parent-teacher conference with her tomorrow night."

*Crap.* Jillian had forgotten about that dreaded chore. "Nice to meet you, Mrs. Brothers," she said. The other woman shook her hand with an insincere smile, then, apparently having written her off as unimportant, became absorbed in the supermarket gossip tabloids proclaiming to have the latest in compromising celebrity photos.

Mr. Brothers stepped in front of his distracted wife and put his hand uncomfortably low on Jillian's back. "Jonathon's doing quite well in school this year." He spoke in a low voice close to her ear. "I'm happy my son is in your class. I look forward to working closely with you. For Jonathon's benefit, of course."

The man made her skin crawl. She tried to move away from his hand, which was moving farther down her back, but she couldn't go far, as her exit was blocked by her shopping cart and her purchase was still being rung up.

"Miss H. used to be my teacher." Billy said as he placed a bag filled with groceries in her cart. "She was one of my favorites. She's really good."

"I'm sure she is," Mr. Brothers said. God, now he was leering at her.

Jillian could feel the heat rising in her cheeks. She couldn't think of a civil way to make him stop this ridiculous come-on. She couldn't walk away; she hadn't paid for her groceries yet. She didn't want to offend the man — although he seemed to have no problem offending her — because she had to teach his child for the rest of the year and would no doubt have to see him again, and as soon as tomorrow's conferences at that. But she sincerely wished he would take his hand off her ass.

Billy pulled the cart out of the checkout lane and stepped to her side. "Do you need help carrying these groceries to your car, Miss H.?"

"Yes, I do, thank you, Billy." She jumped at the offer. Any excuse to get away from Mr. Brothers was a good one in her book. She pulled out enough bills from her purse to pay the cashier, then all but ran from the store, Billy following, carrying two lightweight bags that she could have easily handled herself.

When they were out of earshot, Billy spoke up, his voice terse. "That guy's a creep."

*Lecherous old man*, she wanted to correct him, but she was supposed to be a role model. "He's the township supervisor, Billy. You shouldn't speak badly of him." But she couldn't be nice for much longer, and when she reached her car, she made a wry face. "But, yeah, he is sort of creepy, isn't he? Thanks for rescuing me back there."

Billy smiled and shrugged. "No problem, Miss H."

Jillian raised her hand to lightly touch the bruise around his left eye and hoped he hadn't gotten into a fight at school. Not that she would expect that of Billy, but boys would be boys, after all. "What happened to you?"

He brushed off her concern, but she noticed he straightened and puffed out his chest at the attention she gave him. "Oh. That. It's nothing. Got clobbered in gym class. Someone threw a mean elbow during a basketball game."

She winced in sympathy. "How do you like high school, besides the flagrant fouls?" She took the bags from him and put them on the front seat of her car.

He shrugged. "It's all right. Twelfth grade is a lot harder than fifth grade."

Jillian nodded in agreement. "I'm afraid so. Any favorite classes?"

"Auto Shop and Chemistry," he said instantly, breaking into a wide, toothy grin. "First I get to build things, and then get to I blow things up."

Jillian laughed. He was a typical boy. "Well, you'd better get back to work. Thanks again." As she drove off, she saw him in her rearview mirror waving until she drove off the lot.

# CHAPTER EIGHT

## MONDAY, SEPTEMBER 25

JILLIAN LOVED CHOCOLATE CUPCAKES. CHOCOLATE ANYTHING, for that matter. Katie Bittens was celebrating her fifth birthday and, in true kindergarten form, brought the little desserts for everyone in class to celebrate. She made sure everyone knew how hard she had worked helping her mother decorate them by adding the pink candy sprinkles on top. She pranced around the room, gleefully setting a cupcake in front of each child and finally Jillian, all while wearing a pink fairy princess costume — complete with elbow-length gloves, tiara, and wand — that she had received as a birthday gift Sunday and refused to leave the house without. "I put the sprinkles on," she announced to each and every child. "They match my princess dress. See? I'm a princess!" She twirled in her skirt, then anointed each child with her wand.

Jillian had made her wait until the end of the class to pass out the treats, knowing she would lose control of her students from the resulting sugar highs. They were bounding around the classroom enough as it was.

"Teacher!" MacKenzie Knightley, the resident tattle-tale, called out in a voice that meant she was about to rat out another student. "Zack put his fingers in my cupcake!"

"I did not!" the accused youngster replied, wiping his chocolate-stained hands on his pants.

Laughing, Jillian wiped both of them off with a paper towel and helped them gather their things to go home.

She sat back in the chair behind her desk and licked chocolate icing off her fingers as the last of the students left. She had an hour before the first parents arrived for conferences. Each family was allotted ten minutes to come and speak about their children, and with fourteen students in her class, that meant she had about two and a half hours of conferences looming ahead of her. She hated to do it, but at least this year she only had one class to put up with; last year conferences had taken two nights. Conferences were always hard, forcing her to break out of her shell and talk to strangers, but the first conferences of the year were by far the worst. She had to establish a rapport with new families every September. The thought left her paralyzed her with fear she struggled to overcome. *Just let it be over soon.*

By seven-thirty, she was tired and trying not to be cranky. Despite her dread, most of the conferences went well. Many of the parents were easy to talk to and expressed sincere interest in their children's education. Jillian was especially pleased that two mothers offered to be chaperones for the upcoming cider mill field trip without being asked, taking what she considered the burden of begging off her shoulders. With a sigh, she looked at her list of remaining parents and her crankiness increased. They were the parents of Jonathon Brothers and Emma Stone. She rolled the kinks out of her shoulders and tried her best to appear cheerful as Mr. and Mrs. Stone walked into the classroom and stood in front of her desk. He sported a crisp Armani suit and she wore enough glittering diamonds to open her own mine. They didn't seem to notice the chairs she had set out for them.

"Well, Miss Hobart, tell us. Is Emma a good student?" Mrs. Stone said. She sounded bored.

Jillian was too tired to stand to be eye-to-eye with the couple and stayed in her soft swivel chair. "Emma is a wonderful student, just like her brother. She's very smart and—"

"Yes, I know," Mr. Stone interrupted. "Has she been giving you any problems?"

"No." What kind of question was that? Emma was the quietest in her class and a model student. "She painted this today, I thought you might like to take it home." She pulled out a sheet of paper depicting a house and stick-figure family in bright paints. The child had drawn herself in sunny yellow, her parents in oppressive red, and her older brother in a deep blackish-blue.

Mrs. Stone snatched it from her without comment, folding it and shoving it inside her Louis Vuitton purse. Now the paints would chip and fall off, ruining the picture and, as Jillian uncharitably thought Mrs. Stone would be more concerned about, the inside of her expensive purse. Jillian pretended not to notice and continued speaking. "She's on par with her age group and eager to learn—." She was cut off again when Mr. Stone interrupted.

"On par? Are you saying our daughter is average?"

Jillian blinked at the forcefulness of the man's tone. "She's right where she needs to be for her development level." Under the table, she twisted the ring on her finger with rapid jerks.

"No child of mine will be called merely average. I pay a lot of money for Emma to attend school here, and I expect an exemplary education. Not an average one. Please see to that, Miss Hobart." Mr. Stone turned on his heel and stormed out of the room, and his wife followed, after a haughty glance at Jillian.

Jillian pressed her thumb and forefinger against the bridge of her nose. *Some people never change. There's no pleasing them no matter what I do.* She wanted a glass of wine and to sleep for a week. But she had one more conference to go.

When Simon Brothers walked in five minutes later, he was alone and dressed as if he came straight from the golf course in an argyle sweater and bright blue pants. Jillian's nerves were already frayed, and seeing him without his wife as a buffer made her want to crawl under her desk.

"I'm sorry Tiffany couldn't come with me tonight, but she just couldn't miss Brazilian gem night on the Home Shopping Network." He grinned salaciously. "Whatever my love wants, she gets."

"I'm sorry she couldn't be here," Jillian said in all sincerity.

"Call me Simon. I insist."

"Alright," she said with no intention of doing do. With shaking hands, she shoved her hair behind her ears, then took a deep breath to settle her nerves. "I enjoy having Jonathon in my class."

"I enjoy you being his teacher." He pulled a chair up to sit next to Jillian instead of across from the desk from her. "How is my boy doing?" He draped an arm over the back of her chair in an overly familiar way and leaned in closer still.

Jillian felt heat spreading across her chest and up her neck from a combination of embarrassment and indignation. If only she could tell him to stop hitting on her, or at least back up a few inches. But that would only make working with him the rest of the year awkward. She pressed her lips together into something she hoped resembled a smile.

The door to her classroom swung open and Antoinette Jones walked in. Jillian was so relieved to see her principal that she almost cried out.

"Mr. Brothers, how good of you to come to our parent-teacher conferences tonight," Antoinette said in her soft voice as he rose to greet her. "We appreciate any parental involvement with our students' education. Please, sit down, so we can discuss Jonathon's progress." She sat in the chair he had pulled next to Jillian, forcing him to move to the chair on the opposite side of the desk.

He appeared a little put out by the interruption but offered up one of his roguish smiles. "There's no problems with Jonathon, is there, for you to be here, Ms. Jones?"

Antoinette smiled brightly. "Not at all. I just like to sit in on these conferences once in a while to get a gauge on the children's progress and to address any concerns from the parents."

Jillian sat next to Antoinette and briefly detailed Jonathon's scholarly achievements, answering Mr. Brothers' questions in a polite but curt manner. She could feel his eyes locked on her during the entire conversation, just as she saw Antoinette kept her eyes on him. With Antoinette in the room, it was easier for Jillian to get down to business. "You son has great potential, but I would like to suggest he be tested for Attention Deficit Hyperactivity Disorder. When he focuses, he does great work, but more often than not he—"

"Oh, he's just a boy," Mr. Brothers cut her off with a dismissive wave of his hand. "That's what boys do. He'll grow out of it. Did you say they'll be going on any field trips this year?"

*Well, now I know where he gets it from,* Jillian thought saucily.

Finally, Mr. Brothers took his leave and Jillian heaved a sigh of relief. "Thank you so much, Antoinette, for coming in when you did. He was making me uncomfortable."

Antoinette nodded. "I've noticed that before, so I made it my plan to be here when he was. Sorry I wasn't here sooner."

"Oh, your timing was perfect!"

Antoinette's eyes narrowed. "Did he try something inappropriate?"

"No! Not at all." Jillian said. They were not even one month into the school year and she had to deal with the man until June. She didn't want to make the situation any worse by accusing a politician of anything unseemly.

The principal didn't look like she believed her, but didn't push the subject. "Well, why don't you go home. It's been a long night. I'll walk out with you."

***

*She belongs to me. Everything about her is mine.*

He had to make her see that. But she wasn't paying any attention, not any more, not like she used to. Not that he hadn't tried. He'd done everything he could think of to make her notice him, been as nice as he possibly could be, and still *nada*. But he would change that now.

*No more Mr. Nice Guy.*

Sitting alone in the darkened room, the only light from a glowing screen of a laptop computer, he spread open two books before him and read. The first book, his prize, his souvenir, motivated him. The second book, stolen from the library because he couldn't risk having his name attached to it on the check-out records, gave him all the answers. Then he saw the name. It was perfect. She was perfect.

"Three little kittens," he whispered, then laughed at how easy it would be. He was smarter than all of them. Humming to himself, he turned to his computer and began to type.

Soon she would be his, and they would live happily ever after.

# CHAPTER NINE

WEDNESDAY, SEPTEMBER 27

"I HAVE THREE APPLES," JILLIAN ANNOUNCED TO her class, who was giving her their rapt attention. She held out each apple one at a time while she counted them. "One, two, three. But what happens if I eat one of the apples?" She took a big, crunchy bite out of a Granny Smith, causing a ripple of giggles in her audience. The tart taste reminded her it was the apple Peter gave her last week, and she smiled as she wiped a dribble of juice from her chin. She took another bite, then placed the apple on the desk behind her and held up the remaining fruit. "Now how many apples do I have left?" She felt a surge of pride when most of the class shouted out the correct answer.

She was explaining that this concept was called subtraction when the classroom door opened and Antoinette walked in, dressed in brought, outlandish colors, as usual. Jillian felt invisible next to her. "Just a moment, class," she said as she turned to speak with the principal.

"I wanted to verify your attendance records for today," Antoinette said quietly. She sounded worried.

Antoinette's obvious anxiety rubbed off on Jillian. Personal verification of attendance by the principal wasn't common practice. "Domenic Rubino and Katie Bittens are absent today. Domenic has the chicken pox, so I guess it's going around and Katie has it too."

Antoinette shook her head. "No one called Katie in as absent, so we called her home. The housekeeper insists she put her on the bus, and the bus driver says she watched her get off the bus on the corner in front of the school. We've called her mother, and neither she nor the step-father has picked her up."

Jillian's hands balled into nervous fists that she hid in the pockets of her navy pencil skirt. She kept her voice low so she wouldn't scare the students. "Did you call the police?"

Antoinette shook her head. "I wanted to check with you first, just in case there was a mistake. But I'm calling them now. Don't worry," she added when Jillian's face paled. "We'll find her."

Returning to her class, Jillian tried to focus on the math lesson but found it difficult. She pictured the child wandering off the school grounds and getting lost or hit by a passing car. Then she remembered what happened to Joey and knew the lesson was over. Unable to concentrate and therefore unable to properly continue her math lesson, she passed out worksheets with apples in various amounts the children could color to combine math and art. She kept them inside for recess, playing Duck Duck Goose before their afternoon snack of graham crackers and apple juice.

When class was over, she followed them out to the parking lot and watched to make sure the children either got onto their proper bus or into a car with their parents. Several sheriff deputies' vehicles were in the parking lot, behind the buses. She hurried back to her classroom to find Antoinette waiting for her, and standing with her were Deputy Anderson and Peter in his official capacity. Seeing him for the first time since their disastrous date, she was self-conscious and unsure how to act around him. She decided to play it cool and ignored him. Taking refuge behind her desk, she shuffled stacks of paper as an excuse to keep her gaze off Peter.

"We've searched the grounds and have K-9 units out sniffing along the perimeter of the school," the deputy said, "but we think she got into another vehicle right away because they're not picking up any scent."

"Her parents still haven't heard from her?" Jillian asked.

Peter shook his head. "No one has. Once she got off that school bus, she vanished."

She frowned and twisted the ring around her finger, not sure if her anxiousness was because Katie was missing or Peter was so near. "That doesn't make any sense."

"No, it doesn't." Peter rounded the desk and walked toward her. "You said the intruder last week took your day planner, and it had the names of all your kids in it, right?"

She nodded. "Yes, it had names, addresses, allergies—." She stopped, stunned by sudden realization, and clutched Peter's arm. His bicep was thick and hard. Her hands lingered there a little too long, and when she realized she still held him, she quickly pulled back. "Oh God, that's how he knew Joey was allergic to peanuts, isn't it? That wasn't an accident, someone meant to harm my kids? And they're using my planner to find them?"

Peter glanced back at Deputy Anderson, who scribbled in his notebook. "It's possible."

Jillian turned away so he wouldn't see how afraid she was. He started to follow her, but Antoinette asked him a question and he had to turn back.

Needing to keep busy, Jillian walked to the back door that led to the playground. The parking lot where buses picked up students was about 10 yards to the right. She knew Deputy Anderson said a search of the playground had been completed, but she felt useless and, worse, helpless. Pushing open the door, she walked onto the asphalt school yard. A cool early fall breeze tousled her hair and she pushed it out of her eyes with an absentminded swipe. She didn't know what she was looking for, but couldn't stay cooped up in that classroom. She had to do something or go crazy.

She headed toward the first place she thought a child would go: the playground. It was empty now, no laughing children on the slides, teeter totter, or monkey bars. Closest to her classroom was the swing set, eight swings with black rubber seats attached to long metal chains. Draped across the second swing was an article of clothing one of the children left behind, and she went to retrieve it to add to her Lost and Found box.

She thought it was a scarf at first, but the climate was still too warm for anyone to be wearing a scarf. She was more confused when she discovered it was a glove, and it was not cold enough to be wearing those, either. Then she saw the piece of paper attached to

the glove with a safety pin. It was a paraphrase of a popular Mother
Goose nursery rhyme.

*One Katie Bittens*
*she lost her mittens*
*and she began to cry.*
*Oh mother dear,*
*I sadly fear,*
*My mittens I have lost.*
*What, lost your mittens,*
*You naughty Bittens?*
*Then you shall have to die.*

The typed note was signed in a large, sloppy scrawl, "Father
Noose."

Jillian felt as if the breath had been kicked out of her. The pink
glove was part of the princess costume Katie received for her birthday
and had been wearing ever since.

Her body went limp as she read the note, and she leaned against
the metal frame of the swing set for support. She ran through the
possibilities. The deputies searching the playground hadn't found the
note, which meant it was placed there recently. Which meant this
Father Noose was nearby. Which meant, so was Katie.

Frantic, she looked around, hoping to see the girl standing near
the fence separating the school yard from the surrounding cornfield,
laughing and waving her fairy princess wand like nothing was
wrong.

The only thing she saw waving were brown, withered
cornstalks.

*It would be easy to hide in there*, her mind whispered.

"Peter!" She screamed, dropping the glove back onto the swing
and dashing toward the fence. She glanced over her shoulder when
she heard him holler, "Jillian?" His broad shoulders filled the doorway
of her classroom, but he seemed so far away. "I found a note!" she
shouted. "I've got to find Katie!"

Wishing she were wearing jeans and sneakers instead of this long,
tight skirt and her mules, she hiked the skirt up around her hips and

delicately but quickly climbed the tall chain-link fence separating the two parcels of land. Launching herself off the top rung, she landed on all fours but recovered and took off like a sprinter, rushing headlong into the cornfield.

The towering stalks closed in around her. She knew she could get lost in the labyrinth of identical corn stalks, turning brown and dry at the end of the season. But still she ran on, calling Katie's name, looking for anything that might lead her to the child. The brittle husks slapped at her face, scratching her and drawing blood. When she stopped to catch her breath, she heard pounding footsteps and the rustling of drying leaves. *Oh Jillian, you idiot.* Was the kidnapper in here with her? Spurred on, she turned and rushed back in the direction she thought she came from, but couldn't be sure. It all looked the same. After only a few steps, she collided into outstretched arms and a hard body. Screaming, she flailed at the man with both hands, aiming for his eyes.

"Stop it. Stop." Peter, breathing hard from running, wrapped his arms around her in a bear hug of restraint, pinning her arms to her sides. "What the hell do you think you're doing?"

Coming to her senses, Jillian tried to catch her breath and not to think about how good Peter's chest felt pressed against hers. "I thought you were someone else."

"Exactly my point." His face was dark with fury, and she couldn't look at him because she knew that anger was rightfully aimed at her. "What if it wasn't me who found you?"

She decided to ignore the dire possibilities. "There was a note on the swing, a threatening note, and I thought maybe he was still here somewhere, hiding—"

"And you decided to confront him alone and unarmed in the middle of a corn field?"

"He took Katie. I had to do something," she shouted. She almost sobbed with the feeling of helplessness and terror for poor Katie.

Peter stiffened. "Who's 'he'?"

The adrenaline drained from her body and she let her head drop against his shoulder. "Father Noose. That's how he signed the note."

He released Jillian, but took firm hold of her hand and marched her back through the maize maze. Deputy Anderson was calling his name as they emerged, holding up a clear plastic bag containing the glove and the note.

"We've got a sick one here, boss," he said. He stood under the fence and caught Jillian around the waist, helping her down as she climbed the chain links.

Peter followed her without assistance, then took the bag and read Father Noose's note. "We need to get the prints off this. Did you touch it?" he addressed Jillian, his voice still stern.

"The glove, yes, but not the note," she replied meekly.

"Good." He handed the bag back to the deputy and snapped out orders. "Get this to the lab ASAP, then get someone else out here to go over this playground again, and make sure they do it right this time. And make sure the first person you question is the child's father."

"Got it." Aaron jogged off to do Peter's bidding. The tone of Peter's conveyed his irritation and left no room for argument.

"Which one?" Jillian asked as she sat wearily on a swing, pushing herself back and forth with her feet in the dusty sand.

Peter looked at her, his eyes still hard. "Which one what?" The tone of his voice told her he was still irritated with her.

"Father. She has two. Well, a father and a step-father."

Peter offered her his hand and pulled her to her feet. "I'll need to see her school file."

Jillian led him to the principal's office, where two uniformed deputies approached her. "Ma'am, we need to ask you a few questions."

She looked at Peter, who nodded. "Go ahead. I'll talk to the principal."

***

It was dark when the last of the detectives finished questioning Jillian. Even after repeatedly going over how she found the note, she had the distinct feeling the detectives didn't believe her. How did she find something no one else had? It worried her, but she realized they had to cover every possible theory. She also knew she wasn't the only one being questioned. Wally, Antoinette, and several other teachers with classrooms near the playground were also questioned. No one admitted to seeing the girl or knowing how the note was placed.

Deputies and teachers were heading toward their cars. She spotted Mike among the teachers retained for questioning. Peter was still on the school campus, having personally conducted a second and apparently fruitless search. As she stepped outside, he took her arm, escorting her past the small crowd to the parking lot.

"I don't like the idea of you being alone tonight," Peter said.

Yet another man thought her helpless. "I won't be. I called Donovan, and he and Tina are already at the house. They're staying with me tonight."

"Good. Then I don't need to worry as much." The tenderness in his voice conveyed he was no longer upset with her, and touched her. She bristled at it just the same.

"I'll be fine." She stubbornly yanked her arm from his grasp and she dug into her purse for keys. Peter leaned down to glance in her car's windows to make sure one was lurking inside. She noticed what he was doing and frowned. "I said I'll be fine."

"I know. But I can't help it. It's what I do." He straightened and faced her. "I wish the circumstances were different."

She couldn't look at him; she didn't want him to see the sadness in her eyes. "So do I."

"If they were different, I'd think about kissing you right now," he said.

She spun and stared at him. She had misunderstood, thinking he was merely offering condolences about the missing child. Her gaze wandered to his mouth and she wondered if maybe he would kiss her anyway. Too late, she realized she said it out loud. She froze, horrified at what she'd said, and backed away from him, stammering an apology. "I, um, I'm sorry. Forget I said that," she mumbled.

Peter gently took her arm, pulling her closer. He cupped her face with his hand, lightly tracing his thumb along the sharp red welt a cornstalk left on her cheekbone until she shivered, then tipped her head up toward the starry night sky. His breath was warm against her skin, then his lips were hot against her mouth. He lightly pressed his lips against hers, caressing. His kiss was soft and sweet, a testing, tasting kind of kiss, but it burned a trail of fire straight down to her toes. Her hands went to his shoulders to steady herself when she thought her legs would buckle under her. Closing her eyes, her breathy sigh melted into him as she relaxed against his body, tilting her head to invite him closer, and returned the kiss with a passion that surprised her almost as much as her request did.

His hand moved to cup her neck, and she felt his fingers tighten, pulling her closer still. With a shaky breath, Peter suddenly broke off the kiss and took a step back, releasing his hold on her. Weak-kneed and trembling, Jillian stumbled back a few steps. He stared at her, a serious, penetrating gaze she could feel in her bones, then he took a deep breath and smiled. "I'll do that better next time, when I see you Friday for our date," he said.

She had to remind herself to breathe. His touch left her shaken and her whole body burning. *It gets better than that? Is that possible?* She felt herself blushing again and was glad it was dark. Maybe he wouldn't notice.

With a squeal of rubber on pavement, a compact car sped by them, too close for comfort. Peter yanked Jillian hard against his side a scant second before the battered and rusty Honda's side-view mirror clipped her back.

"Who the hell was that?" Peter scowled into the dark after the vehicle.

Jillian sighed and closed her eyes. "Mike. He must have seen … us." She still couldn't describe what had just happened, but she knew Mike wasn't going to be happy about it. She hadn't yet found the opportunity to tell him the truth about why she refused to go out with him.

"He's got balls to drive like that in a place swarming with cops," Peter muttered, and signaled with his arm to get a deputy's attention.

Jillian lay her hand on his arm, pulling it down. "Don't. He's just mad at me. Ticketing him will only make it worse."

Peter glanced down at her and frowned. "Why is he mad at you?"

*Because I blew off his offer of a date. Because he probably saw you kiss me and he's jealous.* Jillian bit her lip and stepped back. *Like I can tell him any of that.* "It's nothing," she mumbled.

He dropped the subject but was still frowning. "If you say so. Get in your car and head home. I'll follow you to make sure you get back okay."

She rolled her eyes. "You don't need to do that."

"Humor me," he said with a smile, lightly brushing a finger under her chin.

Who could say no to that? Grumbling under her breath about presumptuous knights in shining armor, Jillian climbed into her car and drove off, and Peter pulled out behind her. When they reached her house a few minutes later, he waited until she parked her car and opened her front door, then honked and waved before he drove away.

Tina and Donovan were waiting for her in the living room, snuggled up together on the couch in front of the television, watching an old black and white movie.

"I've always liked a man in uniform," Donovan said with a dreamy look in his eye.

"Sergeant Dack does wear that uniform well," Tina remarked.

"Stop it, you two," Jillian said as she kicked off her shoes and joined them on the couch, wedging herself between her two friends. She knew they were only trying to cheer her up, but wasn't in the mood for their matchmaking. No way was she telling them that he kissed her, and certainly not that she enjoyed it.

They ignored her. "I think the military uniform is best, Navy in particular. It's the hat," Donovan said with a nod.

"Nah. It's the UPS guy. The guy who makes deliveries to Pop's restaurant, man, he's nice in his uniform." Tina swooned melodramatically.

Donovan was appalled. "UPS? Are you serious? With those horrid shorts?"

Tina shrugged. "That's the best part."

# CHAPTER TEN

FRIDAY, SEPTEMBER 29

PETER HAD A WRITTEN REPORT ON his desk at six a.m. Aaron apparently came in well before his regular shift to finish it. It was a short report so far, but there was enough in it to interest Peter.

Bleary-eyed, Aaron walked in with two mugs of steaming coffee while Peter read the document. "Good reading?"

"Best seller," Peter mumbled as he reached for the mug Aaron set before him without looking up. "Mom and step-dad have iron-clad alibis. Marcie Bittens-Rosenblum and Max Rosenblum were both at work."

"Yeah, and each had half their offices as witnesses," Aaron said, sitting in the chair opposite Peter's desk, and yawned widely. "But the biological father, well, he's a fun one. Not only did he not have an alibi, but just seemed to not really care his daughter is missing."

"Anything to get out of paying child support," Peter said.

Aaron shrugged. "Maybe. I'm not saying he did it or anything yet."

"Of course not." Peter shook his head. "Innocent until proven guilty and all that. But all he said was he was home sleeping, alone, when all this went down?"

"He works the graveyard shift the Ford Stamping Plant. But that's about all he would tell me. Said he wouldn't say anything else unless there's a warrant."

Peter decided he didn't like Katie's father, even if he turned out to be innocent. "Well, we can accommodate him. When Judge Jefferies gets in, we'll just get ourselves a warrant if it will make Mr. Bittens happy. Did he happen to say why he didn't want to talk?"

"Something about being hassled by his ex-wife. Thinks she's doing this to cut his visitation or up his child support payments, and doesn't believe his daughter is really in any danger." Aaron snorted. "Said he'll believe that when he sees the body."

Peter closed the folder over the report. "Give the man a Father of the Year Award," he said, his voice dripping sarcasm.

"You think he had something to do with it?" Aaron asked as he took the manila folder.

Peter nodded curtly. "The note was signed 'Father Noose.' I'm going to guess the word *father* isn't a coincidence. The note also mentions the mother. If it was an acrimonious divorce, the ex might be trying to get back at the child's mother." He sipped his coffee. "Revenge isn't pretty."

"Nope. So…" Aaron started, the craftiness in his voice immediately putting Peter on alert, "are you ever gonna tell me about that date with the teacher?"

"No." Peter wasn't one to kiss and tell. But mainly he didn't want to talk about it because he didn't want to feel guilty about it. He questioned the sanity of his decision to go on another date with Jillian when he would only end up hurting her. As a child Peter watched while his father destroyed his marriage, alienating his wife and children so he could be a better deputy, then the best deputy, working his way up to Undersheriff, all in the name of being elected Sheriff. The only time he saw his father lately was at work, discussing either criminal intent or political intent. He saw how it hurt his mother, and vowed never to do that to a woman, to his children. If being Sheriff meant being alone, so be it. He'd rather not have a family at all than have a miserable family.

But that didn't mean he couldn't take a pretty girl to dinner once in a while. For the first time that morning, he smiled.

\*\*\*

Notes were sent to parents explaining the need for everyone to be extra vigilant. Sheriff's deputies stepped up their patrols of the surrounding area. But still no one heard from Katie Bittens or her alleged abductor.

Jillian tried to ease her students' fears. They had some idea of what was going on, hearing it either from their parents or on the playground. She made sure to inform them of the dangers of talking to strangers and what to do if they were approached by someone they didn't know. The deputies were focusing the investigation on Katie's father, which would mean no other children would be harmed and her lesson, while important, would be thankfully unnecessary, but she wished she could be as easily reassured as her students.

She felt like she was always looking over her shoulder, expecting to find someone watching. She kept the students inside for recess all week, but finally relented when their pent-up energy made it next to impossible to teach them anything. She kept them close on the playground, chasing after them if they wandered too far away for her comfort level, hovering as she tried to watch them and her surroundings all at once. Antoinette told her she was overreacting, but she couldn't help it.

To make matters worse, Mike was no longer speaking to her. He was polite when necessary, ready with a simple and rather curt 'hello' when other people were present, but walked away if any further conversation was required or attempted. She knew he saw Peter kiss her and knew she should have told him the truth, but that didn't give him the right to act like a jealous teenager. If he didn't want to talk to her, she was fine with that – she almost preferred it – but she wished the tension between them wasn't so thick. It only added to her feelings of anxiety and guilt.

She felt so bad she almost cancelled her second date with Peter. The thought of having fun while her children were suffering sounded callous, but Donovan had talked her out of breaking the date. When Peter arrived to pick her up at seven-thirty, she barely managed a smile and didn't speak on the ride to the Italian restaurant in Romeo. The owners had plastered their front window with "missing" posters of Katie Bittens, and she had to look away from the little faces that seemed to stare at her accusingly.

Peter, following the hostess, led her through the crowded restaurant to a table topped with flickering candle and a vase holding a single, drooping yellow rose. He ordered them each a glass of Montepulciano red wine while Dean Martin crooned in the background, then waited until the glasses were set on the table before he spoke.

"It's not your fault."

With shaking hands, she organized a saucer full of sugar packets by color. Anything to keep from crying. "I feel so helpless."

He took her hand, interrupting her nervous organizing, caressing it gently with his thumb, making her shiver and almost forget why she was upset. "I know. So do I. But you have to believe me, there's nothing you could have done. No one saw what happened."

"That's what Donovan said." She sipped her wine and let it relax her. "But I just wish I could do something."

"Yeah, well, just as long as you're not running into cornfields anymore."

She cringed at the memory. "That was pretty stupid, huh?"

He grinned when she smiled sheepishly at him. "Yeah. Commendable, but stupid."

The waitress came for their order. Peter got the all-you-can-eat spaghetti special with extra meatballs, while Jillian ordered the chicken fettuccini. When the waitress left, Peter tried to steer the conversation to more cheery thoughts, but Jillian kept coming back to the topic at hand.

"It must get hard, dealing with all this evil all the time," she said. Peter's answer was delayed when the waitress brought their salads. Finding she didn't have much of an appetite, she nervously pushed a Kalamata olive around her plate with her fork. She was too wound up to eat; the anxious nerves that left her a little queasy whenever she thought of Katie were bad enough, but now she also had to contend with the bewildering way her stomach fluttered every time she looked at Peter. "How long have you been with the Sheriff's Department?"

"Since I graduated college, so—" Peter thought a moment "—fourteen years."

"That's a long time."

He nodded. "I didn't even realize it had been that long. Guess it's true what they say about time flying."

"You like it then."

"Wouldn't trade it for the world." He shrugged. "It's in my blood, you could say. My father's the Sheriff."

"I thought so." She pictured the opportunistic politician, always ready to kiss babies in the name of shameless self-promotion. The joke was he'd attend the opening of an envelope if he thought it might support his reelection bid. "If it weren't for the last name, though, I wouldn't have known. You're so ... different."

His fork stopped in mid-air and he stared at her for so long, she had to look away. She thought he was upset and was about to apologize when he said, "Thank you." He sounded sincere. His smile was genuine, and devastating.

She blinked and tried to find her voice. "So I take it he wanted you to join the department?"

Peter shrugged. "Yeah, but I was planning on it anyway. What he really wants is to groom me to replace him." His smile was gone, she noticed with disappointment.

The waitress returned with their main dishes. Jillian lay her fork down, no longer able to pretend she had an appetite. "Is that what you want?"

Peter was unable to reply because of the meatball in his mouth. After swallowing, he said, "No where to go but up, right?" His voice sounded upbeat, but somehow she wasn't convinced. "Dad's been showing me the ropes, taking me out on all his daily campaign stops when I'm not working on a case."

"You do that a lot?"

"Seems like that's all he does lately. He's been so busy with the campaign, he hasn't handled an actual investigation in three months. Not even a traffic ticket." He frowned as he paused to shove another meatball in his mouth. "He's a politician, not a cop." He said the last words under his breath, more to himself than to her.

Knowing she was pushing but curious, Jillian delicately asked, "And you're a cop, not a politician?"

His eyes flickered for a moment, but then his smile returned, making her feel warm. "Right." She knew he didn't want to talk about his father any more when he changed the subject. "How long have you been a teacher?"

"Nine years total, but only six at Cray Charter School. Have you dealt with many missing children cases?" Uncomfortable talking about herself, she quickly brought the conversation back his work, and to Katie.

He shook his head. "Yes and no. Most of them around here end up being runaways, or ugly divorces where the non-custodial parent takes the kid."

"You think that's what's happened here?"

Peter spoke carefully. "Possibly. Most of those cases have happy endings. If there is something fishy, it's just a complaint about someone lurking around bus stops, and the guy's usually caught before anything bad happens." He polished off the last of his spaghetti and snatched the olive from her plate, popping it into his mouth. He stared at her for a long moment, making her fidget, before he spoke. "Enough of the depressing talk. Finish up, I want show you something."

She picked out one last piece of chicken from her pasta while he paid the bill, then followed him out to his truck. He didn't say where he was taking her, but the ride was short. He stopped at a park with wooden benches and walking trails that led to a Japanese-style bridge spanning a narrow burbling creek. Dusk had settled, and the stars were starting to come out. He took her hand to help her from the truck, and didn't let go as he led her toward the bridge and pointed out constellations in the evening sky. She felt the spark of electricity at such a simple touch, and when he smiled down at her, she looked away, blushing.

Nuzzling into her soft hair, he whispered into her ear, "See that one up there? That's the Big Dipper."

His attempts to impress her made her giggle. "Everyone knows the Big Dipper, Peter."

Encouraged by her laughter, he said, "Okay, sure, but have you ever heard of the Medium Dipper?"

"No." She laughed at him, and he smiled back at her, their eyes locking for what seemed an eternity. Her breath caught in her throat as she stared up at him.

"Yeah, neither have I," he said, breaking the moment.

Laughing, he laced his fingers with hers and gave her hand a little squeeze. She felt giddy. He leisurely led her over the bridge and toward the tree line along the edge of the park. Crickets chirped in the grass, chiming in with the frogs singing in the water.

A chill hung in the air, and when Jillian shivered he put his arm around her shoulders and pulled her close. Smiling up at him, she leaned against his warm body and wrapped an arm around his waist for lack of a better place to put it. It felt so comfortable, so natural, to talk with and touch him. Normally she'd be what Donovan liked to teasingly call a 'shrinking violet' — a term she hated — timid and nervous with a man so near, near enough to touch. But not with Peter. She was starting to feel completely at ease with him, which ironically made her uneasy if she dwelled on that strange new fact. She tried to think of something to talk about so she wouldn't dwell on it.

"I haven't been here before," she said.

"It's new, the city's attempt to make everything bigger and better. It was a vacant lot a few weeks ago," Peter said. "They're putting in a little strip mall on the other side of these trees."

"Like we need more of those."

Peter shrugged. "Can't stop progress."

They walked down a narrow paved trail that meandered into the trees and looped back around to the entrance of the park. The lights of the shopping center glinted through the thinning leaves and reflected off the creek to their left. It was pretty, but something wasn't right. Jillian stopped and tugged on Peter's arm, forcing him to stop as well.

"What is that smell?" She wrinkled her nose as a rancid stench accosted her nostrils.

"It's probably the Dumpster out behind that strip mall." He peered through the trees at the lights illuminating the back entrance of a coin-operated laundry.

"Ew. Let's get out of here." She put one hand over her nose and breathed through her mouth as the smell became overpowering.

Peter pivoted on his heel to walk back in the direction they came from but suddenly froze where he stood, eyes wide as he stared into the trees.

"Jillian, go back to the truck."

"Why?" She was puzzled and a little crestfallen, wondering why he seemed to be abruptly ending their date. Again. Story of her life. Maybe dating wasn't all it was cracked up to be. Maybe there was still time to become a nun.

He pulled his keys from his jeans pocket and pressed them into her hand as he spoke. "Go back to the truck now and wait for me inside. Lock the doors." His voice changed; he sounded so severe. Like a sergeant. Startled by the strength of his command, she looked up at him but his face was unreadable, his eyes trained on something just over her shoulder.

"Peter, what—." And then, despite his best efforts to prevent it, she saw it too, shimmering ghostly white in the light from the full moon and the shopping center floodlights, lying along the side of the creek bed. Feral animals and time had already taken their toll. She took an involuntary step backward, bumping into him. "Oh my God."

He pulled out his cell phone with one hand and gave her a little push on the small of her back with the other. "Go," he said, gently this time.

It was all the motivation she needed. She fled, stumbling blindly, running as fast as she could from the image of the pale, limp body and wide, unseeing eyes of little Katie Bittens, her face frozen forever in a silent scream.

# CHAPTER ELEVEN

THE NAUSEA PASSED, AND JILLIAN WAS surprised she had been able to keep her dinner down. She had never seen a dead body before and knew the horrifying image would stay with her for as long as she lived. She sat huddled in the passenger seat of Peter's truck, the doors locked and her head between her knees, for what seemed liked hours when a rapping on the window had her bolting upright with a startled yelp. Peter stood outside. He rapped again. "Let me in."

Relieved, she pressed the button to release the locks and Peter climbed in. He sighed and, closing his eyes, lay his head back on the seat's headrest. He looked drained and suddenly several years older.

"It was Katie." Jillian knew without being told.

"Yes," he answered, sounding desolate. "I'm sorry."

She debated with herself, wondering if she really wanted to know, before she asked the obvious question. "What happened?"

Peter opened his eyes and looked at her. "That's for the coroner to decide, but it looks like she was strangled."

She shouldn't have asked. Even with the hand she clamped over her mouth, she couldn't muffle the whimper she made in response.

He started the engine. "I'm taking you home. The sergeant on duty can handle things without me." They drove in silence for several miles before he spoke again. The lightness in his tone sounded forced. "We don't seem to be having much luck with this whole date thing."

Her heart lurched, but she saw a teasing glint in his eye. She offered him a weak smile. "I never was very good at it."

"Hey, at least it's not boring." He reached across the seat to squeeze her knee in a gesture of comfort. It took all her effort not to burst into tears.

Willing herself to stay calm, she took a deep breath and stared out the side window, watching the street lights pass by in a blur. "What was she doing out here?"

"It's about, what, five miles from the school? That's not too far. Could be near where the, um, suspect lives."

She knew he meant to say something more sinister, like *murderer*. "Why would he leave her near his house? Wouldn't that be suspicious?"

"Yeah, but it wouldn't be the first time that's happened. People have been known to bury victims right in their own back yard."

She shook her head, appalled. "That wasn't a back yard, or even a yard. It was right out in public. Poor Katie."

Peter squeezed her leg again. She put her hand over his and held on tight.

Distraught, Jillian began whispering to herself. "What's that?" Peter asked.

"Sorry. I was … never mind. It's morbid." She shuddered. Releasing Peter's hand, she crossed her arms over her chest to ward off the sudden chill and looked away, berating herself for letting him hear her nervous rambling.

"Tell me."

She hesitated. "For some reason, that rhyme with the glove popped into my head."

"Father Noose's note? Huh."

"What?"

"That name. It's not a reference to a parent. It's a play on Mother Goose, isn't it?"

She thought about that for a moment, then nodded and repeated the verses, louder this time.

"Say that again!" Peter demanded.

"Hmm? Oh. The rhyme. There's the verse he left, about kittens losing their mittens. But he changed the last line. It should be, 'Then you shall have no pie'." She couldn't bring herself to say the words Father Noose used. "In the other verses, they find their mittens, then the mittens get dirty, and they have to wash their mittens." She shook her head. "I don't know why I thought about it. Like I said, it's morbid."

Peter was silent for a long moment. "They had to wash their mittens," he said slowly.

"Yeah. It's just a silly rhyme."

"Maybe not. She was found behind a Laundromat."

She turned in her seat and looked quizzically at him. "She was in the creek."

"Which is behind the laundry."

"So?"

"It's in the rhyme. The kittens, or Katie Bittens, had to wash mittens. He left the glove, in lieu of a mitten, to go with the rhyme, so maybe he used the laundry the same way." He snorted in derision. "He thinks it's funny." His head snapped to look at her when she gasped loudly. "What?"

"I remembered the last lines. 'Oh mother dear, did you not hear, our mittens we have washed. What, washed your mittens? Then you're good kittens*! But I smell a rat close by.*" She stressed the last sentence and shuddered.

Peter nodded. "So do I."

# CHAPTER TWELVE

MONDAY, OCTOBER 2

PETER PULLED HIS SQUAD CAR UP to the curb in front of Jillian's house and watched her work as he climbed out. Her coppery hair was pulled back in a ponytail and her cheeks were flushed with the exertion of pushing an oversized and outdated lawn mower across the lawn. Her hips swayed as she walked with long, purposeful strides. She was beautiful. Shaking his head, he pushed the thought from his mind. If he kept thinking like that, he was going to get himself in trouble.

Pivoting the mower around a towering elm tree to head back in the other direction, she saw him and turned off the motor. He could tell by her eyes she was both exhausted and confused, probably wondering why he was there. So was he. *I should have called first*, he thought. He knew she went to Katie's funeral that morning and thought she might need a shoulder to cry on, but it appeared she was coping just fine without him. Unsure how she'd react to his unannounced presence, he was grateful for the mirror-tinted Ray-Bans that hid his expression. He leaned back against the wheel well of the car, one foot casually crossed over the other.

"Hope I'm not interrupting anything," he called.

"Not really. I hate mowing." She swiped at stray grass blades stuck to her forehead and walked toward him. "Is something wrong?"

"Yes," he said, then mentally kicked himself when panic flashed over her face. "The sweet and sour chicken is getting cold."

She squinted at him, the smooth skin of her forehead wrinkled. "What?"

"Dinner." He held up a brown paper bag. "I've got a few minutes, so I wanted to try to spend some time with you where I wouldn't need to file a report afterwards." His smile deflated at her confused look. "But you're busy." Of course she was busy. So was he. What was he doing here? He didn't have time for dating. He'd only end up hurting her. Yet here he was, wooing her with Chinese food like a moron.

"Oh." She hesitated at first, fidgeting with the hem of her ratty college sweatshirt, but then she smiled up at him and his worries melted away. "Well, I'm a little dirty, but we can sit on the porch."

Grinning, he pulled off the sunglasses and hooked them over his uniform shirt pocket so he could admire her long legs and round butt as she bent over to rinse her hands with the garden hose. Then he pushed away from the car and joined her on the tiny slab of cement she called a porch. Digging into the bag, he pulled out two white take-out boxes and passed one to her. He sat next to her, his elbows on his knees, and shoveled food into his mouth with a plastic fork. She ate slower, trying to balance the box with one hand while carefully eating small bites with chopsticks he thought to grab at the last second.

"This is great, Peter. Thanks."

"You're welcome." He hesitated, wondering if he should bring up an unhappy subject. "How was the funeral?"

Jillian turned her head away, but not before he saw tears well up in her eyes. "It was lovely," she said, sadness evident in her voice. "They had five pink balloons at the cemetery, one for every year of her life, and they let them go at the end of the service." Her voice cracked, and she set the half-eaten take-out box on the ground.

*Nice going, Pete. Ruined her appetite* and *made her cry*. He shook his head. Aaron was right: he had no idea what to do with women. He changed the subject as nonchalantly as he could. "So help me figure something out." He paused to stick a pineapple chunk in his mouth. "I thought you rented this place."

"I do." She sent him a confused glance.

"Then why are you mowing the lawn? Shouldn't the landlord do that?"

She shrugged. "I just needed something to do to keep busy today. But I do this all the time now. When my hours and pay at the school got cut, I negotiated to lower the rent if I did the yard work."

"Impressive." He nodded his approval.

Shaking her head, Jillian said, "Not impressive. Just self-preservation."

He grinned at her, appreciating her streak of stubborn independence. He thought about how much he wanted to kiss her again and lowered his gaze to her mouth.

"What?" she asked, wary.

"What what?" he replied mischievously.

She turned her head and stared down at her feet. Was she blushing? "Stop looking at me like that," she mumbled.

Peter set his empty take-out box on the porch next to her hip. "You know, it occurs to me, I never gave you that kiss I promised you Friday." She was definitely blushing now. And damn if that didn't turn him on.

For a long moment, she didn't say anything, and he wondered if he'd pushed too far. "No," she said finally, her voice soft, still staring intently at her feet, "I don't believe you did."

He moved forward then, placing two fingers on her chin to tip her face toward him, forcing her to look at him. Gazing into her sad green eyes, he leaned in and gently took possession of her mouth. She gasped as if surprised, but then leaned into the kiss. He closed his eyes and found himself thinking it was just as he promised her it would be: better than before, better than he could have imagined as his lips cruised softly over hers. He moved his hand from her chin to cup the back of her head, pulling her closer. He felt her hand on his chest, clutching at the fabric of his shirt as she fell against him. With a low moan, she parted her lips and allowed him to touch his tongue to hers, and suddenly the kiss was hot and hard. He couldn't get enough of her, and pulled her closer still until she was almost in his lap.

His cell phone unexpectedly vibrated in his pocket, startling him out of the kiss. *Damn.* Reluctantly moving away, he pulled it out and looked at the screen. His father. *Double damn.*

"Sorry," he said to Jillian as he answered the call. "Hello?"

"Peter, where are you, boy? I've been waiting with basted bread for you over here."

"What?" Peter blinked. He was used to his father mangling his metaphors, but his mind was elsewhere and that one confused him. "Do you mean baited breath?"

"Yeah, sure, whatever. We're supposed to speak at the Sterling Heights city council meeting in forty-five minutes. You've got places to be, son, people to meet, elections to win!"

Peter scowled, the reminder obliterating the memory of Jillian's soft, plump, yielding mouth. So far work had interrupted every single attempt he had made to see her. That should tell him something.

He saw Jillian's eyes widen as she watched him. "Is everything okay?" she asked.

He nodded and tried to make his expression neutral. "Everything's fine, sweetie," he said, not wanting her to think the call was about the Father Noose investigation.

"Sweetie?" Patrick bellowed on the other end of the line. "I've been called a lot of things in my life, but I can't say I've ever been called that, not by my son anyway."

"I was talking to Jillian," Peter muttered, then plowed ahead, hoping to change the subject before his father could interrogate him. "Where am I meeting you again?"

His father didn't take the hint. "Jillian? That woman who drove your squad car to save that kid? Ah, right, yeah, I see. Well, then, I won't bother you, son. I'll get out of your hair. Take your time." He hung up.

Peter stared at the phone. That was possibly the least talkative his father had ever been. What the hell was he up to?

Jillian leaned in toward him, looking up questioningly, her lips once again within range of his, distracting him. "Who was that?"

"My father." Taking advantage of her closeness, and wanting to end on a good note for once, he kissed her again. She tasted sweet, like the pineapple from dinner. It was easy to fall right back into the kiss – too easy. But his father kept popping into his brain, putting a major dent in his enjoyment of her. He pulled back. "I've got to go."

Her eyes were closed, but flew open at his words. "What?" She blinked, confused, and he noticed her breathing was ragged. So was his. "Why?"

He asked himself the same question. Dismissing it, he tried to regain his train of thought and offered her a slow smile. "I'm still on duty. I've got to get back to work." He stood to leave, but stopped and swore. He looked at her over his shoulder. "But I'll be back."

She bit her lip and looked away, and his nagging doubts returned. But his smiled widened when she replied in a soft voice, almost a whisper, "Good."

# CHAPTER THIRTEEN

TUESDAY, OCTOBER 3

JILLIAN WAS CORNERED IN THE HALL near the teachers' lounge by Mike, who questioned her about the funeral and criminal investigation. Most of his focus was on the rumor that she was present when the body was discovered. It was not something she wanted to discuss, but Mike was relentless in his quest for every gory detail.

"It's too bad this psycho's targeting your kids. Although, I suppose if I had been offered the job, they'd be *my* kids. Hey, Tristan!" He interrupted their conversation to speak to a boy passing them. "Great pitching this season. You've got a great arm. You'll play Little League again next summer, right?"

The boy grinned. "You bet! Thanks, Coach G.!"

Mike returned his attention to Jillian. "But, hey, anyway, are the rumors true? I heard part of her face was eaten away by foxes and raccoons," he said.

Her stomach lurched as his graphic questioning brought back an all-too-vivid memory of Katie's body in the creek, and she decided there was no better time than the present to apologize for blowing off their supposed date. Not a pleasant subject, but it had to be better than decayed corpses.

"Mike," she began, hesitating as she searched for the right words. "I think I misunderstood you the other day. I didn't realize you wanted to go out that day and I ended up making other plans instead. I'm sorry."

He smiled and leaned in as if they were sharing a secret. Their foreheads almost touched, he was so close. "That's alright. How about I make things cut and dry for you this time? I'd like to take you to dinner tomorrow night. Say, five o'clock? There's a little deli that opened out on 26 Mile Road in Washington, in that new strip mall near the historic Octagon House. I head they have great corned beef."

*Corned beef? Is he serious?* Her stomach made another threatening roll. "Oh, um, I don't know," Jillian stammered. This wasn't going as well as she had hoped. "See, the thing is, um…"

Mike moved away quickly, tension back with a vengeance. "Oh. I get it."

Surprised and a little ashamed by the accusation in his voice, Jillian tilted her head down, casting her eyes away. "Get what?"

"You're seeing that cop, aren't you?"

She felt herself flush. *How did he figure that out? Oh yeah, the parking lot.* She remembered that night, and that first kiss, which led her to remember the second kiss, and the flush was no longer one of embarrassment. Then she caught Mike glaring at her, and she stammered, "Oh. Well. Not seeing, exactly."

"What, exactly, then?"

She was torn. On one hand, he deserved the truth. On the other hand, it was none of his damned business. With a sigh, she went with the truth. "We've only been on a couple dates." *If you could call them dates.*

Mike's features contorted into a pout. "Obviously, you prefer him over me?"

How was she supposed to answer a loaded question like that without hurting his feelings? "I like you, Mike, but, as a co-worker and a—"

"So we're just co-workers, then? Fine," Mike snapped. "I can be a co-worker. That's what I've always been. I hope your children enjoy Library Time this afternoon. I understand the kindergartners get a big kick out of it." He picked up his coffee mug and stalked away before she could utter another word.

He hadn't allowed her to finish her sentence. She would have called him a friend as well, but she decided it was probably for the best. If he really were a friend, he would have reacted better to her announcement. Rolling her eyes in exasperation, she headed to her room to prepare for class.

***

Moving with brisk strides down the hallway of the school, his top lip curled into a sneer as he thought about all the stupid little brats who stood between him and Jillian, taking up all of her time and attention that could be better spent on him. But he knew how to fix that now.

Hearing the clicking footsteps of high-heeled shoes echoing on the tile lining the hallway, he slunk into the lavatory and quietly closed the door behind him. The antiseptic scent was familiar to him. He towered over the miniature sinks and urinals specially tailored for boys five feet tall and under. He thought about her to pass the time. Her voice was low and soft and breathy, a real turn on, just like that whore who answered the phone when he'd dialed that 900-number late at night and made him so hot. Just thinking how Jillian sounded when she said his name was making him hot. He needed to think of something else, to focus. *Jillian is wearing that fuzzy brick-colored sweater I like so much today. It's one of my favorites. I love the way it clings to her round, plump breasts, making them look so soft and inviting…*

He realized he was breathing heavily. He was letting himself get distracted and shook the fog from his mind. Focusing on the present, he smiled as he played his plan over in his mind. The rhyme was perfect, better than before, and he was feeling cocky because everything was going so well. It had been surprisingly easy to kill the stupid whiny girl. He thought it would be hard to do, because he didn't have a problem with kids in general. It wasn't part of his original plan, but once it came down to it, he couldn't wait to get his hands around her throat, if only to shut up her incessant babbling about being a goddamn fairy princess.

*I took her right from under their noses without anyone being any the wiser, and I can do it again. Today. It makes me feel powerful. No, omnipotent. Yes, that's a better word. Godlike. No one can stop me.* His blood surged with thoughts of the power he had and how he would use it. Jillian would be so impressed with his power, she'd be begging him to fuck to her. He imagined her on the floor, on her knees before him, telling him how hot she was for him, and he trembled. Oh yes. No one could take her, or anything else that belonged to him. She was his now.

***

The students were little terrors. In order to attend Katie's funeral the day before, Jillian had requested a substitute teacher, who had allowed the children to paint, play with modeling clay, and generally do nothing resembling education. Jillian tried to present her Michigan geography lesson, showing them with a large, colorful map that showed how the two peninsulas looked like a mitten and a bunny-rabbit, but they were having none of it, restless and giddy as they were. Glad it was nearing the end of the afternoon, she announced Library Time, where the children could to run amok with the intent of checking out books their parents could read with them at home.

Several students were overjoyed about the prospect of finding new books to read. Allen Etter, the brightest in her class, was first in line, standing a whole head taller than the rest of the students. "Yay! The libary! Miss Hobart, can we go to the libary now?" He pushed his constantly sliding glasses, its thick lenses comically enlarging his eyes, back up his nose.

She ruffled his curly red hair and tried not to chuckle as she corrected his mispronunciation. "It's *library*, Allen, you're missing an R. And yes, we can go now. Walk, please!" she added when he took off like a shot down the hallway.

She followed them to the library, separated from the enclosed classrooms by a maze of hallways. As soon as the kids saw the huge cardboard cutout of the Cat in the Hat, they ran toward the shelves and started arguing over who would take home which book.

"There's plenty of books for everyone. If you don't get what you want, you can try again next week," she reminded them as she walked down an aisle where three boys were arguing over their book, each grabbing an edge and pulling in a three-way tug-o-war.

"Read this to me, Teacher," MacKenzie Knightley pleaded with big, round, puppydog, brown eyes. Jillian got down on her knees to be eye level with the girl and started to read her the opening lines of

*Madeline* when the electricity went out and the room turned black. There were no windows in the enclosed room, making it feel like a tomb. The children, frightened and disoriented, started screaming, and as she tried to adjust her vision to the inky darkness, she heard the librarian, a petite, elderly woman, call out for calm.

"It's alright, kids," Jillian said loud enough to be heard over the din. "Everyone stick together. Find the nearest person and hold hands. I'm coming around to find you all." *Good thing I'm not claustrophobic,* she thought as the darkened room closed oppressively around her. She tentatively felt her way forward and found Tyler Watson and Allen, and made them hold hands with MacKenzie, who had been clinging to her tan moleskin skirt in terror, creating a train. "Hold on and follow me," she commanded.

She followed the plaintive sounds of crying children. She felt a little better when the librarian announced she had Emma Stone and Jessica VanDysen. "We're by my office, dear," she called out. "I'll stay here with them."

"Thank you, Mrs. Keding." Rounding another stack of books, Jillian added a wailing Clare Peck to her train, caught Jonathon Brothers by the shirt collar as he ran by, then tripped over something on the floor and fell to her hands and knees just as the lights flickered back on.

"See, everything's alright," she said in a soothing voice as she rose up from the floor. The children instantly quieted, aside from some sniffling. Looking around to account for the children, she noticed the book she had tripped over. The pages were scrawled in red crayon. Incensed that one of her students may have defaced public property, she said, "Okay, who wrote all over Mother Goose?" Then her brain registered what the book was and what the scribbles said and her blood ran cold.

*Father Noose was here.*

"Oh God, no," she whispered as a sudden, paralyzing fear gripped her. Looking up, she quickly counted children gathered around her. Even with the known absences, she came up short and, with dread in her heart, picked up the book. Scanning the rhyme, her breath caught in her throat, then came out in a scream.

"Robynne!"

# CHAPTER FOURTEEN

PETER BURST INTO THE OFFICE, THE run from the parking lot leaving him panting, his eyes dark and full of fear. He had only heard the basics when the radio dispatcher called for backup. He recognized the school as Jillian's and hoped it was just a coincidence. But there was Jillian, sitting in a straight-backed armchair in the principal's office, her arms wrapped around her torso, anxiously rocking back and forth. Principal Jones stood behind her while a pair of Sheriff Department detectives peppered her with questions. "I got here as fast as I could. What happened?" he demanded of Jillian.

She looked away from him, but not before he noticed how pale she was.

"Thanks for coming, Sergeant," the younger of the two detectives said. His badge showed his name was David Livernois. "We were just about to ask Miss Hobart how she knew the missing girl's name was Robynne Smolenski." He sounded cocky, which must have annoyed Jillian. It sure annoyed him.

"I know all my students' names," she said.

The second detective, Bob Lewandowski, whose unkempt beard and rumpled uniform made him appear much older than his partner, was more patient than his partner and reworded the question. "But how did you know she was the one who was missing?"

"She's not here, is she?" she snapped.

Peter knew she was struggling to remain calm because he was doing the same. Why weren't they out looking for the girl, instead of sitting here asking her stupid questions?

Ms. Jones patted her shoulder. "Why don't you just tell them what you told me," she said.

Jillian motioned to the book on the desk before her, open to a page covered with blood-red crayon. "The rhyme told me."

"She's not making any sense," Livernois said, slapping his hands on his thighs in frustration.

The principal's head snapped up, her soft voice sharp. "She's in shock. I think she has every right to say whatever she wants."

Peter leaned over the two detectives' shoulders so he could see the book. As he read the words scrawled across the pages, his whole body tensed. "I think she's making perfect sense," he said. Using a tissue so he wouldn't leave fingerprints, he gingerly picked up the book to take a closer look.

"Don't bother. Every kid in this school has had their paws on that book. We're not gonna get any useful prints off it," the first detective said, shaking his head.

"I'll follow procedure just the same, Detective Livernois," Peter said sternly, eliciting a sheepish look from the younger man. "As I was saying, what Miss Hobart says does make sense. Have either of you thought to look at the title of this particular rhyme?"

"It's one of a million kids' books from the library, a bunch of meaningless nursery rhymes," Livernois said with a dismissive wave of his hand.

"Remind me to send you back through forensics training," Peter said through gritted teeth, then tossed the book into Livernois' lap. "The name of the nursery rhyme is *Who Killed Cock Robin.* The child's name was Robynne. I don't think it's a coincidence. Read it."

Fidgeting under his sergeant's glare, the detective started reciting the words. "Who killed Cock Robin? I, said the sparrow, with my bow and arrow, I killed Cock Robin. Who saw him die? I, said the fly, with my little eye, I saw him die. Who caught his blood? I, said the—"

"Enough," Jillian said weakly. She covered her ears with her hands and closed her eyes, as if trying to block it all out.

Her fear set off something primal in Peter and he clenched his fists at his sides, struggling to maintain a professional demeanor.

*This is business.* "Where was the patrol car during the blackout?" he demanded.

Detective Lewandowski spoke up. "Deputy Ciamantaro had just completed a drive-by not ten minutes before, Sergeant."

Peter paced in a circle around the group as he spoke. "No more drive-bys. I want someone posted here permanently. I want them here before school starts to sweep the building before students arrive, and remain on the premises until the last student leaves. Understood?"

Both detectives agreed, while the principal vigorously nodded her approval of the plan.

"What about her?" Livernois tilted his head in Jillian's direction, his voice still accusatory.

Peter stopped pacing and looked at her. Her face was pale and etched with guilt and fright. He made a snap decision. "You two are done here," he said. "I want to check in on Deputy Anderson with the girl's parents, and then I want to ask Miss Hobart a few questions. Alone."

After Livernois and Lewandowski filed out of the room, Peter pointed at Jillian and ordered her to stay put until he got back. Then he asked Ms. Jones to direct him to a cramped conference room before ordering her to stay with Jillian.

Opening the office door, Peter slammed into the teacher he recognized as Mike Georginidis. He had been standing close to the door. Too close.

"Whoa. Sorry, sergeant." He shoved his hands in his pockets and walked off, in a hurry.

Peter watched him leave, unsure what to make of the man's actions. Was he eavesdropping or just walking by at the wrong moment? He put his thoughts aside when he heard raised voices. Opening the conference room door, he was accosted by angry shouts. "You have got to be kidding me. We were both at work when this happened, because you yourself called us there, but you think somehow we managed to kidnap Robynne while we were at work?" The girl's father, his face red, berated Aaron, who tried unsuccessfully, in a much quieter voice, to calm him.

"No, sir, that's not what—"

The mother didn't let him finish. "And our own daughter! Never mind we were 20 miles from here. She's our daughter! Why would we kidnap her when she was due to come home in half an hour anyway? That's just absurd."

"Mrs. Smolenski, I was just—"

"When we drop off our daughter, we entrust these school officials with her safety. They failed us, but you're not talking to them. It's that teacher's fault. She was supposed to watch her. Robynne's the second child in her care that's gone missing. Maybe you should be talking to her."

Peter swore to himself. He didn't like where this conversation was heading. If these two were thinking like that, so was everybody else.

Aaron spoke quickly, his words meshing together in his rush to be heard before he was interrupted again. "We will speak with them ma'am but it's routine to question the family members as well."

"This is preposterous! I want to speak to your superior!" Mr. Smolenski hollered, leaning over the table to shove a finger into Aaron's chest. "I'm going to have your badge for this."

If the situation weren't so serious, Peter would have laughed at the look on Aaron's face. His jaw was clenched, and his smile not cordial so much as it was simple bared teeth. He looked like he wanted to throw these people through the wall, and Peter didn't blame him. Peter knew he would never act on such a violent impulse, and also knew he had lost control of the situation. He stepped in while Aaron fidgeted in discomfort.

"I'm Sergeant Peter Dack. You can speak to me, sir." He stood behind the still seated Aaron, his arms crossed over his chest.

"The Sheriff's son? Good, finally someone who can do something," Mr. Smolenski said, and Peter tried not to cringe at the reference and its implications. "Do you realize this man has accused us of kidnapping our own daughter?"

Peter saw Aaron shake his head ever so slightly. "Well, sir, if he followed our established procedures, and I'm quite sure that he did because he is one of Malcolm County's finest, I doubt very highly that he has accused anyone of anything at this point. As a member of the Sheriff's Department, Deputy Anderson has to make sure all bases are covered as part of a thorough investigation, and that does include interviewing any and all family members who may have had recent contact with the victim." He kept his voice firm but quiet, forcing the irate man to shut up and listen. "I would think you should be glad that we are pursuing all possible avenues in order to find your daughter, including talking to you. That is, of course, unless you have something to hide." He stopped and regarded them with impassive eyes.

Mrs. Smolenski gasped, and her husband stammered and stuttered, too stunned to offer a coherent reply.

Smiling tersely, Peter continued. "I assume you will cooperate fully with Deputy Anderson for the duration of this investigation." He motioned for Aaron to join him. Excusing himself, Aaron stood and followed Peter into the hall, closing the door behind him.

"Damn, you're good," Aaron said.

"That's why I'm the sergeant. Did you see the note?"

Aaron shook his head. "There was another note?"

"Well, not an actual note this time, but a calling card, I guess you could call it. Father Noose strikes again."

"No shit. Well, that blows your theory out of the water, doesn't it?"

"About Todd Bittens? Probably." Peter didn't like that one bit. "That probably means the Smolenskis are off the hook, too, but keep up the questioning anyway. Might get something out of it."

"You mean besides a headache?" Aaron said.

Peter's lips almost twitched into a smile. "Better you than me."

Shaking his head, Aaron rejoined Robynne's parents in the conference room.

Peter returned to the principal's office. He found Jillian sitting on a leather couch, her head in her hands, while Principal Jones sat next to her, leaning in close, speaking in tones too low for him to overhear. The principal saw him, and, patting Jillian on the shoulder, left her office and closed the door behind her to give them privacy.

Even once they were alone, Jillian would not look at him. Her eyes darted from the desk to the wall behind him to her feet, but never directly at him. He sat next to her and tried to take her hand, but she shifted subtly, just enough to place her hand out of reach. He knew he was being rebuffed, but he sat patiently and waited for her to speak.

After a few minutes of his silent staring, she spoke up. "They think I did it."

"Why do you say that?"

"Those detectives made a point of telling me no other teachers have had a problem. Only my kids go missing. Why is that?" She spared him a quick, sideways glance before returning her gaze to her feet.

Peter kept his face impassive. "It's all part of routine questioning. They have to consider everyone a suspect at first."

"And you're their sergeant." She said it so quietly, almost a whisper, he had to strain to hear the words.

Realization dawned on him. "Ah, and you think I blame you, too." When her body stiffened, he knew he had his answer. "If I thought it were you, I wouldn't be here talking to you. Besides, I was with you when some of the things happened: the cookies and then when we found Katie." He watched her shudder at that memory, and suppressed the sudden, distracting urge to hold her. "I don't think you have a bone in your body that would allow you to harm a child," he said softly.

She finally lifted her eyes to his. "Are you saying what happened to Joey with the cookies is related?"

He shrugged, trying to dismiss a vague, haunting feeling in the back of his mind. "Everything is a possibility right now. It could just be coincidence and bad luck. But the Muffin Man bothers me. Isn't that a nursery rhyme? There seems to be a pattern forming, and that would fit."

As he spoke, he noticed she closed herself off even more. She drew her knees up almost to her chin and wrapped her arms around her legs in a tight little ball. Cursing himself, he put his arm around her. "I didn't mean to scare you."

"You didn't. I was already scared."

The pain and sadness she tried to hide dulled the usual sparkle in her emerald eyes, and he made a snap decision, despite his better judgement. "I'm taking you home." Prepared for a fight, he was pleasantly surprised when she didn't argue. She simply leaned into his embrace and said, "Okay."

\*\*\*

Exiting the principal's office with Peter trailing her, Jillian was surprised by the commotion in the hallway. Many parents already heard of the most recent abduction and came to the school, anxiety-ridden, to take their children home. She saw families of several of her current and former students hustling out of the building, children in tow, including Simon Brothers, who was leading his son Jonathon out the front entrance. She was glad he was in too much of a hurry to notice her. She didn't have the energy for him at the moment.

Robynne's parents rushed past her, Mr. Smolenski ushering his crying wife out by the elbow. She expected them to be terrified over the apparent kidnapping of their daughter, but she did not expect the hot glare of pure hostility she received from them. She stopped short in the middle of the hallway, too stunned to move, as the couple's angry eyes seemed to bore holes right though her.

"Hi, Miss H.!"

Dazed, Jillian searched through the hordes until she found the face addressing her with a friendliness that seemed absurd, considering the circumstances and the mood of everyone else around her. "Billy? What are you doing here?"

The boy tossed his head toward the little girl standing beside him, making his many silver earrings bounce. "The high school lets out at two-thirty, so Mom made me drive down here and pick up my kid sister before I start my shift at the Shop'n'Fresh." He tugged playfully on his sister's pigtail. "Ready to go, shrimp?"

Emma Stone fidgeted, then smiled with admiration up at her big brother. "Don't call me shrimp, doodoo-head."

Billy grinned. "C'mon, shrimp, I mean Emma. Mom said she'll go crazy until she knows you're home. Bye, Miss H." He stepped around Jillian to lead his sister toward the exit, but instead ran headlong into Peter. "Sorry, man. Hey." He squinted up into Peter's face as if trying to remember something. "Aren't you that guy who saved Miss H. from that mugger dude? I didn't know you were a cop."

"Yes, he is," Jillian answered for Peter. "It's lucky he was there, isn't it?"

"Yeah," Billy said. "Lucky." With one last glance at Peter, he walked off. Emma waved and ran after her brother, the girl's short legs scrambling to keep up with his long strides.

Peter insisted on following Jillian home, pulling the car behind hers into her driveway. Exiting the vehicle, he didn't immediately follow her into the house but popped the trunk, pulling out a gym bag, before he met her at the front door.

"What's that?" She eyed the bag with suspicion.

"Extra clothes. In case I get dirty during an investigation, or go to the gym after my shift." He followed her into the house and dropped the bag on the floor next to the door.

Confusion made her forehead wrinkle. "This is not a gym."

"I don't think you should be alone, so I'm staying tonight. When I can't be here, I want someone else to stay with you, one of your friends or your parents."

She was torn: should she be grateful or pissed? "I don't need a babysitter," she replied, and couldn't help but wonder where he intended to sleep.

Ignoring her protest, he walked into her narrow kitchen. "What's for dinner? I'm starving."

Knowing she was defeated, for the moment anyway, she sighed and followed him, only to find him raiding her cupboards. "Help yourself," she said sardonically as he tore open a bag of Doritos.

"Don't mind if I do," he said with a lopsided grin that almost made her forget she was annoyed with him. He stuffed a handful of chips into his mouth as he sat in a chair at the kitchen table. "Look, I know you're not happy with this arrangement, and Lord knows, neither am I—"

"I can take care of myself. It's Robynne you need to be worried about. Wait. What?" She stared at him as his last words sunk in.

"— but I'll feel better if I know you're safe." He had continued speaking as if he hadn't heard her. "I don't know why this guy is targeting your students, and until I do, I plan on keeping a close watch on you. Whether you like it or not."

She knew he was watching as she gathered ingredients for a quick dinner. She admitted to herself she was glad he was here, but was not about to tell him that. Because he certainly wasn't jumping for joy over the prospect. "I never said I didn't like it," she mumbled.

He laughed. "You didn't have to. I can tell. You think I'm being that white knight again." He stood and put his arms around her waist from behind. "But I'm not leaving."

His actions surprised her, but she didn't pull away. Instead, she closed her eyes and leaned back against him, feeling safe for the first time in what felt like days, and something else just as rare: warm and fluttery and desirable. It was disconcerting and she didn't know how to react to it. "Then you'd better go change. Dinner's in ten minutes."

As promised, she had cavatappi pasta and zucchini tossed with garlic and olive oil ready when he returned. He exchanged his sheriff uniform for jeans and a blue sweater that she couldn't help but notice matched his eyes. He inspected a wrought iron wine rack in the corner. "Got a corkscrew?" He asked as he selected a bottle.

She dug one out of a drawer, then peeked at the bottle he set on the table. "Oh, Pinot Noir. A man after my own heart."

He winked at her. "Is it that obvious?"

She would have dropped the brightly colored pasta bowl, shattering it on the floor and ruining perfectly good food, had he not taken it from her trembling hands. "Um … that's not really what I … uh." He smiled at her flustered stammering and set the bowl on the table next to the wine. Then he leaned toward her and she was sure he was going to kiss her. She stared up at him, frozen. "Stop worrying," he whispered against her lips.

The telephone on the wall rang, making them both jump. Laughing, Peter answered it because he was closer. "Hobart residence."

After a moment of silence, he replaced the receiver. "No one there."

Jillian nodded, glad the subject was changed. Her heart still beat in her throat remembering how close he had been to her. "Stupid telemarketer computers. That happens all the time. So much for the Do Not Call Registry, huh?" She sat at the table and helped herself to a large portion of pasta.

Peter looked at the phone suspiciously. "Don't you have Caller ID?"

She shook her head. "I got rid of it to save money."

He looked at her a moment with a studiousness she couldn't define. Was that a 'cop' look? It was a fast change from the 'kiss me' look. She preferred the latter. He poured two glasses of wine then helped himself to the food. "This is great," he said between mouthfuls. "I'll have to invite myself to dinner more often." He grinned when she laughed and rolled her eyes at him.

He helped her with the dishes after dinner, then followed her into the living room, where she sank onto the black chenille couch and closed her eyes with a soft moan. She was bone-tired, and now that she had stopped moving, stiffness and soreness from stress became apparent. She lifted a hand to the back of her neck and started rubbing out the kinks.

"You look tired," Peter said. "Maybe you should go to bed."

Dropping her hand to her lap, she opened her eyes and sat up straighter. He was staring intently at her again. It was not the cop look. "I'm fine," she lied.

"Right."

She decided to ignore the sarcasm in his voice. "I just wish there was something else I could do for Robynne. We should go out in the search party."

He shook his head. "You're too close to it. You'd make yourself sick searching. And you can deny it all you want, but you're tired." He moved a red pillow from the couch to sit beside her and ran his hand comfortingly down her back. "And tense. Geez, you're stiff as a board. Turn around." He shifted on the couch so he was facing her.

She looked warily at him. "Why?"

"So I can rub your shoulders."

"With those hands? You'll snap me like a twig," she blurted, then blushed. She really needed to think before she spoke when she was around him.

"I can do a lot with these hands," he said, low and slow, with a smirk that made her cheeks redden further.

With one last dubious glance, she turned her body on the couch so her back was to him. He kneaded her shoulders, his hands warm and strong but gentle, rubbing out the days of tension and fear.

Jillian tensed even tighter. His touch sent a rush of heat over her body and air clogged in her lungs. *It's just a massage*, she told herself. She took a deep breath and forced herself to relax. His persistent fingers melted away her defenses as quickly as they did the knots in her muscles. She almost forgot about Robynne and the other children as she relaxed under his skilled hands. Tilting her head to give him better access to a particularly painful spot on her neck, she moaned low in her throat as the tightness disappeared.

"That feels so good," she said softly, arching her back with a sharp intake of breath when he touched a tender spot between her shoulder blades. "Right there." Her tension returned tenfold when Peter gently brushed his lips over the exposed soft skin under her ear.

The electrifying surge through her body made Jillian gasp and jump up from the couch. Startled back to reality, it dawned on her how she was acting. She was appalled that after what had happened, Peter might think she was interested in anything other than the friendly comfort of the offered massage. She was, she was starting to realize, but she didn't want him to think that. She desperately tried to think of something to say to change the subject. "I want to go to bed," she announced, then realized too late she was making matters worse. "To sleep. Alone," she added quickly. *Oh, that was smooth.* Peter just grinned at her, his head crooked to the left as he watched her with obvious amusement. Nervous, she backed away from him until she bumped into the coffee table and could go no farther. "Good night," she said, her voice too loud. "There's an afghan on that chair if you get cold." She turn and ran to her bedroom, closing the door behind her and leaning weakly against it. *Real smooth.*

# CHAPTER FIFTEEN

S UNLIGHT STREAMED THROUGH THE FRONT WINDOW over the couch and Peter's face. Grunting, he turned restlessly on the couch he slept on. It was too short and too narrow for his large frame, but he had managed to get a few hours of shut-eye. The bright sun put an early end to his efforts.

Knowing he wasn't going to get any more sleep, he kicked off the afghan and dragged himself off the couch, stretching his long, lean body lazily. Grabbing his jeans from the arm of the couch, he pulled them over his boxer shorts, then wedged himself on the floor between the couch and the coffee table to start working out for lack of anything better to do. He didn't want to start the shower or turn on the television and risk waking Jillian, who needed the sleep. She had been under too much stress lately, and he wanted to allow her to avoid reality as long as possible. He thought he ruined his good intentions when he accidentally nudged the table, toppling a candle onto the glass top with a clatter. Swearing under his breath, he put it back where it belonged and hoped she hadn't heard it.

Stretching on his stomach, he started a set of pushups. This was more than a usual workout; this morning he used it to work out his frustrations. Professionally, he wanted to catch the SOB who was snatching and killing innocent children and terrorizing Jillian. Personally, he wanted to climb into bed with Jillian during the night and just hold her in his arms. He wouldn't have touched her —

although he wanted that just as badly — but something about Jillian made him want to protect her as much as he wanted to make love to her. It scared the shit out of him. He'd never felt like that about a woman before — he'd never allowed himself.

He had to remind himself why he couldn't get involved with her. Besides the time and energy he allowed his job to suck out of him, he saw, all too often, what the wives of cops went through when their husbands were injured, or worse. It happened just last week, during the jail break, with Sergeant Bryan Whitaker; he had a wife and two young children at home. Sure, he survived, but he caused everyone a hell of a lot of worry in the process. He remembered how tense, how worried Jillian sounded, just thinking that he might have been the one injured. He didn't want to subject anyone to that kind of heartbreak — or himself to that kind of guilt. He knew that made him less than ideal boyfriend material. So instead he put even more energy and longer hours into his work to make up for the social life he voluntarily left behind. He didn't miss it.

Something Jillian had said popped into his mind. "You're a cop, not a politician." He shook his head to clear the thought. It didn't matter. His path was laid out before him, had been for years.

Thinking of Jillian's words made him think of Jillian. Smart and sexy as hell, even if she didn't realize it. Those sparkling green eyes and soft curves and …

With a grunt he quickened the pace of his pushups, trying to push the conflicting thoughts out of his mind.

But then he saw her, standing in the hallway, wearing nothing but a look of utter surprise and a very short blue cotton nightshirt. She was staring at him, mouth agape, eyelids low and sultry. He knew that look. It was a look he tried hard to keep from taking over his own face.

He stopped in mid pushup, arms outstretched and locked at the elbows, supporting himself on his hands. "Morning."

She jumped, his voice startling her, then stared at him wide-eyed for a long moment as her face turned pink. Then with a quick and quiet, "Hi," she turned and fled into the kitchen.

Grinning, Peter scrambled to his feet, following her into the kitchen. She was brewing coffee. He reached over her shoulder to take a mug from the cupboard and waited to pour himself some of the steaming liquid.

His gazed traveled the length of her naked legs down to her bare, high-arched feet. He'd always been a leg man, and damn, did she have great legs. "You're really cute when you're embarrassed."

He knew he flustered her because her hand shook as she replaced the coffee pot to its warmer with a clatter. She blurted out, "You're really hot without a shirt on." Closing her eyes, she sagged back against the counter and groaned. "I can't believe I said that out loud. I'm not awake yet. Sorry."

He braced his hands on the counter on either side of her hips, trapping her. He was so close, he could feel her warm breath on his chest. "No need to apologize," he said, his voice gruff. He stared down at her, no longer smiling.

She opened her eyes and he thought he saw uneasiness flicker through them, but he didn't move. She tried to avert her gaze, but his presence left little else to look at, her eyes moving restlessly from his bare chest to his navel to his feet.

Nervously taking her bottom lip between her teeth, she looked up at Peter through lowered lashes, looking so seductive that he felt dizzy. She took a deep breath and tentatively ran her fingers over his biceps, across his shoulders, down the sides of his torso. His muscles quivered at her soft, hesitant touch. He tolerated the sweet torture for as long as he could, then gave up the fight and swiftly bent to kiss her, her gasp of pleasure when his lips possessed hers further fueling his fire. His hands were light over her body, sliding easily on the soft cotton as they moved down her back to her round bottom. He gently teased her until she stood on tiptoe to wrap her arms around his neck, pressing her curves into his body. Her short nightshirt crept up on her long, firm thighs as she stretched toward him. He responded by pressing her back against the kitchen counter, crushing her to him, molding her pelvis against his. She made an eager sound in the back of her throat and ran her fingers through his hair as he kissed a trail from her mouth to her ear, nibbled gently, then slowly worked his way back to her lips until she was desperately clinging to him, trembling.

His hands slid down her body until they left the safety of her shirt and touched the bare skin of her thigh. She sighed, and the doorbell rang once, then twice, followed by loud banging on the front door. Peter dropped his hands, now balled into fists at his sides, and spun in the direction of the sound, immediately on alert and not at all happy with the interruption.

Jillian leaned her forehead against his back, her breathing ragged. "I'd better get that. Sounds important."

Peter glanced back at her with a stern frown. "Not dressed like that you're not." His voice came out strangled as he panted for breath.

She pulled herself away and walked to the front door, stopping at the hall closet to retrieve a long gray raincoat. Slipping her arms into the sleeves, she opened the door a crack to peer out, then pulled it open wide.

\*\*\*

"Mr. Brothers!" She couldn't have been more surprised had the president of the United States been standing on her porch. She frantically pulled her raincoat closed over her inappropriately attired body.

"Miss Hobart, I am so glad I caught you before you went in to school today," he said as he pushed past her into her home, uninvited. "There's been developments that you must be made aware of, and I took it upon myself to be the one to tell you because you needed to know as soon as possible. You'll thank me, I'm sure, once you hear what I have to say." He took her by the shoulders as he spoke.

"What's happened?" She tried to step back but his hold was firm.

"I came as soon as I heard. I didn't want you to walk into things unprepared. I was only thinking of you." His voice softened. "My dear Jillian, can I call you Jillian? It sounds bad at first, but if you only let me help you, we can work through it, I'm sure." He lifted a hand from her shoulder and captured a stray tendril of her silken hair, caressing it between his fingers.

She flinched away from his touch, stepping backward until she ran against the wall. There was no where else to go. "Heard what?" she replied, more forcefully and with building concern, wishing he would get to the point and talk without using his hands. She drew the raincoat closer, clutching it tightly at her neck with hands that shook.

"Is there a problem?" Peter walked into the vestibule, startling them both when he spoke. Jillian was at first relieved he interrupted, but then blushed when she saw him. Still shoeless and shirtless, he stood with muscular arms crossed over his broad chest sprinkled with curly brown hair. The look on his face conveyed that he had seen the township supervisor's unwanted advance and was not pleased.

Mr. Brothers looked from her to Peter and back again, then took a step back, his eyes first growing wide, then narrowing in disdain. "Am I interrupting something, Sergeant?" he said with a sneer.

Peter put his arm round Jillian's shoulders in a blatant exhibition of possessiveness. "Yes," he said simply.

Jillian coughed.

A vein in Mr. Brothers' forehead throbbed. He puffed out his chest and stood taller as he addressed Peter. "Then I won't keep you. I only came to tell Miss Hobart that parents at the school are calling her conduct into question in light of recent events. They doubt her ability to keep their children safe." He smiled when Peter's features grew stony. "I've spoken with several of the families myself, trying to restore calm. There will be a meeting tomorrow night to discuss the situation. Miss Hobart will be required to attend, of course."

"My conduct?" Jillian said, paling. This was moving too fast and not making any sense. "But I didn't do anything wrong."

He turned to her, his face now full of compassion. "Of course not. That's why I came to see you, to see if I could offer my help. I thought I could go to the meeting with you, to speak on your behalf. I am still a lawyer, Jillian, not just the town supervisor. Let me help you." He stepped closer as he spoke, arm moving toward her hand.

She shoved her hands into her coat pockets, and Peter moved in front of her, blocking the other man's path. "That won't be necessary."

"Yes, well." Mr. Brothers stepped back quickly. "It was merely a suggestion. If you change your mind, let me know."

Jillian nodded. "Yes, thank you."

Offering a last, insincere smile, he nodded and let himself out the door.

Stepping out from behind Peter, she reached a trembling hand out and laid it his forearm. "He thinks I need a lawyer?"

Peter started pacing in a circle around her, moving away from her touch, and she missed his warmth. "For a glorified PTA meeting?" he scoffed. "I don't think so. But I should be there, because I'm willing to bet there are going to be questions about the investigation you won't be able to answer." He was back in sergeant mode again, a switch that Jillian thought was accomplished rather quickly and easily; if he remembered the scorching kiss they just shared, he didn't show it. She wasn't too offended by his abrupt change in attitude for very long; she was busy digesting what Mr. Brothers had said.

"What kind of questions? Why are they focusing on me?" Her voice was shrill with worry and she couldn't stop shaking. It wasn't the same trembling as when Peter kissed her; this was from fear. Fear for her students, fear of having to stand up in front of people and defend herself. "Oh God."

Peter arms dropped to his sides, relaxed now that Mr. Brothers had driven away. "Because they're scared and don't know what else to do. They think they're doing something useful by holding this meeting." He reached out and touched her cheek softly. "Don't think about it yet. Just get through today. You're going to be late for school if you don't get dressed soon."

When she arrived at the school, a sheriff's deputy was already at the building. Deputy Keith Jenkins had been patrolling the campus all morning and would be stationed outside her classroom door while she taught. Jillian immediately felt tense and insecure, the opposite of what she knew the action intended. The idea of a deputy whose entire job was to watch her only made her think all the more of why he was there and what else might happen to require his presence.

Attendance was down more than usual. Less than half of her children came to class, and one mother even insisted on accompanying her daughter Jessica, which Jillian willingly allowed. She wanted to show Mrs. VanDysen, and everyone else who doubted her, that her conduct and teaching ability were beyond reproach and that she should not be held responsible for circumstances beyond her control, no matter how heinous those circumstances were. She reiterated her stance over and over with Tina and Donovan when they stayed with her that night, but they didn't need any convincing. They just let her rant and get it out of her system as they tried their best to cheer her up and prepare her for Thursday's meeting.

# CHAPTER SIXTEEN

THURSDAY, OCTOBER 5

THE SUN WAS RISING OVER THE tops of the gold- and russet-colored autumn trees when Peter pulled his truck into the parking lot of the sheriff's department. He hoped it would be an uneventful day, because the evening promised not to be. Then he saw the man standing in the center of his reserved parking spot and knew his day would be shot to hell, too.

Sheriff Patrick Dack, his uniform straining across the paunch hanging over his belt buckle, stood between the marked parking lines on the asphalt, arms crossed over his chest, looking authoritative and impatient. The last thing Peter wanted this early in the morning, or ever really, was another pep talk on politics. But he could not avoid his father when he was standing right in front of him. Peter sighed and pulled into the spot after the old man moved out of his way. "You're up early," Peter said by way of a greeting when stepped onto the pavement.

"Early bird is bright-eyed and bushy-tailed," Patrick said jovially. Peter did not bother to correct him this time. Not that his father would have heard, because he continued to speak. "Son, you know Election Day is exactly one month away."

Peter nodded. How could he forget? His father had been reminding him for the last nine months.

Patrick clapped a hand on Peter's back and steered him toward the building. There was no escaping now. "And the Sheriff's Number-

One Son is involved in the highest-profile case this department has seen in quite some time. I'm proud of you, son, taking the initiative, heading up such an important case. It feels good to get away from those routine patrols, doesn't it?"

*It feels good?* He envisioned Katie Bittens, dead, and Jillian, pale and scared. Peter pulled away from his father's embrace with disgust. "It's not exactly a vacation."

The Sheriff laughed, oblivious to his son's discomfort. "No, no, but it's good for you, son. This is the kind of crime that will make a lawman's career! When your turn to run for sheriff comes in, say, twelve or even eight years, people are going to remember this! This is your chance. Now's the time to solve this case, catch this son of a bitch, the sooner the better! You've got to give them something to remember you by."

Peter headed to the locker room stripping off his tee-shirt to change into his uniform, hoping his father would get the hint and leave. He didn't. Giving in, Peter sighed loudly and said, "What are you saying, Dad?"

"I'm saying, a bird in the hand is worth a hill of beans. You've been given an opportunity. Don't fuck it up."

Peter winced at his father's vulgarity as he shrugged into a clean shirt. "Thanks for being so concerned about my election bid." *Even though it's not my election you're worried about.*

His sarcasm did not register with Patrick, who paced across the locker room, looking pensive. It was never a good thing when his father got that look. "Of course, it's going to look good for my campaign as well, I can't deny that. Constituents will get into the voting booth and say, 'Patrick Dack, his son solved that gruesome murder. Like son, like father. I should vote for him'!" He smiled proudly.

*Bingo.* Peter shook his head as he buckled his utility belt around his waist. He knew his father was the consummate politician, but this took the cake, exploiting the deaths of innocent children for career advancement. What little respect he still had for his father was ebbing away; obviously he didn't care about the victims nearly as much as he cared about himself. It shouldn't have surprised him, but it did piss him off.

"So, are you here to give me advice on how to solve this case?" Peter suddenly felt tired. Slamming his locker closed with a reverberating bang, he headed out to find some strong coffee. His father trailed him.

"My son doesn't need advice! Peter, you're the best we've got, and I'm not just saying that because I'm your father. I'm sure you're already well on your way to having this be open and shut." He paused while Peter poured himself a cup of joe, shook his head when Peter held the pot up in a silent offer to pour him a cup as well. "But if you are looking for some good advice—" Peter rolled his eyes "—this is what you need to remember. You always have to ask yourself: how will I look on the eleven o'clock news?" Peter cocked an eyebrow at him, and Patrick corrected himself. "How will the department look? People have long memories, Peter. Something like this can, and will, come back to haunt you."

Peter gave up trying to play his father's game, slumping against the wall while he sipped his coffee. "And you."

Patrick frowned. "Yes, and me, if it comes to that. And this whole department. Arnold Wellinger, my opponent, is already asking if I put my son on this so-called Father Goose case so my name would be prominent in voters' minds come November."

"It's Father *Noose*," Peter corrected. Obviously his father was not paying any more attention to the matter than he had to.

"That's what I said," Patrick blustered. "While I admit it's a brilliant plan, I didn't come up with it. You stepped into this one all on your own." He was suddenly very serious. Peter had always suspected that his father's overly friendly, slightly addled personality was just a campaign schtick, and that thought was reinforced when Patrick leaned in close and spoke, clear, deliberate, and stern. It was so out of character that Peter straightened and paid attention. "And now you have to deal with it. This case is going to have repercussions that ripple all the way to the top, and that top is me. I want this over by November. Before November. I want people who are voting to feel safe, not feeling their sheriff can't get the job done. *Don't fuck this up.*"

Peter stared at his father, stunned by his serious turn. "Right."

Hs father grinned, all seriousness apparently easily forgotten.

"So, who's this girl you mentioned on the phone? Judy? Janice? Did I interrupt a hot date?" He winked.

*Crap.* "Jillian."

"Right. You know, having a wife would make you look good in the eyes of female voters."

Peter choked on his coffee.

Patrick slapped him on the back and walked away laughing.

Peter did not appreciate his father's idea of advice, but was starting to appreciate that politics and detective work intermingled more often than not. News of the Father Noose case, and tonight's town hall meeting, had apparently traveled far and fast. His father must have received calls from important concerned citizens for him to be so worried. Patrick Dack rarely paid attention to the northern, rural parts of the county, instead focusing on the more populated, and more profitable, southern half, with two of the top ten largest communities in Michigan, leading to larger voter turnout and, inevitably, larger campaign contributions. If his father was this upset about the investigation, then the investigation was far bigger than Peter had hoped it would ever be.

*\*\*\**

After Tina prepared a hearty brunch of *huevos rancheros* that Jillian barely touched but Donovan devoured, Jillian went to school filled with dread. She tried to maintain a happy face for the few students who showed for class, bringing out their favorite drums, tambourines, and xylophones for an extended music hour. But the stone-faced deputy sitting outside her classroom always brought her crashing back to reality and her anxious thoughts of the impending parent meeting. When the students were dismissed, she didn't go home, but spent extra time in her classroom, reorganizing art supplies and hanging new autumn decorations, brightly colored construction paper leaves and pumpkins. She had a nagging feeling that this would be the last time she would be in her classroom, and she wanted to leave it in impeccable condition. It was the one thing she still had control over. It also gave her something to do to pass the time that didn't involve tearing her hair out.

Walking from her classroom to the gymnasium, many of the staff ignored Jillian or bade her only the shortest of greetings. Already feeling like an outcast, she wondered how much worse it would be once the parents arrived. Only Mike seemed willing to talk to her, giving her a quick one-armed hug and wishing her luck.

The school gymnasium was crammed with people and echoing with noise, as parents with children from all grade levels arrived to have their say. Jillian stood in the wings of the stage facing the gym, out of sight of the crowds' eyes, watching with growing concern the angry throng. It sounded like a witch hunt, and Jillian had a terrible feeling she was the witch.

She was pacing and twisting her topaz ring with nervous energy when she saw Peter, fighting through the pulsing crowd toward her. Despite the urge to go to him, to let him hold her and tell her everything would be alright, she stayed where she was and listened to Antoinette outline what she thought would happen that night. "There are some people here to support you, but most of them are just plain scared and are willing to do or say anything to make themselves feel better," Antoinette said, then paused. "You should know, I've had several suggestions to fire you."

Jillian stopped pacing, unable to take another step, frozen in shock. "Fire me? You can't do that. You can't! I didn't do anything."

"I know that, and I wouldn't fire you. But if I can't get things to calm down here tonight, well, I just thought I should warn you now."

"Warn me about what?" She already knew, but she wanted to hear Antoinette say it.

Antoinette took a deep breath. "I may be forced to place you on administrative leave. Paid, of course," she added quickly. "The union has already approved this option. It won't go on your record, and it won't have any effect on your review or your tenure. But we have to do something, and if that means keeping you away from the school until this dies down, then that's what we have to do. We can't have them all withdraw their children and demand tuition refunds, for which I have also already fielded threats."

"No. No, of course not." Jillian felt light-headed and pressed a hand over her eyes. It was suddenly too warm in here. "I need to sit down."

Peter appeared at her side, taking her elbow to support her and leading her across the stage to a bench.

"Better?" He sat beside her and watched her, concern in his eyes.

*Not really*, she thought, but nodded. "I hate public speaking. Scares me to death." Her voice trailed off as she realized her poor choice of words.

Antoinette nodded in understanding. "You won't have to say a word. Let me do all the talking and everything will be fine."

Shaking her head violently, Jillian started to stand, but slumped back down when she found she was still dizzy. "But I have to defend myself. They're saying awful things about me."

Now Peter shook his head. "You didn't do anything that needs defending. So it's probably best that you don't talk. You don't want to incite the crowd more than they already are. I might be pressed into crowd control if this gets any worse."

She couldn't catch her breath. There didn't seem to be any air. "Not helping," Jillian whispered. She struggled to quash the urges to run and hide.

"Sorry," he said. He began gently rubbing the back of her neck.

"It's time." Antoinette's voice was quiet as she took Jillian's hand and patted it reassuringly. "Once we get this over with, everything will be fine. Just fine." She pushed her way through an opening in the middle of the burgundy curtain draped across the stage that separated them from the anxious crowd on the other side. Jillian heard the loud voices hush, then Antoinette speaking. "Ladies and gentlemen, thank you for coming. I know everyone is under a lot of stress and fear, which is understandable. But please, let's keep this meeting as civilized and professional as we can, and together we can work out something that can be satisfactory to everyone."

Peter took Jillian by the shoulders and forced her to look at him. "You have to be strong. Just go out there like everything is normal."

They both heard Antoinette announce Jillian's name from the stage.

"This is normal?" Jillian squeaked.

Peter stroked the back of her neck in soft little circles, raising goosebumps and giving her ideas that had nothing to do with the crowd beyond the curtain. Parting her lips to help draw in more air, she looked into his eyes imploringly, ashamed at what she was about to ask. "Are you coming with me?"

His eyes flickered briefly to her mouth before holding her gaze, steady and sure. "I'll be right behind you."

She stared at the curtain with dread and uncertainty. Then she took a deep breath and resolutely walked through it.

She was greeted with an eerie quietness as the crowd stared at her from the polished floor between the twin basketball nets of the gymnasium, and almost wished they had booed her instead. At least then she would know what she was dealing with. The silent stares of anger and anxiety all directed at her were devastating, and she wanted to turn and flee. There were only about fifty people, but it might as well have been a million. Her knees felt weak, and she shifted her balance nervously from foot to foot, wishing she had a chair to sit on instead of standing there in front of all these people, watching her with accusatory glares, waiting for her to do something. She felt a rustle of the curtain and then Peter was standing on the stage with them, about a yard to her left, hands clasped behind his back. His proximity quelled some of her anxiety and she was so grateful she almost smiled.

Antoinette spoke, using a microphone so her soft voice could reach into the crowd. "Miss Hobart is here, as is Sergeant Peter Dack of the Malcolm County Sheriff's Department. He may be able to answer any questions that either Miss Hobart or I cannot."

The voices in the audience erupted at once. Jillian could make out individual questions within the cacophony.

"Why isn't she under arrest?"

"Are my children safe?"

"She should be fired!"

"What is the sheriff doing to stop this?"

"Stuff only happens to her students, so she must have done it."

The color draining from her face, Jillian took an involuntary step backward, moving away from the angry mob. Antoinette's gentle hand on her arm stopped her. She looked to Peter, but he remained passive and authoritative, gaze fixed on the crowd.

Antoinette raised her hands in an attempt to alleviate the

noise. "People, please. One at a time." Once the noise dimmed, she continued. "To answer some of those questions, yes, we are making sure your children are safe. A sheriff's deputy is assigned to patrol the campus grounds during school hours, and we have cancelled all outdoor activities, including recess, until further notice. We are bringing in teaching students from the local college to act as extra eyes in the classrooms, and we are looking into purchasing security cameras and metal detectors." Some of the parents quieted, seemingly pleased with the actions.

Others still voiced concern. "Will Miss Hobart be arrested?"

Antoinette deferred to Peter. He addressed the crowd in a commanding voice that didn't need a microphone to be heard. "Rest assured that the Sheriff is doing everything he can to help. Besides the posted officer, we are increasing road patrols in the area. There are several detectives and deputies assigned to this case, myself included. And no, Miss Hobart is not currently a suspect."

The audience was calmer, but still not happy. Some voices still questioned why only Jillian's students were being harmed, and if students in other classes were in any danger. Apparently not satisfied with either Antoinette's or Peter's answers, a voice in the crowd declared Jillian posed a threat to the children and demanded her immediate dismissal. Stung, Jillian started to speak up in protest, but a booming male voice from a cluster of news crews in the back of the gymnasium drowned out her feeble response. "Sergeant, what can you tell us about Father Noose? I understand that's the name being associated with evidence left at the scenes. Is there a serial child killer on the loose, like they had in Oakland County in the 1970s?"

If the crowd had been scared and loud before, it was suddenly ten times worse. Shouting and crying reverberated throughout the room as the crowd began to surge toward the stage. Wide-eyed and trembling, Jillian backed away from the melee until she felt the thick velvet curtain brush against her legs. Antoinette tried to silence the audience, but her quiet voice could not be heard over the din. Then a deafeningly shrill sound pierced the air, instantly silencing the crowd, and all eyes turned to Peter, who had two fingers in his mouth as he whistled into Antoinette's microphone.

"Now that I have your attention." Peter was a commanding

presence, his stance authoritative, his face stern. "Everyone just calm down. I am not at liberty to discuss the particulars of the case, and how you came to obtain your information, which I am neither confirming nor denying, will be thoroughly reviewed." The fierce look he sent the reporter, though startling, was somehow reassuring to Jillian. "However, I will say this. As long as everyone takes basic precautions in their lives, I don't expect there will be any reason to panic." He passed the microphone back to the principal.

Antoinette weakly nodded her thanks to him then sent a sharp look to Jillian that she couldn't define. "I have taken the concerns of everyone, either spoken here tonight or to me in private, into consideration to make this decision. It is not an easy decision, but I realize that for the well being of all those involved, it must be done for the safety and peace of mind of not only our students, but the entire community." She paused and took a deep breath, and Jillian suddenly felt ill. "Before I go any further, let it be clear that Miss Hobart is not accused of any crime, and she has the full support of the staff of Cray Elementary. However, because these concerns are creating distractions that take away from educating our students, who are our first priority, effective immediately, Miss Hobart is being placed on leave. She is not being fired or punished in any way and will continue to receive her salary," she stressed when a murmur ran through the audience, "and when this situation is resolved, she will be welcomed back to teach at this school again."

Jillian had been warned this might happen and knew it was probably in the school's best interests, but she felt like she had been kicked in the stomach. The faces in the audience stared at her, smug. Superior. Laughing at her. Pushing her way blindly through the curtain, she staggered to the back of the stage and leaned weakly against the cold cinderblock wall. Taking deep, cleansing breaths, she willed herself to stay calm, but she couldn't stop shaking.

She saw Peter push his way through the curtain a few minutes later. He headed in her direction, concern creasing his features. But before he could get close, the reporter from the crowd whose announcement had caused a general panic appeared from the wings.

"Sergeant!" The short, young man in a cheap blue suit two sizes too large called, waved a microphone as he ran up behind Peter. "I was wondering if I could get a statement now? And then I'd like to speak to the teacher."

Peter's demeanor instantly changed from concerned to irate. The reporter must have been just has surprised as Jillian because he took a step backward. "This is private property, and you're trespassing. If you don't get your ass out of here right this second, I'll charge you with inciting a riot and throw you in jail faster than you can say 'Freedom of Information Act'," Peter said, towering over the reporter with his hands fisted at his sides.

"I'll take that as a 'no comment'," the journalist stammered as he rapidly backed away.

The anger Peter showed toward the loud-mouth reporter disappeared as soon as he turned back to Jillian. He crossed the room to her in two long strides. "Are you alright?" he asked.

"No," she said, burying her face in her hands. "They think I murder children."

Peter folded his arms around her. "No, they don't. They're just scared."

His tender touch shattered her as she collapsed into his embrace. "I'm not a teacher anymore," she whispered. That was easier to think about than being accused of kidnapping and murder.

"Yes you are," he said quietly, stroking her back as she cried. "You heard Ms. Jones. You'll be back here teaching in no time."

*Right. As long as no other children go missing.* "But what am I supposed to do until then? I'm a teacher, but I'm not allowed to teach. Do you know how much that hurts?"

He kissed the top of her head. "Try not to take it too hard. It's just a job."

"What?" Her head shot up fast, nearly clipping his chin. She pushed away from him and glared with eyes that flashed fire. "Just a job?" Her voice was shrill, and she took a deep breath to steady it. When she spoke again, her voice was a normal decibel but scathing. "You're the workaholic. You tell me. What would you do if you were forced to quit working? If someone said you weren't good at what you do, and in fact were so awful at it that you caused others harm?"

"I'm sorry, I didn't—"

She cut him off, turning away so she wouldn't have to see the concern in his eyes. "And by the way … I'm not *currently* a suspect? Does that mean I will be at some point in the future?" Angry now, she lost the fight to control her emotions and spun to face him, her voice rising. Heads turned in her direction but she didn't care. "Or that I was in the past? Is that why you stayed the other night? Was I under surveillance? You think I'm a serial killer, too?" Having Peter think that about her might even be worse than losing her job.

"No," he said forcefully, reaching toward her. "Jillian—"

She bit back a sob. Pride wouldn't let her show him how much he had hurt her. "Go away."

He dropped his hands to his sides. "Jillian, listen—"

She shook her head and turned her back on him. "Just leave me alone."

He stood there a long while, but she was determined not to speak to him, not to change her mind, not even to look at him. But when he blew out a rush of air and walked away, she felt like a knife had sliced into her heart.

Standing in the shadows of the wings of the stage, Mike Georginidis smiled.

# CHAPTER SEVENTEEN

FRIDAY, OCTOBER 6

ETER'S POLICE RADIO SQUAD CAR CRACKLED to life while he sat on the side of the road in his squad car completing paperwork for an early morning deer versus car accident investigation. "Malcolm-12, this is Dispatch. We have a 10-54 at A-Maize-ing Grace Farms in Cray. Possible match for the 10-65 you've been working. What's your 20? Copy?"

Peter grabbed the mic from the dash. "Ten-four. We're 10-98 here, near 30 Mile and Armada Center Roads."

"Ten-four. Proceed Code Two to location. Be advised, caller is also complaining of 10-91C. Do you need an assist? Copy?"

"Negative, Dispatch. Malcolm-20, Deputy Anderson, is here with me now; he can be my assist. En route to scene. Over." Peter placed the mic back on the radio just as Aaron leaned in the open window.

"Did I hear that right?" he asked in a low voice so the accident victim, still panicked after her crash, would not overhear. "Possible dead body related to a missing persons case?"

Peter nodded. He had a bad feeling about this; the only missing persons case he was working on involved a child in Jillian's class. The natural thought process made him think of Jillian, and he frowned. He missed her, damn it. It had only been one night, but he missed her. He wondered what she was doing, if she was thinking about him. If she would ever forgive him for being a jackass.

Aaron wrinkled his forehead. "10-91C? More injured animals?"

Peter came back to the present. "Yeah. I'm not sure how they relate."

"I'm not sure I want to be your assist on that one," Aaron said. "I've got enough with the 10-91*D* right here." He gestured to the freshly dead three-point-buck he had been volunteered into strapping to the roof of the accident victim's car. She had told him her husband would be furious about the Chevy Impala's smashed front fender, but she hoped to make up for it by serving venison for dinner.

"Meet me there when you're finished here," Peter said. As requested, he drove to the scene a few miles away without benefit of lights and sirens. While it was an emergency, there was no rush. Little he could do now if the victim was already dead.

He realized he was headed to the farm, with it endless acres of corn, adjoining Cray Township Charter Elementary, the last place Robynne Smolenski had been seen alive. An older gentleman in a plaid shirt and grungy overalls met him at the end of a long driveway leading to a turn-of-the-century white farmhouse and a handful of red barns and silos. He shook Peter's hand once he was out of the car. "It's right in the back. This way," Larry Nieder said as he led Peter past the house. "Nice day. Not too cold yet. Wife found it when she went to collect eggs this morning. Certainly was a surprise to her." He spoke matter-of-factly, which turned out to be the exact opposite of his wife.

Mrs. Nieder came running from the house, wringing her hands on her apron printed with thousands of tiny purple flowers. "Oh, Officer, I'm so glad you're here. I've just been beside myself. You just won't believe what I found, it's horrible, just awful, nothing like this has ever happened before! When I called Verna down the road to tell her, she said she'd never heard of it before either!"

*Shit. Nothing worse than a crowd of curious spectators clomping all over a crime scene.*

He was wrong.

A few dozen chickens had already compromised the crime scene, and the body, obliterating any possible evidence with their claws, seed, feathers, and fecal matter. He heard Aaron coming up the gravel drive behind him, forcefully but politely telling several nosy neighbors to keep their distance. Peter shook his head in resignation and went to work before too many more gawkers showed up.

Peter stepped toward the small figure sprawled in the dust, chickens scattering out of his way. He didn't need to get too close to know it was as he thought: the tiny body of a female child lay face up in the dirt, the light brown hair, short stature, and dirty clothing matching the last known description of Robynne Smolenski. The coroner would have to make the final determination, though, just as he would be the one to officially say the glaring red ligature mark around her neck indicated cause of death by strangulation. Purely out of procedure, he squatted next to the body to search for the pulse he already knew wasn't there. The child's skin was firm and cold to the touch, with a grayish pallor. She'd been dead for some time. Probably since shortly after she went missing.

"My poor biddies," Mrs. Nieder crooned as she fussed over her hens. "Leghorns are already such nervous animals to begin with. Usually they avoid human contact, they just don't deal well with strangers at all, so having that poor girl in there is just *traumatizing* them!"

Aaron cringed as a large white rooster with a floppy red comb stood in the center of the tiny victim's forehead, proclaiming himself king of the hill, loud and proud. "I don't know. They seem to be handling it better than I am." Peter thought he looked a little green around the gills, and felt sorry for him.

The woman didn't notice Aaron's distress. "Why, they haven't laid any eggs today, not a single one, since they came out of the coop and found this in their yard. Absolutely traumatized, the poor dears."

"Please tell me that's not our 10-91," Aaron whispered to Peter. "Mentally disturbed chickens?"

"Looks like." Peter nodded in the affirmative before shaking his head in resignation again.

Larry's calm voice penetrated over the squawking of his chickens and his wife. "Didn't see a thing. Chickens put up a fuss around two this morning, but I didn't think nothing of it. They're always making noise about something…"

His wife interrupted. "I *told* you something was wrong when they got fussy last night, but you just wouldn't listen to me. Now their egg production will be affected. We won't have a decent clutch for *days*. My poor biddies just won't be the same after this."

Larry tilted his head conspiratorially to Peter and finished his sentence. "So's she." Peter covered his smile with a cough.

Aaron rejoined the two men after stretching yellow police tape around the chickens' feed station to keep out onlookers. "Think it's the girl missing from the school next door?"

"Yeah." Peter nodded.

Larry spit into the dirt. "Nasty business."

Peter had to agree. "Better call the M.E. out here," he directed Aaron. "And the forensics team. This is going to be messy."

# CHAPTER EIGHTEEN

SATURDAY, OCTOBER 7

RESISTING THE URGE TO LAY ABOUT in her pajamas all day and feel sorry for herself, Jillian took the time to shower and make herself presentable, putting on a chenille black-and-white striped sweater and applying makeup, but it didn't help. She still looked — and felt — pale and weary. She shrugged at her reflection in the mirror and went into the kitchen, where Tina was making breakfast while talking on the phone, tucked between her ear and shoulder.

"Look, you're not getting an argument out of me," Tina said into the phone, then glanced up when Jillian reached around her for a mug. "Got to go. Yeah. See you later."

"Who was that?" Jillian asked after Tina hung up.

"What? Oh. That was Pop," Tina said quickly. "I told him I might be a little late to the restaurant."

Jillian thought that was odd, as it was not even nine in the morning. Dismissing it, she hugged her friend. "I'm sorry if I'm making you late. But I really appreciate you staying again last night. Thanks."

"*No problema, amiga.* So what are you going to do today?" She plunked a plate in front of Jillian.

Jillian took a bite of her breakfast and smiled in bliss. At least she had warm, buttery French toast. It wasn't much but it was something. She tried to sound nonchalant when she said, "I don't know. Maybe I'll clean out my closets."

"That sounds like fun." Tina sounded doubtful.

"Oh, loads. And later, maybe I'll alphabetize my CDs and catch up on my reading. See, being unemployed won't be so bad. I've got a million things I can do now." Jillian smiled brightly, hoping she didn't sound pathetic.

The smile Tina returned was one of pity.

*God, I'm pathetic.* "Stop that," Jillian ordered, to her friend and herself. "I'll be fine. Stop worrying about me."

"Who's worried? Have you seen the nametag for my uniform?" Tina deftly changed the subject.

After washing and putting away the dishes, Tina blew Jillian a kiss and ran out the door to head to work. Jillian stood alone in the silent, empty kitchen. The morning stretched out endlessly before her. Nothing to do but think.

*Peter.*

*Don't think about that,* she told herself.

She pushed aside her feelings of self-pity. Maybe she had overreacted when she told Peter off, but there was nothing she could do about it now. It was so unlike her to react so definitively, but something about Peter brought out deeper emotions in her, for better and for worse, apparently. She was usually the one trying not to rock the boat, and here she had gone and sunk it. She was surprised at how miserable she was without him, and then how much more miserable after she told him never to call her again when he telephoned the night before. But she couldn't dwell on that or she would be … well, miserable. To take her mind off Peter, she worked on the PowerPoint presentation she wanted to show the board of education for her proposed kindergarten program.

An hour later, she hadn't gotten very far. Every time she thought of an important reason to help her state her case, her mind whispered, *What's the point? You were fired.* She was only punishing herself and had to stop thinking about school before she drove herself insane. Giving up on her presentation, she decided to organize her eclectic CD collection instead. She didn't get far with that task either. The second disc she pulled out was one she had forgotten about, probably because it was in the jazz section instead 80's rock. *Maybe this will make me feel better.* The stereo blared *Tall Cool One* while she danced and shimmied around the living room, and she didn't hear the door creak open.

"You really should start locking your doors."

Startled, Jillian almost tripped over her feet mid-boogie. Peter stood in her living room, holding a bunch of mini sunflowers and wearing a silly smirk, and her heartbeat quickened, first from fright, but then faster, from Peter.

"Don't you knock?" Jillian pressed her hand against her chest, trying to keep her frantic heart from jumping out onto the floor at her feet.

"I did, but you probably didn't hear me over the music. I got worried, so I let myself in."

"I'm fine." Recovered from her scare, Jillian scowled and remembered she was supposed to be mad at him. "What are you doing here? I told you not to call me."

"I'm not calling." Peter hesitated, then took a cautious step forward. "Tina called me. She didn't think you should be alone, and I agreed. It's my day off, so today I am your body guard and official cheerer-upper." He looked nervous as he handed her the flowers, which she begrudgingly took from him. "Look. I'm sorry about what I said. That just came out all wrong. I did not mean to insult you or your career."

He was standing in her living room in total defiance of her commands to stay away, the jerk. Now would be the time to accept his apology and maybe even kiss him. But she wasn't going to let him off that easy. "I don't need a body guard."

"Really, it's no trouble at all. I enjoy watching your body."

Jillian blushed and choked back a laugh. She flushed even deeper when she realized what she had been doing when he had been watching her body: flailing around like an idiot. Mortified, she slapped the off button on the CD player just as Robert Plant admonished her to lighten up, but after a moment her lips quirked at the corners. "Sit down."

Letting out a long breath, he sat on the couch and pulled her down next to him, kissing the top of her head.

She sighed and nuzzled against him, and the sadness and hurt she kept bottled inside ebbed away. She couldn't stay mad at him, not when he made her feel so happy and safe. "Tina's a traitor," she mumbled against his neck.

"I forgive her," Peter replied, tipping her head back to look into her eyes.

"I forgive you, too," Jillian said quietly. He smiled and kissed her, soft and sweet. She hadn't realized just how much she missed him, missed his touch, and she drew him closer, squashing the flowers between them.

Too soon, he pulled back, taking the flattened flowers from her lap and setting them on the coffee table. "How are you holding up?"

She pouted. "Apparently not well, if everyone thinks I need a cheering-up committee."

He chuckled and kissed her again, sending shiver down her spine, but her brain would not cooperate with the rest of her body. This time she pulled away. "Have you found anything else about that Father Noose?" She hated to ask, worried the answer would not be to her liking. She leaned back against the couch, moving away from him. "Have they found Robynne?" When Peter hesitated, a wave of queasiness surged through her. Something was wrong. She leaned toward him again, eyes wide. "Is she okay?"

"I'm sorry," Peter said.

"No!" Jillian cried.

Peter put his hand on her knee. "The farmer who owns the property surrounding the school found her. She was out behind a chicken coop." When he paused, she knew he was trying to think of a way to present bad news. "It was the same as Katie. Strangled."

Jillian closed her eyes and covered her face with her hands. "She was just a little girl. So sweet. So … just…" Her voice trailed off as she thought, *Not another one. Dead. It's my fault she's dead.*

"I'm sorry," he said again.

"Poor Robynne." She gasped and dropped her hands into her lap. "Wait. A chicken coop?"

Peter nodded. "Yeah. We don't think the farmer's a suspect, though."

Jillian shot to her feet. "Chickens are birds."

Peter sent her an odd look. "And cows are bovines. Are you alright?"

"And robins are birds." She looked at him, her eyes wide. Her voice held a tinge of hysteria. "And kittens wear mittens that need to be washed."

Peter stood, placing his hands on her shoulders as he peered with concern into her face. "I think maybe you need to lie down."

"I'm not going crazy," she snapped, jerking away. "I'm talking about the rhymes."

Peter didn't look like he quite believed her.

"Father Noose," she explained with exasperation. "The way he, he—" she stumbled over the word, still unwilling to accept it "—killed them is the same as the rhymes. For Katie, it was her glove and a laundry, and now Robynne was left with birds. *Who Killed Cock Robin* is about birds at a funeral."

Peter immediately reverted to investigation mode. "And for Joey, *The Muffin Man* gave him inspiration for a food allergy." Peter began to pace in a tight circle around Jillian as he thought. "Murder in nursery rhymes. What sick bastard would have thought of that."

Jillian dragged a shaking hand through her hair. Maybe if she focused on the history of the stories instead of their current use, she wouldn't feel so helpless. "Actually, that's not strange at all. Most nursery rhymes and old children's stories have a basis in something violent or bad. They were morality tales or even historical references."

"Yeah?" Peter looked intrigued, so Jillian kept talking. It was like teaching, and easier to think about than Robynne.

"Remember *Ring Around the Rosy*? It's about everyone dying in the Black Plague. And *Mary Mary Quite Contrary*, that might be about Mary Queen of Scots and the subjects she had put to death."

"There's a pleasant way for children to pass the time." Peter's face scrunched in disgust.

Jillian was just getting started. Pretend murder was easier to talk about than real murder. "And Cinderella? In the original, her step-sisters cut off their toes to fit into the glass slipper. Most of these stories have been around so long, or tamed down for modern cartoons, know one really knows their true meaning anymore. But a lot of them are pretty violent if you pay attention."

"What about *Humpty Dumpty?*" Peter asked. She knew by the glint in his eye he was teasing her, but she answer anyway.

"It was a cannon in a war that the enemy knocked over during battle."

"Okay, you convinced me." Peter sounded impressed. "So you think this guy's not just randomly quoting nursery rhymes, but Father Noose is plagiarizing Mother Goose to find ways to kill his victims?"

Jillian sank back onto the couch, her burst of energy suddenly gone. She realized just how crazy she must have sounded. *No wonder Peter was worried.* "I don't know. I was just thinking out loud. It's stupid."

Peter sat next to her. "No, I don't think it is. It makes sense, in a sick, twisted kind of way. And right now it's the best thing we have to go on." She turned away so he wouldn't see her despair. But he must have noticed because he changed the subject. "I'm starving. What are you making me for lunch?"

She saw the teasing twinkle in his eye and tried to smile. "Nothing. You're on your own."

"You're going to make me cook?" He slapped his hand against his chest in mock indignation. "Have you ever eaten my cooking? It's horrible."

She giggled. "You seem to have turned out pretty well despite that." *He sure didn't develop that body on peanut butter and jelly.* She realized she was staring at his broad chest, defined so well in his faded green tee-shirt, and quickly turned away, her face burning. She continued speaking in an effort to keep him from knowing what she was thinking. "I have plans this afternoon, so you can do whatever you want until I get back."

"Hell no."

She turned back to him, surprised by the forcefulness in his voice. "Excuse me?"

The teasing was gone from his eyes. "I told you why I'm here. I'm not letting you out of my sight. You're not going anywhere alone."

Her ire rose at the idea of being, once again, thought of as helpless. "I won't be alone. My parents invited me over for burgers. Dad's grilling while it's still nice out."

"Then I'm coming with you."

The thought of introducing Peter to her matchmaking mother was more terrifying than venturing out by herself with a potential serial killer on the loose. "Really, that's not necessary."

"Yes, it is." He nodded emphatically. "Maybe it's time I meet your parents anyway."

Jillian thought she knew why and frowned. "So you can question them about me and what's been going on at the school?"

His smile was sly as he pulled her into his arms. "Nope. So they can question me about my intentions with their daughter." His grin widened when she chewed her bottom lip and flushed.

"You wouldn't think that was funny if you'd ever met my mother."

# CHAPTER NINETEEN

ILLIAN FEARED THE WORST, BUT IF Mary Hobart was surprised to see her daughter bring a man to dinner, she didn't show it. In moments, she had Peter stretched out on a chaise lounge with a beer in his hand on the cedar deck in the back yard of her home in Bloomfield Hills, an old-money town with big-money houses in a neighboring county southwest Jillian's home. She smiled brightly at him while she chatted non-stop.

"I am so glad Jillian has someone to take care of her until this awful kidnapping mess is over. I just cannot believe anyone thinks my Jillian had anything to do with those murders. It's just not right. You know everyone knows she's an absolute angel. We told her she could stay with us, because just like you, I don't think she should be all alone out there in the middle of nowhere, but she's just so stubborn. I'm sure you've noticed." Peter smiled, but was Jillian was mollified when he prudently stayed silent.

"She just doesn't want to be an imposition," her father said as he flipped thick burgers on the grill. He had passed his coppery hair and shining green eyes on to his daughter. "Jilly, go grab the cheese from the kitchen, will you?" Nodding, she moved fast, wanting to return before her mother said something embarrassing.

"Imposition? Please. I'm her mother. How is she imposing on her own mother? She's just stubborn, that's all. She certainly didn't get that stubborn streak from me. I don't know what she's trying to prove, thinking she can do everything by herself when we're right here. We just want to help." She beamed at Peter. "But now she has you to watch over her."

"Mother, please..." Jillian stepped onto the deck and froze as she overheard her mother's last statement and its implications.

"Jillian, I was just telling your sergeant here how happy I am you've finally found yourself a decent, sensible man." She addressed Peter again. "And it's about time, too. We were starting to worry she would never meet anyone. Now if only she'd find herself a decent job in a decent town."

Jillian screwed her eyes shut. She knew she was turning several shades of red. When she spoke, her voice came out strangled and barely audible. "He's not *my* sergeant." She opened her eyes and sent Peter a chagrined look that said 'I'm sorry.' But he was chuckling.

"Mary, don't embarrass our guest," her father said, winking at Jillian when she handed him a plate of sliced cheddar. *It's not the guest you have to worry about,* Jillian thought. Her father continued to speak. "How do you like your burgers, Peter?"

"Medium to medium well is fine, but I'm not picky." Peter stood and joined Jillian's father at the grill. "Mr. Hobart, I was wondering—"

"Doug," he insisted.

Peter smiled and nodded. "Doug. Is there anyone who might have a grudge against your daughter? Maybe a relative or an angry ex-boyfriend I should know about?"

Her mother answered instead, and Jillian squeezed her eyes shut in anticipation of what embarrassing thing she would say this time. "The entire family loves Jillian. I was just talking with her sister, Jacqueline, yesterday, and she agrees with me. Jillian has two little nieces who absolutely adore her. Chloe and Zoe are just the cutest little angels, but I'm sure if Jillian ever has any children of her own, they'll be just as adorable." She smiled at Jillian, who groaned. "As for ex-boyfriends, well, Jillian doesn't date very much, I'm afraid. She's too focused on her work and trying to be independent, I think, and I told her so, but she just won't listen to me. The last man she dated was that teacher from her school. What was his name, dear? Michael?"

"Georginidis?" Peter stared at Jillian. "You dated him?"

"It was not a date, Ma," Jillian mumbled. Baffled by the incredulous look on Peter's face, the emotion in his voice, she couldn't look at him.

She was relieved when her father announced the burgers were done. Everyone followed him indoors to the dining room, where potato salad, baked beans and sliced cantaloupe were waiting to accompany the hamburgers. Her mother continued to monopolize the conversation throughout the meal, questioning Peter on everything from the progress of the sheriff's investigation to his family. Surprisingly, he seemed to enjoy Mary's company, answering all her questions with ease and a smile. But Jillian sat hunched over her plate, pretending to eat and wishing for an earthquake, tornado, anything that would take the focus off her and her imaginary love life. Maybe they could talk about the homicide investigation again. When Mary broached the subject of the length of Peter's last relationship, Jillian jerked to her feet. "Who wants dessert?" she asked a little too loudly and started clearing plates from the table, even though not everyone was finished eating. She almost dropped a plate when Peter winked at her.

When she was at last able to pry him away from her mother so he could drive her home, Jillian couldn't speak, so mortified was she by her mother's behavior. When he pulled up in front of her house, she finally found the courage to talk. "I am so sorry about my mother."

Peter looked confused as he put the truck in Park and turned off the ignition. "Why? I liked her."

Jillian shook her head. "Did you hear her? She practically has us married! She's already counting the days until she can tell her society friends that her son-in-law is the Sheriff."

"You don't want to be married to me?" His eyes twinkled.

"Oh, I, um … what?" Jillian stared at him, stunned by both his question and his devastating smile.

Laughing, he exited the vehicle and rounded it to open her door. He helped her out of the truck and pulled her into his arms when she was standing. "Don't worry about your mother," he said softly into her hair.

She nodded against his chest. "Right. I've got other, more life-threatening things to worry about."

"Don't think about those either." His hand caressed her back.

"Any suggestions on what I *can* think about then?"

His answer was to kiss her, and thinking was suddenly out of the question. She lost all capacity for rational thought when he tenderly bit her plump lower lip, soothed the spot with his tongue, and gently coaxed her back into the kiss. She responded by kissing him back with a passion that left them both panting.

Jillian pulled away and glanced at the front window of her house. She could see the lights and television in the living room, and the fire-engine-red convertible, top up, parked in her driveway. "Tina's waiting for me inside," she said, disappointed.

Peter nibbled her neck when she turned her head. "Then I'll have to come back another time when she's not here." He lifted his head and grinned slyly. "Any way you can kick her out now?" There was laughter in his voice, but she didn't think he was joking.

She pressed her face into the hard curve where his neck met his shoulder, astonishing herself by actually considering his idea. "Don't tempt me."

"Okay." He pulled back abruptly and laughed when she pouted. "I'll call you tomorrow, but you call me if you need anything. Good night." He gave her one last quick kiss before he climbed into his truck and drove away.

# CHAPTER TWENTY

SUNDAY, OCTOBER 8

PETER DROVE DOWN THE TREE-LINED STREET in fashionable Ferndale on Detroit's northern border until Jillian pointed out the cookie-cutter bungalow. Only bright blue shutters and a blue Porsche Cayenne in the driveway made it stand out from the other homes. When he pulled up behind the expensive SUV, Donovan walked out of the house to wave enthusiastically.

Jillian got out of the squad car and waved back. "Thanks for letting me come over. Peter took me to lunch, but he has to go to work for a few hours, and he still thinks I need a babysitter." Peter just smiled and didn't take the bait.

"Oh, so you had a date, huh?" Donovan wiggled his eyebrows at Peter and laughed when Jillian giggled and shyly averted her gaze. "Well, he may think you need a babysitter, but I need a shopping partner, so there is no need to thank me. I am taking you to Somerset Mall for some much needed and deserved celebratory shopping."

Jillian's eyes widened. "Celebratory? Does that mean—?"

"Yes." Donovan interrupted. "I am a free man. Cancer-free, that is. I think that means I deserve something shiny and expensive."

Jillian squealed and jumped into his arms for a hug. Peter wasn't quite as sure how to respond. He hadn't known Donovan was sick, but that explained his too-thin frame and extremely short hair. For lack of anything better to say, he climbed out of the car and stuck out his hand to shake. "Congratulations."

Donovan pumped it eagerly, grinning like an idiot.

But Peter frowned. "She shouldn't be seen in public too much." He knew people were still worried about the abductions and until someone was caught, they would continue to blame her. He worried how Jillian would take any taunting, or even silent, pointed staring, that might be cast her way.

Donovan waved off Peter's concerns. "This is Somerset Mall, not a bowling alley, for Bob's sake. I doubt anyone will cause a scene in Crate and Barrel." He grinned at Jillian. "As a matter of fact, I doubt many people from your end of town get out to Crate and Barrel much. They're more the Sears set, I think."

"Look who's spouting stereotypes." Jillian laughed at him. Her laugh was loud and hearty and genuine, making Peter smile and want to laugh right along with her just from hearing the joy in her laughter.

"Alright, maybe not all of them have a subscription to the John Deere catalog," Donovan conceded, then addressed Peter. "But my point is, nothing horrible is going to happen in a huge mall with tons of witnesses and a Gucci store. And I'll be with her, so she'll be perfectly safe." He flexed his scrawny arms as proof of his ability to protect his friend.

"I feel better already," Jillian said.

Peter was outnumbered and had to relent. "Okay. Just keep your eyes open, and if anything does happen, get out of there."

"Yes, sir." Jillian was mocking him and he knew it. He wasn't used to being mocked.

"Come here," he ordered with a stern look. When she approached him, her eyes meekly cast down, he swept her into his arms and kissed her thoroughly. After a moment's surprise, she clung to his shoulders and reciprocated with just as much zeal. He was just losing himself in her soft, hungry kisses when Donovan cleared his throat.

"That's enough to make a boy jealous," he said.

Peter lifted his head. "Don't even think about it." He smiled as he made the comment. He liked Jillian's best friend.

"Oh be still my heart," Donovan said with a laugh. "Now scoot. I hear Williams-Sonoma calling, and we must answer the call. She'll be fine, I promise," he added in a more serious tone.

Peter reluctantly drove off and Donovan led Jillian to his Porsche SUV. "He is a nervous one, isn't he? Why is he so concerned, anyway? Now I'm not saying I don't appreciate that, anyone who cares about my Jillian that much is automatically on my Christmas card list, but really, darling, it's not you, it's the children we need to be worried about." When Jillian winced, he went overboard with apologizes. "Oh my God. That was tactless, sorry. I'm such an idiot. Forget I said anything. Forget about all of it. We're going to have fun today."

She was glad he dropped the subject. She needed a distraction and knew Donovan would provide it. After the quick drive to the mall – quick because Donovan drove – the two of them burned a path across the marble floors of the trendy mall. Lush ferns and bubbling water fountains created a calming environment to encourage shoppers to spend more money while a space-age moving sidewalk carried people through a covered walkway high above the busy roadway separating the two halves of the mall. Donovan carried several large shopping bags from stores like Pottery Barn, Armani, and Williams-Sonoma. But Jillian held only one tiny bag containing a new color lipstick that she splurged on. She felt guilty even with this small purchase.

Her friend's idea of retail therapy helped improve her mood, but she could not completely shake her feelings of guilt and dread. She glanced nervously around as they walked, Peter's words still ringing in her ears. There seemed to be more people at the mall who recognized her than either she or Donovan expected. A group of high school students walked past, talking and laughing loudly. Some of the teens stopped to chat when they recognized her as their former teacher, including Sara Johnson, Tony Benedetti, and Billy Stone. The kids wanted to know all the details of her leave of absence.

"Oh, I'm *so* sorry, Miss H.," Sara said, her poker-straight blonde hair died black at the tips swaying as she spoke, her kohl-rimmed eyes wide. "It must really, really suck, being, like, *fired* and everything."

"I wasn't fired," Jillian said, trying not to snap or cry.

Tony laughed, making the chains on his black leather jacket rattle. "Are you kidding? It don't suck. I wish I got a free vacation from school."

"Are you scared, Miss H.?" Billy asked in a low voice, leaning in close to be heard.

"Everything is going to be alright," Jillian replied, deliberately not answering the question to spare his feelings and hide her own. She didn't need or want anyone else worrying about her.

"Oh, I know," he said, nodding.

Sara grabbed Jillian's arm. "Well, I'd be scared, too, for sure, if that was happening to me. It's, like, so freaky! I mean, OMG, who wouldn't be totally freaked out?" Sara would have said more, but Billy, rolling his eyes, pressed his hand on the small of her back and steered her away from the adults. "Bye, Miss Hobart," she called over her shoulder.

Donovan linked his arm into hers and gently pulled. She took the hint, thinking he was following Peter's directive to keep her away from crowds. He leaned down and spoke in her ear, his voice low. "That boy was leering at you."

Surprised, she whispered, "Which boy?" She glanced back at the teens, Billy with his arm still around the girl being trailed by Tony, his silver chains clanking as he walked.

"The one with all the metal punched into his face." He sighed wistfully. "I remember when I first fell in love with one of my teachers. Ninth grade, Mr. Silverman, wood shop."

"Billy's a good kid. He had a crush on me when he was in fifth grade. He asked me to marry him."

"Really?"

"Yeah. He gave me a ring from a gumball machine." She laughed, remembering the boy's earnestness and the pale pink paste gem glued crooked on the plastic yellow ring.

Donovan wasn't laughing. "You didn't shatter his hopes and dreams, did you?"

"No. I told him he was too young, that he had to graduate high school first and then I'd think about it." She'd been too afraid of hurting anyone's feelings, same as always, and had tried to let the boy down easily without outright telling him *No*. "He's probably forgotten all about it by now. I know I did."

Donovan spared a glance back at the students, then looked down at her over the top of his thick-rimmed glasses. "Are you sure?"

"That was years ago. I think he's dating that girl Sara now."

He looked doubtful.

She laughed. "Don't let the piercings fool you. They might look like thugs, but they really are sweet."

Donovan sighed. "There is no point in arguing with you, is there. You'll defend your kids until the bitter end." He looked down at her sensibly clad feet. "I was serious about those shoes not being right for a date. Don't you want to wow Sergeant Peter, Jillian?"

She was used to Donovan jumping subjects so quickly, but still looked quizzically at him. "With shoes?"

He laughed. "If he gets wowed by shoes, then *I* should be dating him. No, silly, not the shoes themselves. The right shoes make a woman gorgeous. Those shoes make you look like a teacher."

"I am a teacher." She frowned. "Or at least, I was."

He waved off her self-doubt. "You need at least one pair of stilettos that will make a man stop dead in his tracks and take notice. High heels make the leg look longer and shapelier. It's all about sex, darling." He laughed when Jillian's mouth dropped open in shock. "Stop blushing. I think some cute Jimmy Choo's would be fabulous on you."

"What's Jimmy Choose?" She didn't follow the latest fashion trends.

Donovan gasped melodramatically. "You don't know who Jimmy Choo is? My God, I've got a virgin on my hands."

She leaned into him, glancing around to make sure no one overheard. She adored Donovan, but sometimes — *like now* — his tendency to blurt out whatever popped into his twisted mind made her cringe. "Donovan! Please." She was hardly a prude, but the disapproving look they got from passersby made her feel like a naughty child. Offering them a wavering, nervous half-smile of apology, she pulled him away and waited until he stopped laughing. "I shop at Payless Shoes, not Saks Fifth Avenue."

"Ooh! Saks. Let's go there." He pulled her toward the flagship store at the other end of the mall.

She tugged on his arm to force him to stop walking and look at her. "I'm a part-time teacher, and a teacher on the verge of being fired at that. I can't afford designer shoes."

"Well, *I'm* the co-owner of one of the most prestigious architectural firms in the Mid-West, and I *can* afford them. And since I can't wear them myself, I might as well get some vicarious enjoyment out of it by watching you wear them." He smiled down at her. "It's my treat. After all you've been through lately, you deserve something frivolous and sexy." He started to pull her again in the direction of the upscale department store, but was looking at her and not where he was going and ran headlong into another shopper. "Oh, pardon me!"

The man glared at Donovan with contempt, but his expression softened when he turned to Jillian. "Hello!"

"Mike! Hi!" She tried to sound pleasantly surprised, but knew she just sounded nervous instead. She silently cursed Peter's warnings for making her paranoid. "What are you doing here?"

"Shopping." He held up a Crate and Barrel bag. "I picked up something for my mother's birthday tonight."

Jillian tried hard not to smile when Donovan nudged her and subtly gestured to the name on the bag.

Mike addressed Donovan. "I'm Mike Georginidis. I work with Jillian."

Putting his arm around her shoulders in a possessive gesture, Donovan nodded and spoke in a tone a few octaves below his normal speaking voice. "Donovan Parker. Pleased to meet you."

Mike didn't spare him a second glance. "The kids are all asking about you, Jillian. They really seem to miss you. "

"I miss them, too," she said, and felt the hole in her heart reopen. "What have they been told as a reason for me not being there?"

"Ms. Jones told us to tell the kids you're sick, but I'm pretty sure most of them heard the truth from their parents or on the playground," he said. Jillian pressed her lips together and wondered what that 'truth' was. Mike stepped forward, reaching toward her hand. "It's not the same without you there, Jillian."

Without hesitation, Donovan pulled Jillian closer, protecting her like he promised Peter. With a devilish smile, he kissed the top of Jillian's head. "Ready to go, honey?" The corners of Mike's mouth turned down at the familiarity Jillian shared with him.

Jillian was torn between discomfort and amusement.

"Sorry, I didn't mean to keep you," Mike muttered. "See you around, Jillian."

"Bye." When she thought Mike was out of earshot, she fell against Donovan with side-splitting laughter. "Think he believed you?"

Donovan vainly buffed his nails on his shirt. "I should get an Academy Award for that performance. Now, let's go find something to make Sergeant Peter fall madly in love with you. If he hasn't already, that is."

\*\*\*

He blended into the crowds at the mall, inconspicuous, just another shopper on a lazy Sunday afternoon. He hadn't expected to find her here, but it was an added bonus that pleased him, until he saw whom she was with. His eyes narrowed as he regarded them, tormented by angry thoughts he tried to keep suppressed.

*Look at him. Who does that skinny fairy think he is? Does he think he's fooling anyone? Touching her. Kissing her! Confusing her to turn her against me. First the cop, now him. How dare they. She's mine, she should* know *by now that she's mine.*

He scowled, furious that his vision of perfection was being sullied. He focused his energy on the lanky man with her, laughing with her. Laughing at him.

*She must know, but he's confusing her. They're all confusing her, trying to get her to give them what belongs to me. She's too sweet and pure to know better. She's too nice, and she'll just go along with their plans to make her imperfect and ordinary without even knowing what's happening to her. She'll never even realize she's ruined. But I can fix it. Everything will be better when she's with me. Once she's mine, I'll make her pure again, and she won't want anyone else. Not the whiny kids, not the cop, not the skinny fairy, not anyone else but me. Just me.*

He formulated a new plan in his head, figuring out the quickest way to eliminate his new rivals for Jillian's affection.

# CHAPTER TWENTY-ONE

ONOVAN PULLED HIS SUV INTO JILLIAN'S driveway just as the clouds opened up with a downpour. Dashing from the vehicle to the house, Jillian saw Tina's red sports car zip down the street and pull in behind Donovan's SUV. She jumped out of the car and joined her friends in the porch, out of the rain. Her brown eyes were twinkling merrily. "Quick, let's go inside. I have something to show you." She glanced down at Jillian's feet, which were sporting red leather Jimmy Choo slingbacks with a three-and-a-half-inch spike heel. "Whoa, great shoes, J! They're hot! Did Donovan pick those out?"

"Don't you think I could pick out something like this myself?" Jillian pouted as she unlocked her front door and led her friends inside.

"No." Tina laughed.

"I do have great taste, don't I?" Donovan bragged.

Tina rolled her eyes. "I've got a little something for you too. Wait til you see this." She pulled a package out of her voluminous black purse and handed it to Jillian.

"Um, thanks?" Jillian looked uncomprehendingly at the slender cylinder ensconced in a clear plastic blister-pack, but Donovan peered over her shoulder and whistled.

"Weaponry. That, Tina darling, is the sign of a true friend. It beats shoes any day."

Jillian was so startled she dropped the package. "It's a weapon? What is it?"

Donovan caught it. "Mace."

"Pepper spray?" Jillian was still surprised.

"Hell, yes," Tina said. "If there's a whacko stalking you and your kids, I want to make sure you're protected and able to defend yourself."

"I can't use this!" Jillian warily eyed the package Donovan held out, not wanting to touch it.

Tina stuck her hands on her hips. "If someone's coming after you, you bet your ass you can." She pointed at the top of the tiny canister. "If anyone gets in your way, point this at him and press this button. Stops 'em dead in their tracks." She lowered her voice to a whisper. "Just don't let the cop know you have it."

"The cop?" Jillian blinked. "You mean Peter?"

"Are you playing tonsil hockey with any other cops I don't know about?"

Jillian ignored her friend's baiting. "Why can't I tell Peter?" *What's she getting me into now*, she thought warily.

"Just trust me on this." Tina snatched the package from Donovan when they heard a knock on the front door. "Is that him? Quick, give it to me." Standing on tip-toe, shoved it onto the top shelf of Jillian's pantry, hiding it behind a box of croutons.

Donovan answered the door and led Peter, shaking raindrops out of his hair, into the kitchen. "The second shift's here, so I'll be heading out," he said, leaning over to peck the cheek of Tina, then Jillian. "Call me later, darling. Let me know how those shoes work out for you." He winked on his way out, and Tina followed soon after.

Jillian took the opportunity to start heating a few teaspoons of olive oil on the stove to make dinner. Peter held up a plastic bag. "I stopped at that farmer's market out on Van Dyke, picked up some of the last fresh corn." He loosened the tie to his uniform as he rounded the counter and stepped into the kitchen, then froze, staring slack-jawed with a stunned expression.

"What's wrong?" Jillian asked in alarm, whipping her head around to look behind her to see what Peter was staring at.

"New shoes?" he asked, his voice husky, his gaze fixed on her legs.

She remembered Donovan's words and smiled. Despite the blush that crept over her face, she felt more daring than usual in her sexy new footwear, so she pivoted and bent her knee, showing off more leg. "These old things?"

Swallowing hard, he lifted his head and gazed into her eyes. "Tell Donovan he has good taste."

It was the second slight that day against her fashion sense, but she ignored it. "You really like them?"

Peter's answer was to grab her around the waist, yanking her body hard against his. The heels gave her added height and she found herself aligned with his body, eye to eye, mouth to mouth, hip to hip. Peter took advantage of her increased elevation and ravished her with a hot kiss that left her breathless, his tongue forcing into her mouth, rough and demanding. Her fingers dug into the muscles of his back as his hands roved over her jeans to her hips and up, under her violet silk blouse to touch bare skin on her stomach, across her ribs, and higher.

When she pulled back to catch her breath, Jillian struggled to remember how to speak. "So, um, is that a yes?"

"That's a yes." He dipped his head and kissed her again.

A timer on the stove beeped and with a startled gasp, Jillian pulled back again. She was trembling and had trouble forming a coherent sentence. "I, ah, the stove's on." She tried to turn away, but Peter, his arms wrapped tight around her waist, wasn't relinquishing her yet. He nibbled her earlobe and her entire body shuddered in response. "I mean it. I don't want the pan to burn."

"Okay." He rested his forehead briefly against hers. Reluctantly, he stepped back. "Can I help?"

She occupied herself with the hot frying pan, but her hands were shaking and her pulse racing. *Does he know what he did to me? I can't even remember what I was going to cook.* Her face was flushed, but it had nothing to do with bashfulness. "Um, you can make a salad, I guess. There's stuff in the fridge and the pantry."

She pulled salmon from the refrigerator, so Peter rummaged through the pantry. He paused, then spun and spoke so forcefully that Jillian jumped.

"What the hell is this?"

She chewed her bottom lip when she saw what he held: the package Tina said she was supposed to prevent him from seeing. "Nothing," she said quickly, and tried to grab it away from him, but he held it above his head, out of her reach.

"Where did this come from?" His voice was stern as he automatically reverted to investigation mode.

"I have no idea," she said innocently, and it was the sort of truth. She didn't know where Tina bought it.

"Bull."

She never had been a good liar. Sticking out her chin in stubbornness, she said, "Tina gave it to me, for protection. She's worried about me." Even though she doubted she'd ever use it, now it was a matter of principle, and she tried to guilt him into giving it back. But he wasn't budging.

"Damn, this is ten percent pepper spray. Jillian, the legal maximum in the state of Michigan is only two percent. You can't carry this."

She fisted her hands to her sides and faced him down. "There's a crazed sicko out there killing my students, and you're getting on my case for trying to protect them, and myself?"

He spoke slowly, his voice becoming deeper as he tried to reason with her. "This is illegal and you know it."

"Am I under arrest? Maybe you'll arrest Tina, too? Better get us off the streets now, we're dangerous." Irritated, she turned away and slapped the fish into the hot pan. Sizzling oil spattered out in protest.

Placing his hands lightly on her shoulders, he turned her around until she was forced to look at him. He glared in frustration despite his gentle touch and soft voice. "No, I'm not arresting you, but if you ever use this on someone, you could be. Jesus, this stuff could really hurt someone!"

She pulled away. "What else am I supposed to do if this Father Noose guy comes after me? And why are you worried if *he* gets hurt? I need to be able to—"

Her protestations were cut off when Peter dropped the Mace and tackled her.

Peter wrapped his arms around Jillian's waist and brought her roughly with him to the hard linoleum floor behind the kitchen counter. She heard a loud, reverberating crash and screamed, clutching his chest, her breath coming in fast, shallow gasps. He covered her body with his and his head with his hands, protecting them from any flying debris.

"What was that?" Jillian cried.

Peter placed two fingers gently over her lips in a gesture that she would have considered endearing had she not been mindless with fright. "Shhhh. Just a minute," he whispered. He remained there long after the last tinkling sound of glass echoed, listening for the telltale signs of something sinister. No explosions, no hiss of inflammatory elements, no ticking. Silence.

Slowly he raised himself up to peer over the countertop into the living room. His brow furrowed quizzically.

"That's not a bomb," he said, his voice filled with bewilderment.

Her heartbeat returning to normal, Jillian rose to her knees to get a look as well. She glanced from Peter to the broken living room window and back again. She tried not to sound like she was teasing him when she replied, "No. I believe it's a gourd."

A small orange pumpkin, not more than six inches in circumference but solid, lay among the shards of glass on the carpet.

He turned to Jillian, his eyes narrowed in suspicion. "Are you laughing at me?"

"No." She bit her bottom lip to keep from doing just that.

He glanced away from her back to the shattered window. "You're laughing at me," he muttered.

She did break out into giggles then, more as a release of pent-up nervous energy, earning a semi-stern glare from Peter. She stood to walk into the living room and picked up the produce, trying to avoid the wind-lashed rain that sprayed in through the gaping hole in her home.

She stopped laughing when she spotted the hand-written note tied around the fruit's woody stem. Lightning flashed in the sky, illuminating the living room and casting an eerie glow.

Peter went to her when her teasing smile crumbled and the color drained from her face. "What is it?"

She handed him the pumpkin and wrapped her arms around herself, shaking. "It's from him."

He read the short note aloud. " 'Peter, Peter, pumpkin eater. Has a girlfriend but he can't keep her.' It's signed Father Noose." He swore under his breath. "He knows where you live."

Jillian had trouble grasping the note's meaning. "But he's threatening you."

"No." Peter shook his head. "My girlfriend."

Her back stiffened. The indignant anger she felt moments before was back, along with a sadness so heavy it felt like it was crushing her chest. *He hasn't made any promises. We've only been on a few dates, for God's sake, and not very successful dates at that,* she told herself. She tried to keep the disappointment out of her voice but failed miserably when she said, "You have a girlfriend?"

He didn't answer right away, but waited with a slow, wide smile. Some of her anger cleared. "Oh. Right. He thinks I'm your girlfriend," she said, nodding but still not happy. Still he was silent. She blinked and her mouth dropped open as the pieces fell into place in her mind. "I'm your girlfriend?"

Slowly pulling her toward him, Peter's voice was husky as he said, "Which would make me your boyfriend."

His kiss was warm and gentle and undemanding and she never wanted it to end, but she pulled back with a start when a cold wind from the window swept over her back and reminded her of the note. "If it says you can't keep me, then it's a ... a ..."

"A death threat," he finished for her solemnly. "But I intend to keep you." He kissed her again, not as gently this time, and she let him. "I'm not leaving you here alone. You're coming home with me tonight."

An acrid smell greeted their nostrils just as the fire alarm blared in their ears. Black smoke billowed from the stove. "Might as well. I burned dinner anyway."

While she rushed to move the pan off the stove, Peter drew his gun from the holster at his back and made a perimeter check of the house. But whoever threw the pumpkin was already gone. When he returned, Jillian had disposed of the ruined food and disabled the fire alarm.

"Does this mean I get to keep the pepper spray?" she asked sweetly.

# CHAPTER TWENTY-TWO

A FTER INFORMING HER LANDLORD OF THE broken window, making a report when a deputy came out to investigate, and boarding up the shattered window with plywood from the shed in an attempt to keep the rain out of the living room, Jillian was hungry, tired, and wet. It was past midnight when Peter finally pulled his truck into the driveway of his little ranch-style house at the top of a steep, a tree-lined street in Utica, twelve miles to the south of Jillian's home. Despite its relative proximity, it was far removed from the rural feel of Jillian's home. While the downtown district was rather small and old-fashioned, the town itself was cramped with large homes and businesses popping up between the century-old buildings. Even at this late hour, the roads were heavy with traffic.

Drained, Jillian drifted in and out of sleep in the passenger seat, her head resting on the window, her even breathing causing it to fog over.

"Jillian. We're here," Peter whispered, softly touching her shoulder. She jerked and it took her a startled moment to figure out where she was. Drowsily, she picked up the duffel bag at her feet and followed Peter into his house.

Peter flicked on a light near the entry and illuminated his home. When Jillian's eyes adjusted to the bright light, she decided the cozy house couldn't have been more than seven hundred and fifty square feet. From the foyer, she could see the living room, dining area, part of the kitchen, and a short, narrow hall leading to the opposite end of the house. Its furnishings were Spartan, as if he hardly spent any time there. A large-screen television and a dark green couch were the sole features to the living room, while two vinyl-padded barstools shoved against the kitchen counter served as the dining room. He led her down the hall and flicked a light switch in a room on the right. It was his bedroom, the tight space taken up by an oak dresser and a king-sized bed draped in a green-and-white striped comforter. The single window had blinds but no curtains. Based on his sparse interior decorating — and now that she thought about it, his taste in civilian clothes — she made a wild guess that his favorite color was green.

"The bathroom's across the hall. Good night," Peter said from the corridor as he backed out of the room and started to close the door behind him.

"Wait." The reality of the night's events had come crashing down around her, her tired mind exaggerating the details, and suddenly the idea of being alone in a strange place terrified her.

"Yes?" Peter inquired, coming back into the room.

Jillian nervously shuffled her feet on the carpet. "Don't leave."

He took a cautious step forward. "You want me to stay with you tonight?" He spoke slowly, deliberately. Jillian knew he was giving her an out.

Chewing her lip, she nodded and looked down at her hands, twisting her ring with nervous energy. "I don't want to be alone."

Peter took a deep breath and nodded, then slowly let his breath out. "Okay. If you're sure. I'll just go lock up and be right back."

Pulling her pink satin nightgown from her duffel bag, she quickly changed and flicked off the light, then climbed into bed and pulled the sheet up around her chin. Thunder exploded over head, and she jumped, nerves on edge. She curled into a tight ball, facing the door, waiting. Tired as she was, she couldn't fall asleep until she knew Peter was safely by her side.

A few moments later, he came in and quietly closed the door. He stripped out of his damp uniform down to his green plaid boxers then lifted the covers to slide in beside to her. His body was long and strong and warm, and she leaned into him, laying her head on his shoulder and wrapping her arms around his torso, taking the warmth and the protection he offered. In his arms she felt safe again, and something else; the simmering attraction she felt toward Peter intensified by lying with him in his bed, something she was too frightened to have anticipated. Too reserved to act on her desire, she only nuzzled closer against him. Her heart pounded so loudly, she was sure he could hear it.

He moved closer, gently stroking her hair until she stopped trembling. Finally, he whispered a gruff "Sleep tight" as he leaned in for a good-night kiss. His lips brushed hers, quick and light. And then again, lingering this time. Jillian responded by clutching at his shoulders as she melted into him. Peter broke the kiss and pulled back, nuzzling into her hair, his breathing deep, his eyes closed.

She frowned, almost disappointed that Peter would rather sleep. *What did you expect?* she scolded herself. *You put him on the spot, asking him to stay.* "Good night," Jillian said softly.

Peter sighed. "To hell with chivalry," he said, and she gasped in surprise when he recaptured her mouth in a fierce kiss.

Suddenly they were locked in a hard, hot, passionate embrace, lips, tongues, teeth, and hands eagerly exploring every inch of each other's bodies: the firm muscles of his back, the soft curve of her hip. She was trembling again, and this time it wasn't all from fear. When her fingertips hesitantly touched him through the cotton of his boxers, he groaned and rolled over, taking her with him so he lay on top of her, supporting his weight on his elbows. He caressed her hair and face as she moved restlessly under him, trying to touch all of him at once. Rearing back on his knees, his hands slid down her body to the hem of her nightie, gripping it tight as he began to pull it up. A flash of panic, and Jillian's breath caught in her throat, her hands trembling when she grabbed his. He paused.

"Are you okay?" he whispered, intently searching her eyes. "Do you want me to stop?"

"Yes. No." She almost laughed at the confusion on his face. Her attraction to him was undeniable, as was the desperate need now throbbing in her. Swallowing hard, she decided she wasn't going to suppress it any longer. He represented protection and pleasure and tonight she wanted both.

Her hands went to his shoulders to pull him down for another long, hard kiss. Her tongue touched his, her teeth nibbled gently, and Peter resumed pulling her off her gown. He disengaged their lips only long enough to yank it over her head; she wore nothing beneath the cool satin. "You're beautiful," he whispered reverently as she lay naked beneath him, her coppery hair fanned out on the pillow and framing her face like a halo. She tried to answer, but all that came out was a low, throaty moan when he brushed his thumbs tenderly over the tips of her breasts, sending a hot wave of need through her, making her shudder.

Then he pressed his body onto hers, and she moaned again at the feel of his bare chest against hers. She arched and rubbed against him, skin on skin, letting her sensitive nipples be tickled by his coarse brown chest hair as she traced her foot, she hoped seductively, along his calf. They kissed again, wild now, until he broke it off again to blaze a trail down her neck, across her shoulder, and lower, tasting every inch of her body. When his warm mouth closed around her erect pink nipple, she cried out and curved her body into his, giving in to her needs.

His tongue and mouth teased and sucked while his hands reached lower, skimming down her torso to her hips, pulling them roughly against him, then lower still, caressing between her thighs and finally into her hot center. She begged him to stop then in the same breath demanded more, her hands clutching helplessly at the bedsheets while he touched, teased, and tasted. Her blood boiled and her breath stopped as he tormented her, her body trembling with need and her head twisting back and forth on the pillow as the tension wound higher and higher, tighter and tighter until it snapped and the raging sensations shattered within her.

Looking smug, Peter took his time working his way back up her quivering body. Smiling, Jillian wrapped her arms around his neck to pull him closer. He used the opportunity to kiss the soft skin under her ear. Feeling bold, her hands traveled to his boxers and, curling her fingers around the elastic band, pulled them down over his hips as he growled with a deep hunger. He helped her by wiggling out of them, and they pressed their hot, naked flesh together. She could feel him trembling. His groan was one of both triumph and need. "God, I want you," he whispered against her mouth. "I've wanted you for so long."

Her lips curved into a smile under his. "Me, too," she replied, realizing she meant it, as she arched toward him, pushing against him, coaxing him until he was nestled between her legs and just barely nudged into her, so close yet tantalizingly out of reach. With a soft sigh, she took her teasing a step further and twisted her hips around him. He grunted and, chest heaving, pulled back before he reached the point of no return.

"Geez." He groaned, his voice gritty as he laid his forehead weakly against her shoulder. "Not yet, sweetie." His hands were unsteady as he paused to tear into the drawer of his nightstand, fumbling blindly while she clung to him, lavishing hot kisses on his chest. Finding what he was looking for, he took a moment to make sure the condom was securely in place then gently lowered himself back onto her writhing body.

Pushing her thighs apart with his knee, he drove into her with a long, low groan. Running her hands into his thick, dark hair, she gasped with surprise and pleasure and arched up to meet him, letting him fill her, her long legs instinctively wrapping around his lower back to pull him closer still.

"Jillian," he whispered as he slowly, rhythmically, began to thrust against her. He was so gentle, so tender, she wanted to cry from the beauty of it all. His hand fisted into her hair and he gazed into her eyes, clouded with passion. Jillian could barely breathe as wave after wave of rapture consumed her, and she quickened the pace of their dance in a desperate quest for more. Her mind could only focus on one thing now.

*Peter.*

His name became an ascending mantra in her mind until she lost her mind completely. When she gasped and sobbed out his name, her body tightening around him convulsively, he buried his head into the delicate curve of her neck and with a muffled shout collapsed on top of her.

Breathing heavily, Peter nibbled the hot skin on the column of her throat. Jillian was too blissfully exhausted to do anything but softly caress his shoulders.

He raised his head and captured her lips in a fast kiss. Gathering her in his arms, he rolled onto his back and pulled her with him until she was cuddled against his side. He kissed the top of her head and she sighed, content, her head resting on his shoulder, her arm draped across his chest.

Satiated and still dazed, she felt her heartbeat gradually returning to normal. Their lovemaking had been both earth-shattering and beautiful. As her brain started functioning again, she was stunned by the realization that she had fallen in love with Peter. She had no idea when that happened. She clamped down on her heart, determined not to get it broken. He was more interested in his career than in dating; he'd never have time for a real relationship, and she'd never ask him to stop doing something he clearly loved. She understood that, but couldn't compete with it. *This is just a fling*, she told herself, *just a matter of two people, pumped up on adrenaline and fear, pushed together by circumstance and working out their stress in a mutually beneficial way.*

*Right?*

Her lips curved down into a frown as she rubbed her cheek over his shoulder.

"Hey, sweetie." His voice was gruff as he trailed his fingers down her spine, causing her to shiver and snuggle closer. "How ya doing?"

She pushed the too-serious thoughts away and offered him a timid smile, tilting her head to gaze into his deep blue eyes. "Perfect. I'm perfect," she whispered.

He grinned and wiggled his eyebrows. "Sure were."

With a giggle, she hid her face against his chest.

He chuckled then yawned loudly. Taking it for a hint that he wanted to sleep, Jillian started to roll away, but his arm locked around her, preventing her from moving. She looked up at him with a drowsy smile, and they fell asleep wrapped in each other's arms while the rain drummed steadily on the roof.

# CHAPTER TWENTY-THREE

MONDAY, OCTOBER 9

**B**EFORE THEY ARRIVED BACK AT HER house early the next morning, Peter insisted on making a detour to the sheriff's department. He spoke with his superiors, including his father, to tell them to get a replacement for his regular patrol duties. Until further notice, he would be spending the majority of his working hours on the Father Noose case; that was the party line, but his main intent was to protect Jillian. The pumpkin in her window drove home the point that her students were not the only targets of this killer. In fact, Peter now wondered if her students may have been just a convenient path to Jillian.

Aaron had already filled the department heads in on the basics from the previous night, and because Peter had earned a staunch reputation as a hard worker, putting in longer hours than most while rarely taking vacation or sick time, his request was readily granted. For once it didn't hurt that his father was the Sheriff and wanted the case solved as soon as possible — even if it was for purely selfish reasons — or that he himself was an obvious future candidate for the position.

The older man did manage something that resembled a fatherly discussion to caution his son about the perils of becoming personally involved with a case before granting his permission, which surprised Peter. He hadn't told him about the full extent of his relationship with Jillian, not yet fully understanding it himself. But his father was clearly more perceptive than he gave him credit for. He didn't disapprove of the relationship in general, but in terms of his reelection bid, signs of favoritism by his staff, and his son in particular, would not be appreciated by his constituents. Peter half-heartedly denied his father's accusations, not caring to discuss his personal life with a man who never before seemed concerned with his personal life. Still, he knew the advice was relevant, even if Patrick was concerned only about himself.

Peter wanted to make it painfully obvious to Jillian's stalker, and anyone else interested, that she was protected, so he swapped his truck for a marked sheriff's cruiser and donned his uniform. He would not technically be off duty, but rather had simply reassigned himself. A workaholic to the core. Although the more time he spent with Jillian, the more he was willing to cut himself some slack.

By the time they arrived at her house, her landlord was already inspecting the damage. He suffered from male pattern baldness but was apparently prepared to fight it to his dying day. What flaming red hair he had on the sides of his head he grew long and coaxed it upwards, so it stood on end and framed the top of his shiny dome in defiance of gravity. Peter thought his brave attempt at youth left him looking like a particular television clown icon minus the floppy shoes. His aging hippy wife, with a braided ponytail and layered beaded necklaces, was also there, along with an insurance agent in a standard cheap blue suit. Two men in dark clothes and baseball caps were gingerly unloading a sheet of glass from a truck, preparing to install it in the gaping hole left by the vandal the night before. Peter stayed near Jillian's side the entire time the men worked, protecting her from both potential murderers and roving eyes.

Jillian fidgeted as he draped an arm over her shoulders in a show of possession, obviously uncomfortable with Peter's public displays of affection. He noticed her flush deepen when the landlord smiled at them with approval.

When the workers and the landlord finally left, the new glass securely in place, Jillian went into the kitchen to fix lunch. They never got the chance to eat dinner the night before, and had skipped breakfast in her haste to get back home and inspect the wreckage in daylight. The light on her answering machine was blinking, so she hit the button to listen to messages while she cooked.

As she pulled plates from the cupboard, Peter came up behind her to plant little, nibbling kisses along the side of her neck. "We're alone now," he whispered into her hair. He had missed the opportunity to repeat last night's stellar performance because of her rush to get home and was trying to make up for lost time now. He didn't want to let go of her. He'd never experienced such intense passion as he had with Jillian, and knew it was different because it was with her. He'd been with his fair share of women, but never had any of those encounters made him pine the way he did for her. His heart beat faster just looking at her, and her touch made him tremble. He didn't understand it, but he didn't want the feeling to go away.

Peter wrapped his arms around her waist, splaying his fingers wide over her soft belly to pull her back against his chest as he nuzzled into her hair. Abandoning the plates, she sighed and leaned back into him, tilting her head to one side to give him better access to her earlobe, and raised one hand back to run her fingers through his hair. She melted against him and his whole body tightened in response, coiled tight with a need that was new and somewhat disturbing. He'd had her less than ten hours ago, and already was aching to have her again. He was debating the pros and cons of taking her right there on the kitchen floor when Tina's lilting voice emerged from the recorder. He had a hard time concentrating on the voice as his hands cupped Jillian's breasts. "Hey J, it's T. Just calling to check in. You must have turned your cell phone off — again. So hey, I drove by the house this morning, and it looks like your windows are boarded up. What's up with that? Call me! *Hasta!*"

A male voice was next on the machine, sounding nervous and whiny. "Hello, Jillian. It's Mike. Georginidis. From school. Just called to say hi. Maybe see if you'd like to go see a movie or something."

Peter felt a surge of jealousy, but it was quickly doused when Jillian tilted her head back so she could reach his lips with hers. Movies were out of the question. He forgot all about Georginidis.

When the third message started, neither one of them was paying much attention. But suddenly Jillian jumped back from the recorder so fast, the back of her head rammed hard into Peter's nose. He yelped in more surprise than pain, rubbing his nose to make sure he wasn't bloody, before noticing she stared, terrified, wide-eyed, and pale, at the answering machine. He listened attentively to the tinny recording of a little girl singing sweetly.

*Alouette, gentille alouette, alouette, je te plumerai.*

Jillian was trembling and breathing hard as she stepped back further from the phone.

Peter glanced between her and the phone. "What is it?"

Jillian's voice was surprisingly calm and quiet as she pointed to the machine with a shaking hand. "It's a French nursery rhyme."

He drew a quick breath and glared at the machine. He knew who left the message; the only person it could be was Father Noose.

He strained to listen to the recording, somewhat muffled, probably caused when a phone receiver was help up to a music player, distorting the true sound. The foreign words were unrecognizable to him. Instead he focused on the background noise, faint but distinct. A roadway, cars zooming by. He guessed the message was sent from a payphone, and knew better than to hope they would be able to trace the caller. "I don't speak French. If it was German, maybe I could help you, but I don't know what she's saying."

"I do." She sang softly along with the chorus, her voice cracking with emotion. "Loosely translated, it means pretty lark, I'm going to pluck out all your feathers."

"What a sick joke," he said, then watched her already pale face turn ashen as the song went into another verse. "What else is it saying?" he demanded.

"The rest of the song," she whispered. "It's all the other things he's going to … pluck off."

The fear in her eyes made him furious. "Son of a bitch."

*Je te plumerai les ailes, et les ailes, et les ailes, et le cou, et le cou…*

"Wings, neck … he'll pluck off its neck. Oh God." She fell into a nearby kitchen chair.

"Where does the sick bastard come up with this stuff?" Peter said, rubbing the back of his own neck in agitation.

"That's how the song goes," she said, her voice weak.

"So the French are sick bastards, then."

"*Je te plumerai les yeux* … Oh, God, my eyes!" She covered her face with her hands.

Peter knelt beside her, his hand on her shoulder. "You think he's talking about you?"

"It's on my answering machine, isn't it?" She pressed the heels her of hands into her eyes as if she were trying desperately to keep them contained in their sockets.

Peter stood and slapped the off button before the cheerful voice could start another sickening verse. "Most of the rhymes were linked to kids taken from your class, but nothing's happened to you yet." This new rhyme, however, combined with the previous night's pumpkin, made him wonder how long it would be before something did.

Now that the song longer tormented her, Jillian dropped her hands and shook her head. "What else could it be?" Apparently she'd come to the same conclusion.

He shrugged, then his face brightened. "What was the name of the last kid?"

"Robynne Smolenski."

"And the rhyme that went with her?"

She closed her eyes. "I don't remember."

"Think." He shook her shoulders to force her to focus.

"A bird. Oh God."

"What?"

"*Who Killed Cock Robin.*" She clutched him, but he didn't flinch when her fingers dug sharply into the muscles of his forearms. "What if … what if he's not using the rhymes for finding ways of *how* to kill them, but he's using them for choosing *who* to kill?"

Peter nodded, feeling confident for the first time, even if that confidence was slim. "Their names are in the rhymes."

"I don't know. Robynne might be obvious, and *Three Little Kittens* could have been changed to *Bittens.*"

He gently pried her fingers away and began to pace around her again, taking long strides as he thought. "Okay, so we need to come up with a list of all names used in nursery rhymes and compare that to the list of your students." He paused. "Weren't their names in that planner stolen from your classroom?"

Jillian's eyes widened. "Yes." She jumped up to play the message again, fast forwarding over Tina's voice to get to the song. *Alouette, gentille alouette.* "No. Oh no."

"What?"

She turned to face him, worry etching lines in her face. "Allen. It's Allen Etter." She sagged against the counter. "Some of the children tease him at recess because he wears glasses. But he's just a sweet little boy."

Peter supported her with his arm around her waist, hoping she wouldn't faint, and flipped open his cell phone and hit the speed dial button. When Aaron answered, he ordered him to get to the Etter residence ASAP, and to inform the deputy on duty at the school of the possible threat. When he hung up, he muttered an obscenity. "He's playing with us. With you." He patted her shoulder absently, then stopped and looked at her. "When does your class start?"

"It's not my class anymore," she said sadly.

"Yes, it is. What time?" he repeated.

"Twelve-thirty."

"It's eleven-twenty now." He grabbed her arm. "Let's go."

She stumbled after him as he pulled her along. "Where are we going?"

"Allen's house. I need to make sure everything's okay, and I am not leaving you here alone." He was surprised she didn't protest. Until he shoved her in the back seat.

"Can't I sit up front?"

He shook his head. "Not during official business."

She crossed her arms over her chest. "I've driven this thing on official business, but now I have to sit in the back?" The tone of her voice let him know she was joking, but only a little.

He picked up the radio and commanded dispatch to send him directions to the Etter residence. In just a few seconds, his onboard GPS system beeped to life. He aimed the car toward the directions provided, turned on the lights and sirens, and hit the accelerator. Then he answered her question.

"I want you involved in as little of the investigation as possible, and sitting up front makes you look involved. But I can't leave you, either. That message might just be a ploy to get you alone, if I leave or if you were to go running to the child's house."

She nodded, but he saw her roll her eyes.

"We need to compare your kids' names to other nursery rhymes so we can alert those parents before he hurts anyone else," he said.

Weary, Jillian leaned back into the car seat. "That's impossible. Robynne was an obvious name, I suppose, but kittens to Bittens and Allen Etter to Alouette are a real stretch. We'll never figure it out. It's not like he's using easy ones like Jack and John…" she stopped, eyes wide. "Jonathon Brothers!"

Why was that name familiar? "Simon Brothers' son?"

She nodded. "His name *is* a nursery rhyme, *Frère Jacques*. We sing it in English as, 'Are you sleeping Brother John'." She leaned forward to emphasize what she was about to say. "Simon is a nursery rhyme name too, *Simple Simon was a Pie Man*."

Somehow that didn't surprise him. "I was thinking more along the lines of Simon Says, if we're using kids' games."

Her eyes widened with surprise. "You think the township supervisor is Father Noose?"

Peter shrugged and turned the wheel hard to the left. "I don't know. But he has access to the school, shows up at convenient times, and so far his son has been unharmed despite the rhyme-name connection." He frowned. "And he knows where you live. He showed up unannounced Wednesday, remember?" His frown deepened into a scowl. "He's got something for you, doesn't he?"

She turned away but he could still see the revulsion on her face in the rearview mirror. "He's tried to find an excuse to touch me every time I see him. Not just the other day, but at school, too. Oh, and that time I ran into him at the grocery store."

He'd never considered himself a jealous man, but Peter was furious now. He didn't have time to tell her his thoughts about Brothers and what exactly he'd like to do to him, because they turned on to Birch Way, the Etters' street. Cutting the siren, he hopped out of the car and strode up the driveway, almost forgetting to let Jillian out of the back seat. He raised a long leg to step over a discarded bicycle with training wheels, tipped on its side, its main front wheel still spinning idly.

Jillian touched his arm. "Peter, watch out!"

He stopped mid-stride and looked toward where she pointed. On the ground beside the bike lay a child-sized pair of glasses. Peter had almost crunched them underfoot.

"Allen wears glasses," Jillian whispered, then softly sang, "*Je te plumerai les yeux…*"

"Stay here," Peter commanded, then jogged to the front door of the Etters' home. He pounded on it until Mrs. Allison Etter opened it, looking surprised to see a harried sheriff's sergeant on her porch.

Peter explained, without going into too much detail, that he had a credible tip that her son might be in danger. "Where is he now, Mrs. Etter?"

The woman waved a shaking arm toward the front yard. "He's riding his bike up and down the sidewalk before he has to go school."

Peter hesitated, then nodded toward the overturned bike. "No, ma'am, he's not."

It took a few seconds for that information to set in, then Mrs. Etter ran screaming out the front door, her hands tearing at her curly red hair. "I just left for a minute! The phone rang and I went to answer it…" She knelt to pick up his glasses, one of the lenses cracked.

"Who was on the phone?" Peter asked as he watched Aaron's squad car race toward them.

"No one," she sobbed. "No one was there."

*Yes, there was.* Peter's jaw clenched. He knew exactly who called: the same person who left the mocking message on Jillian's machine.

Aaron joined them and Peter tried to fill him in above the mother's wails of grief. Peter knew Aaron was good with women, and sure enough within moments Aaron's gentle coaxing had the woman's crying under control.

Peter stepped away to look at the bike. The woman was quiet now, but he could swear he could still hear crying. Tilting his head toward the distant sound, he saw Jillian streak by him in a blur, running past the house and into the back yard. He had forgotten about her while he investigated the scene. "What the—" he muttered, jerking his head up to follow her movement.

"Peter!" She shouted as she darted by. He reached out to stop her but she was too fast.

"Damn it, I told her not to run into any more cornfields," Peter said. He jumped up and rushed across the long yard after her. Aaron trailed after him, leaving a bewildered Mrs. Etter crouched over her son's bike. Peter's heart lurched as he rounded the corner of the house and saw Jillian disappear into long, overgrown reeds leading into deep woods.

Only a few seconds behind, Peter dove into the underbrush, his feet sinking into black muck, fully intending to chew Jillian out. But then the reeds parted and he stopped short. Jillian sat in a muddy clearing, cradling the missing boy in her lap, gently stroking his head and rocking him.

"It's alright, Allen. Please stop crying," she said in soothing tones.

Finding Jillian, and the boy, safe made Peter almost weak with relief, and his shoulders sagged as he let out a long breath.

The child — his tee-shirt, jeans, and Sponge Bob sneakers wet and muddy — started crying again when he saw Peter and Aaron. "Are those policemen going to arrest the man who hurt me?" he said, clinging tight to Jillian, large chunks of her hair and red shirt balled into his tiny fists. Cursing under his breath, Peter exchanged worried glances with Aaron.

Peter crouched beside Jillian, putting an arm tight around her waist both to help her stand and to feed the overwhelming urge to hold her, to convince himself she was safe.

"You're hurt?" she asked the boy in a quavering voice.

"My leg hurts," the boy sniveled. Jillian pulled up his torn pant leg. Blood flowed sluggishly from a gash on his left calf.

They slogged though the weeds toward the house and found Mrs. Etter, impatiently wringing her hands and crying. When she saw Jillian held her son, she ran forward to claim him. "Oh, thank you, Miss Hobart! Allen, honey, are you alright?"

The boy sobbed even harder when he spotted his mother. Stretching out his arms, he was passed from Jillian to his mother, to whom he clung tightly.

Peter waited while Mrs. Etter assured herself her son was in satisfactory condition. He kept one hand, comforting and secure, on Jillian's shoulder while Aaron addressed the child.

"What happened to your leg, big guy?" Aaron asked.

The boy wiped his arm across his nose. "I hurt it when that man dropped me."

Jillian and Allison both blanched. "What man, honey?" his mother asked.

"He took me off my bike," he said, his lower lip trembling with unspent tears. "I didn't want to go with him, because Miss Hobart said don't go with strangers, but he took me. I don't like him, he's mean."

Peter looked back toward the woods, his restless hand settling on the butt of the handgun tucked into his belt holster. Aaron must have noticed, because he said, "Go on. I can handle this," in a low voice only Peter could hear. "I'll call for backup."

With a single nod, Peter turned and jogged back into the thicket, hoping he would be the one to find the alleged kidnapper so he could be alone with the son of a bitch for just one minute.

***

By the time Peter returned from the wilderness, covered in mud and briars but otherwise empty-handed, reinforcements had arrived. He determined the culprit abducted Allen from the front yard and tried to make his escape through the untamed land in back when he apparently heard his siren. He guessed the guy decided it would be impossible to make a quick getaway with the squirming, crying child in tow and the cops so close, and abandoned the boy in the woods, leaving Allen, extremely nearsighted without his glasses, lost, bloodied, and frightened.

Peter heard Aaron coaxing information from the child. "Do you remember what the man looked like, Allen?" Aaron asked.

"He was really tall. He had on lots of black clothes." They were on the back patio, where Allison sat on a picnic bench, still clutching her son to her bosom. Allen struggled to turn and face Aaron, speaking solemnly. "He swore. He said the S-word two times! He's going to get in trouble for that, isn't he, Mama?"

Allison choked, laughing and crying all at once. "Yes, baby, he is."

"He messed up," Peter said.

Aaron glanced up at him. "How so?"

"Out of his element. Everything else took place at the school, safe, known. This was entirely unknown," he said, sweeping his arm toward the yard and wilderness beyond. "And he probably didn't expect us to figure out the nursery rhyme so quickly."

At Aaron's confused expression, Peter explained the message on Jillian's answering machine. They walked from the back yard into the front as they spoke, and saw chaos reigning as several more sheriff's cars and an ambulance were joined by a growing mob of curious neighbors, including the annoying television reporter from the school. Peter also muttered the S-word.

"We need to go," he said quietly to Jillian, jerking his head in the direction of the reporter. He wondered how he got here so fast.

Nodding, Jillian made her brief but heartfelt goodbyes to the Etters before following Peter to his vehicle, circling around the crowd of bystanders to avoid the media.

Only once they were in the confines of the car, both in the front seat this time, did he let loose with his scolding. "You scared the hell out of me, woman. I thought we discussed this before. When I said I didn't want you running off into any more cornfields, I was speaking metaphorically, not specifically. I do not want you running off, period. I want you in my sight at all times. Are we clear?"

She nodded, but didn't speak.

Peter started the engine and drove off, but was not content with her stony silence. "Are we clear?" he repeated, with more force than the first time.

"Yes," she said, her voice a soft squeak that turned into a heart-wrenching sob.

Peter stared. He hadn't thought he had been all that severe. He pulled to the side of the road and cut the engine. Leaning over the center console separating them, he cupped her face in his hands, wiping hot tears from her cheek with his thumbs. "Hey. Hey, what's this now? Allen's fine. In fact, you're the reason he's fine." That only seemed to make her cry harder, confusing him further.

"I know he's fine," she finally sniffed. "I'm relieved. That's why I'm crying. I was so worried, Peter. I thought, not another one. I didn't want another child hurt. My children. I feel responsible for them and what's happening to them. And then when I found him..." She trailed off and turned away, hiding her face again. "I'm babbling. You must think I'm an idiot."

"No." He ran his hand over her hair, trying his best to comfort her, wanting to do more for her. Wishing he knew what to do. "It's okay," he whispered.

"I know. I'm fine." She took a steadying breath and offered him a lopsided, wet, thoroughly unconvincing smile.

Nodding, feeling less restless now that she wasn't crying, he pulled the car back onto the road. Jillian looked out the window and her forehead creased in confusion. "Where are we going?"

"The Romeo library," he replied. "I want to check out whatever nursery rhyme books they've got. We've got to try to figure this guy out, what's he going to do next."

They received odd stares from patrons in the library. "Why are they looking at us like that?" Jillian whispered. With a grin, Peter tugged a twig from her mussed hair. She gasped and looked down at her clothes, caked in drying mud. "Oh God. I hope we don't run into someone I know," she said, hunching her shoulders as she tried to hide behind Peter, whose attire wasn't much better.

Fortunately, they did not, and after taking several books containing Mother Goose, Grimm's Fairy Tales, Aesop's Fables, and other collections they could find, Peter drove back to her place.

Jillian immediately looked more relaxed. She announced she would take a shower to rinse off the mud before whipping up something to eat. Hungry as he was, Peter stopped her. "No. I just brought you back to pack another bag. We shouldn't stay here. I think we should go to my place again tonight."

"Why? The window's fixed."

"That lousy reporter was at the Etters. Won't be long before he shows up here, too. You don't need to deal with that."

"So I won't answer the door." She crossed her arms. "Peter, why are you so worried? I want to take a shower and—"

"I'd just feel better." Peter stared deep into her green eyes as he took her hands. "Stay with me."

She stared back a moment, biting her lip, before she gave him bashful smile. "Alright. Yes."

He felt the tension leave his shoulders. "Great. We'll stop by a McDonald's drive-through on the way. I'm starving."

It took her only a few minutes to pack an overnight bag, but Peter was waiting impatiently by the door. He started to head out when she remembered something. "Oops, be right back. Go ahead and start the car. I'll be out in a second." She turned and ran back inside.

\*\*\*

Slinking down out of sight behind an overgrown shrub half a block away, he watched the cop exit Jillian's house and start the engine of the police cruiser with a roar.

*The cop's leaving. Finally. He's getting in my way. He's stealing her from me. He thinks he's so smart. He's using her to get to me. Only he doesn't know it's me. He never will, because I'm smarter than him. I'm smarter than all of them. He has to resort to using Jillian to get to me. That's not being very nice to my Jillian, using her like that, but I'll make him pay for that. Soon.*

*Now that he's leaving, now that she's alone, I'll make sure "Sergeant Peter" never gets in my way again. Once he's gone, and the skinny fairy's gone, then everything will be mine again. She will be mine again. Like she's supposed to be.*

*Just like in those pretty little children's stories.*

*Happily ever after.*

*Forever.*

He turned and darted off behind a row of houses before the sergeant could spot him – and before Jillian ran out of the house to join Peter in the car.

\*\*\*

Less than an hour later, while Jillian luxuriated in a hot shower in Peter's bathroom, he skimmed the library books, trying to think like a psychopath. Instead, he was just perplexed by poem after nonsensical poem, wondering if the children they were written for even understood half of them.

Peter shook his head with a laugh. *And they say cartoons are gratuitously violent.* They seemed to have it all: religion, violence, maybe even sex. He couldn't imagine any discerning parent reading these to their five-year-old, let alone expecting their child to understand them. He sure as hell didn't.

A knock on the door brought him out of his thoughts. Opening it a crack, he saw no one, so he opened it wider and stepped onto the porch. He thought it might be neighborhood kids pulling a prank, but then he saw the flicker of a tiny orange flame on the corner of his porch. The flame was from a black candle, the only thing keeping a white sheet of paper from fluttering away in the breeze. Reading the words on the note, he sucked in his breath, then cursed.

*Dack be nimble*
*Dack be fast*
*Dack had better*
*Watch his ass.*

He blew out the candle before the flame ignited his porch, then ran inside to grab grilling tongs and plastic bag to pick up the evidence without marring any fingerprints. Securing the items, he stalked inside, shutting and locking the door behind him. A terrifying new thought entered his mind: it wasn't just the students who had names like nursery rhymes. His last name, *Dack,* easily stood in for *Jack,* and he was pretty sure there were a couple poems involving Peters, as evidenced by the pumpkin. But what chilled him to the bone was Jillian's name. He knew very well of one rhyme in which the name *Jill* was prominently featured.

Hearing the shower stop, he stashed the evidence in the hall closet so Jillian wouldn't see it and worry.

Jillian came out wearing tight, faded jeans and an even tighter amber-colored tee-shirt, her still-damp hair pushed behind her ears and hanging straight to her shoulders. All traces of makeup were scrubbed from her face to reveal how tired and drained she was, with shadows under her green eyes. Her wet hair reminded him of the first day he met her, standing in the pouring rain, and how much he had wanted to kiss her then. And how much more so he wanted to now.

He wasn't going to let that rhyming bastard hurt her.

He waited until she was comfortably seated on his couch before he brought up his new theory. "Maybe we're going about this all wrong. Maybe it's not about the kids per se. What if this is all just a means to an end?"

She yawned. "What do you mean 'per se'? What are you talking about?"

"He's a stalker trying to get someone's attention. Your attention." He certainly had hers now. Her eyes widened, and she sat up straighter. "The investigation's been focused on the kids all this time, but I think that's just a ruse. You're no longer teaching, which is probably what he wanted all along. There's no more kids to take you away from him, so now you have that time to focus solely on him. He succeeded, at least until the next distraction came along."

She stood abruptly, grabbing his hands. "The next distraction? Who? What happened?"

So much for not worrying her. He cleared his throat before he continued. "Well, me. There was the pumpkin."

"What else?" she prompted.

Sighing, he opened the closet door and showed her the latest note. "I just found this on the porch."

She paled as she read the words, her shaking hands causing the baggie to vibrate. "He's threatening you again?"

Peter nodded tersely as he took the note back. "Because I'm in his way. I'm redirecting your focus."

She sank back onto the couch, hugging herself. "But who? Who wants my attention so badly?"

"Well, I've thought of a couple people I'd like to get alone in a dark alley."

"Who?"

"Simon Brothers is on the list. After that, it could be anyone, but Mike Georginidis might be interesting to talk to." The teacher had been hanging around too much for his liking. He told himself it wasn't jealousy.

"No, not Mike," she started to defend him, then paused in thought. "Well, maybe. He always was jealous about my job. We applied for the same one, but you knew that."

Forgetting about the note on his porch, Peter regarded her through narrowed eyes. "No, I didn't know that."

She fidgeted under his serious gaze. "Oh. We were both teaching fifth grade a couple years ago. We worked together a lot, lesson plans and stuff. When the previous kindergarten teacher retired, we both applied for it. I got the job. He didn't. Obviously."

"Why did *you* get the job?"

She pouted. "Thanks. Kick a girl while she's down."

"Why didn't Georginidis get the job?" Peter corrected.

"I guess because I have a Master's degree, and he doesn't. But he was still pretty upset that I was picked over him."

Crossing his arms over his chest, Peter stared her down. "How upset."

She nervously twisted her ring. "About as upset as you are now that I didn't tell you this before?"

His scowl turned into a reluctant smile, and he shook his head. "I'm not upset. But yes, you should have told me."

"What do we do?"

"You do nothing. I'll talk to Aaron and my father about it, bounce the ideas around a bit." She had a stubborn set to her jaw and looked ready to protest, so he kept speaking before she could. "I didn't want to tell you any of this because I knew you'd just worry more. Stop worrying."

"Right. Sure." She rubbed her arms as if cold, although the room was toasty warm.

He knew he shouldn't have told her about the note and made her worry again, but there was nothing he could do now. "Why don't you watch a movie or something, relax? I want to get out of my uniform and all this mud."

"Okay," she said noncommittally, standing to look at a collection of DVDs stacked next to his television. It was the stuff of manly men: war movies, raunchy comedies, car chases, Monty Python. Her tired face brightened when she came across a familiar title. She pulled *The Big Red 1* from the pile. "Can I watch this?"

He squinted at her. "You like war movies?"

"Not generally. But I remember when I was a kid watching it with my Dad whenever it was on TV, and I still like to watch it whenever I come across it."

He knew he was staring at her with a comical, lopsided grin, but couldn't help himself.

"What?" she asked, shifting her gaze away. "Can't a girl watch things blow up? It's not like you've got *When Harry Met Sally* here."

*Can she be any more perfect?* He handed her the remote then, still grinning, left to change and take a shower. He spent a longer time than usual under the jets of hot water, not only because of the caked-on mud, but because the shower smelled of warm vanilla-scented soap – of Jillian. The only thing better than Jillian's scent with him in the shower would have been Jillian with him in the shower. Her soap and shampoo bottles balanced in the corner of the tub were less of an annoyance than he thought they would be, and signified a permanence he considered seriously, if briefly. By the time he came back to the living room, having discarded his uniform for jeans and a Detroit Lions sweatshirt but retaining the standard police-issue gun against the small of his back because it made him feel better, she was sound asleep on the couch while Lee Marvin shot Nazis in Technicolor.

Sitting beside her curled and dozing form, his hand resting casually, familiarly, on her hip, he watched the rest of the movie and started falling into a comfortable, relaxed state that brought him close to napping himself. He was startled by a knock on the door. He hadn't been expecting visitors. A quick glance out the window revealed it was dusk.

Reaching around to take the .40 caliber Glock semiautomatic pistol from his belt, he opened the door a crack and peered out, back pressed against the wall and gunbarrel pointing safely up. He wanted to make sure it wasn't that bastard Father Noose leaving another note, or that bastard television reporter looking for a comment on the Etter incident. Actually, he wasn't sure which would be worse. Seeing nothing, he yanked the door fully open and jumped into the door frame, knees slightly bent and gun extended before him in a shooter's stance.

"Holy mother of God." Aaron choked on the words, stumbling backward off the porch. He was out of his uniform and wearing civvies of blue jeans, matching denim jacket, black tee-shirt, and snakeskin boots. A motorcycle helmet was tucked under one arm.

He quickly recovered his balance and said, "Dude, what's with the gun? It's not very hospitable of you, is it?"

"Sorry. I was half expecting Father Noose or the damned TV news crew."

"Wouldn't mind shooting a couple reporters. Scared the shit out of me, though."

Peter reholstered and stepped aside to usher him in, feeling a little foolish, but just for a moment, because he only been concerned with protecting Jillian. "I do have a phone, Opie," he chided.

"Your point?" Aaron grinned and slugged Peter's shoulder in greeting. "I was riding my bike one last time before I put her away for the season and saw your car parked out front. So where's Jillian?" Peter, rubbing his shoulder where Aaron hit him, tilted his head to the sleeping form on the couch, so Aaron lowered his voice. "Got something out of the kid thought you might like to hear."

"Good," Peter said. "I've got something for you that you won't like one bit. You go first." He led Aaron into the kitchen so they wouldn't disturb Jillian, and fished two beers from the fridge.

"The kid recognized the kidnapper," Aaron said as he twisted the top of one of the bottles.

"He knows him?" Peter set his beer, now forgotten, on the counter and pounced on Aaron's announcement.

"No, he *recognized* him. The kid swears it's the same guy as the Muffin Man. Even had on the same hoodie."

*Crap. They* are *all connected.* "Can he ID him? Did we get a description?" Peter paced around Aaron as he fired off the questions.

Aaron shook his head. "No. The kid's five. He's smart enough to know it's the same guy, but we can't get anything useful out of him other than a tall white male between the ages of eighteen and forty, wearing a black hoodie."

"Tall?" Peter ran the list of suspects through his head. He wouldn't consider either Georginidis or Brothers particularly tall. If he remembered correctly, he was taller than both of them.

Aaron shrugged. "To a three-foot-high five-year-old, everyone's tall." He chugged half the Heineken in two long gulps. "Your turn, boss. And stop that pacing, will you? You're making me dizzy."

Peter retrieved the candle and note and passed them to Aaron, charging him with logging them as evidence at headquarters. Aaron whistled quietly when he read the note. "Someone's not happy."

"I'm sure as hell not," Peter replied.

"Coulda fooled me," Aaron said, a slow, sly grin forming.

Peter raised an eyebrow. "What do you mean?"

Aaron took another swig of the beer. "Lately, you've been a lot happier than I think I've ever seen you. I think she may have something to do with that." He jerked his thumb in the direction of the living room, and Jillian. "Am I right?"

"No," Peter snapped. But even as he made the denial, he figured what his friend said was probably the truth.

Aaron, having made his point, let the matter drop and the conversation, fueled by beer, turned to whether the Detroit Lions would ever be good enough to make it to the Super Bowl. Their discussion became loud and heated.

"Is everything alright?" Jillian called as she padded barefoot into the kitchen, rubbing sleep out of her eyes.

Peter moved off his stool. "Fine. Sorry, did I wake you?" She nodded, and he wrapped his arms around her as she closed her eyes and nuzzled against his neck. *Yeah, maybe Aaron knows what he's talking about.*

"Should I come back later?"

Jillian jumped when Aaron spoke, pushing out of Peter's arms and turning pink. "Hi. Um. I didn't know you were here." Aaron appraised her with a knowing leer, and her blush deepened.

Peter just laughed. "I was about to throw some chicken on the grill. Want some?"

The three enjoyed an evening of food and laughter, much needed after the weeks of stress, but exhaustion caught up with Jillian once again and she started to fall asleep while eating. Peter spied her head nod and jerk more than once, and ushered Aaron out before he half-carried Jillian, stumbling with fatigue, off to bed.

# CHAPTER TWENTY-FOUR

**P**ETER WAS AWAKENED BY THE SOUND of rain pounding on the roof from yet another storm. It was past eight o'clock in the morning, and the latest he could remember sleeping in years. He held Jillian responsible for that. Smiling, he glanced over his shoulder to where she still slept curled up against his back and realized Aaron was right: he was happy. He wanted to wake her to make love to her, but she looked so peaceful, her deep, even breathing telling him she was still sleeping soundly, pure exhaustion having taken its toll. She looked so perfect in his bed; not just soft and beautiful, but right, like she belonged there.

The harsh ringing of the phone on the nightstand next to the bed brought him out of his pleasant thoughts, and Jillian out of her slumber. She sat up while he spoke on the phone, and he enjoyed the way her body moved when she stretched like a lazy cat. A soft, curvaceous, beautiful lazy cat.

"Get dressed. We have to go in to the station," he told her as he hung up the receiver.

She leaned against his bare chest, tilting her head back to look at him, her eyes still half closed with sleep, looking inviting and sexy as hell. "Do we have to?"

A smile played at the corners of his lips as he considered what he would rather be doing. "Yes. Come on." He playfully pushed her out of bed.

169

The sky was drab and dreary, but the rain had stopped falling. Peter was impatient to leave, his workaholic habits not easily broken, so he went to start the car while he waited for Jillian. The crisp chill in the air made him shiver, and he zipped his jacket up to his chin.

Jillian finally rushed out the door, dressed in faded jeans and a pink cashmere cardigan hanging open over a lacy camisole, still trying to pull her hair back off her forehead with little daisy-patterned barrettes. She banged on the passenger-side window when she realized the doors were locked. "Let me in, Peter."

After she was buckled in, Peter pulled the squad car backward out of the driveway. As the vehicle bounced over the curb, the glove box popped open and a piece of yellow construction paper fell into Jillian's lap. "Must not have closed your glove box tight," she said, picking up the paper.

"I wasn't in my glove compartment recently," Peter said, giving it a sideways glance as he shifted out of Reverse into Drive and stepped on the gas pedal with a heavy foot in his rush to get to the station. He heard her gasp. "What?"

Her voice came out in almost a whisper. "It's another note. From him." She read the word aloud for Peter.

*Dack, not Jill, went down the hill*
*to crash and drown in water,*
*Dack rolled down and broke his Crown,*
*and Jill will tumble later.*

He glanced at the paper she held but quickly returned his attention to driving. Something was wrong; the car wasn't handling like he was used to. He pressed the brake pedal and frowned.

The car lurched. "This can't be good." Peter said through clenched teeth.

Jillian waved the paper. "No, it isn't good at all. It means Father Noose broke into your car!"

"That's not all he did," Peter said as his heartbeat escalated. "The brakes aren't working."

"What?" Jillian dropped the note and clutched the passenger assist handle above her door.

He flicked on the lights and sirens, hoping it would alert innocent bystanders to get the hell out of the way. It was still early, but a few people were already on the street. A startled pedestrian jumped back onto the curb mere seconds before Peter ran him down. Drivers pulling vehicles out of their driveways slammed on their brakes to avoid a collision. The Crown Victoria careened down the steep street through the neighborhood as he struggled to maintain control. He instinctively stomped on the brakes again, and the tires squealed and the vehicle lurched, but it didn't stop. In fact, it seemed to be *gaining* speed, even more than he would have expected just from coasting downhill.

Swearing, grasping desperately for any idea, tried prying his foot under the accelerator pedal, thinking it was jammed, but nothing happened. He didn't dare turn off the engine. That would only disable the power steering, and since the brakes were of no help, he needed everything that still worked at his disposal. Even after many hours of county sheriff-mandated instruction in defensive driving, Peter found the speeding car almost too much to handle. It zoomed past other automobiles on the road as it headed down the hill. At the bottom was the Clinton River, swollen and rapid from the recent precipitation. He swore again as he had a horrific vision of plunging the vehicle into the cold river and Jillian drowning. If the impact didn't kill her first.

Jillian opened her eyes long enough to notice the car's trajectory. "Peter! The river!"

"I know," he said, bleakly. "Hold on."

He yanked hard on the steering wheel and prayed the power steering would obey his command and not give out like everything else. To his relief, the vehicle veered to the left. Now instead of the river, it was aimed at a furniture delivery truck parked along the river's edge. He stood on the brakes again, even though he knew his efforts were moot. It was an automatic reaction fueled by habit and fear.

Jillian's terrified scream was cut short as the cruiser slammed into the cab of the truck, the deafening rending of metal echoing in her ears. Front air bags deployed immediately, exploding giant nylon pillows into their faces as the impact sent Peter and Jillian pitching forward toward the dashboard. The angle of the collision combined with forward speed kept the vehicle in motion; it lifted off its back wheels and crushed the passenger side into the trailer. The door frame buckled, the window shattered, and glass sprayed all over the inside of the vehicle. The vehicle finally came to a stop, wedged hard against the truck.

The air bag deflated just as quickly as it had opened, and Peter sat stunned, laying his forehead against the steering wheel as he tried to catch his breath, coming in deep, ragged gasps. He took mental inventory of himself and decided he was alive; the sharp pain in his knee told him so. He snapped his head up and let loose with an angry string of vulgarities. A shallow moan caught his attention and shut him up mid-expletive.

Jillian lay limp against crushed metal and plastic. "Oh God. Jillian!" He reached across the armrest console to touch her. Gently turning her face toward him, he smoothed back her disheveled hair to reveal a trickle of blood oozing down her forehead from her scalp, above her right temple. "Oh God, please, no. Jillian! Are you alright?"

"My head hurts," she mumbled without opening her eyes. Her weak voice was barely audible.

Sagging with relief, he closed his eyes and rested his forehead on her shoulder. He hadn't killed her. He would never be able to live with himself if he had. "You love her, damn it," he said to himself. "Deal with it."

He wanted to pull her from the mangled wreck and hold her to convince himself she truly was all right, but knew better than to try to move her after such a horrific accident and risk injuring her further. Instead he radioed dispatch for assistance, his requests more like commands as he shouted with barely restrained panic. Hearing a commotion, he looked out the shattered window to see a crowd gathering. "Call 911," he yelled at the nearest person before returning his attention to Jillian.

A short, wiry man in his forties with permanent grease stains under his fingernails yanked opened Peter's door. "You okay, man?"

Peter waved him off, not taking his eyes off Jillian. "Stand back," he muttered.

The man removed his NASCAR jacket and handed it to Peter. "Put that on her," he said. Peter grabbed it and draped it over her torso, then tersely nodded his thanks.

"What happened?" The man looked back and forth between the totaled car and Peter.

"I don't know." Peter knew he was being curt, but he didn't care. All he cared about was Jillian.

"I'm a mechanic. Danny," the man introduced himself. "I saw your brake lights go on, but you didn't stop."

"No, I didn't," Peter snapped. His voice turned gentle when he addressed Jillian, caressing her face. "Can you hear me, Jillian? Oh, baby, I'm so sorry. Say something, please." She only groaned. "Where the hell is the ambulance?" Peter yelled.

"Chill out, man, she'll be okay."

"Oh God..."

"Look," Danny said. "I'll stick around. I might know what happened. I've seen this before on the racetrack, I think. Looks familiar. Yeah." He stepped back to look speculatively at the wrecked car, nodding. When he turned back to Peter, he opened his mouth to speak but stopped and stared, agape. Peter didn't care that Danny noticed the tears glistening in his eyes.

"They're coming," Danny said softly as sirens sounded in the distance. "It'll be alright, man."

\*\*\*

*NO!*

The word echoed in his head, over and over, as he helplessly watched the car careen down the street toward the river, just like it was supposed to. It was almost perfect. Except that Jillian was in the damn car with the fucking cop. What had he done? How did she get there? What was she doing spending the night at his house? *She wasn't supposed to be there!*

Not thinking about himself, he jumped from his hiding spot behind a hedgerow as the car sped by. He briefly saw Peter's grim face and Jillian's frightened one. His heart wrenched in his throat as he pictured Peter dead, bloody, mangled, and drowned, which was a pleasing image in and of itself until he saw Jillian right there along side him, her beautiful ivory skin marred by ugly, gaping wounds.

He cringed when the vehicle slammed into the tractor-trailer, held his breath for what seemed like forever until he heard cop shouting for an ambulance. He let out his breath in a rush, knowing Jillian must still be alive. But then the anger came upon him so swiftly, he had to restrain himself from rushing down the hill and pummeling the fucking cop right there. *She wasn't supposed to be in the car! That wasn't part of the plan. That bastard cop messed up all my plans lately, first with the crying brat on the bike, and now this, ruining my perfect plan and almost getting Jillian killed like that. It's all his fault!*

Suddenly weak, he sat on the cool, wet grass and took a few deep breaths. He needed to rethink his strategy. He had to move forward faster than expected now. The fucking cop would pay for getting in his way. The fucking cop would be sorry when he realized Jillian belonged to him.

# CHAPTER TWENTY-FIVE

THE DRAB BEIGE HOSPITAL ROOM OVERFLOWED with bright, fragrant flowers. Tasteful arrangements with carnations, ferns, and tulips from Antoinette Jones, Jillian's parents, and her sister in Grand Rapids were paired with colorful autumn bouquets from other well-wishers. They were all overpowered by the elaborate display prominently featuring calla lilies and Birds of Paradise that Donovan sent. But the flowers Jillian kept by her bedside were a straggly bunch of daisies Peter bought in the gift shop downstairs.

Peter's uniform was sagging and wrinkled, the tie loosened and the top shirt buttons undone, after spending the last twenty-five hours in it. The grizzled stubble on his jaw was thick from going without shaving. He had stayed in the hospital with her all night. He didn't eat, and certainly couldn't sleep in the uncomfortable unpadded chairs, as he kept watch over her, berating himself over and over for letting her get hurt. Five stitches closed the gash on her head, her torso was bruised where the seat belt cut into her, and she had a mild concussion. Peter had only jammed his knee into the dash and refused medical treatment, convincing himself it was only temporary. It was stiff and swollen and he limped when he walked, but he didn't care. It was not nearly as important as Jillian.

She was sitting up in bed now, alert and talking to visitors, telling everyone she just wanted to go home. He knew she hated all the attention; she had pulled the bed sheet up to her neck to conceal as much of the puke-green, open-backed, modesty-be-damned hospital smock, and herself, as possible.

When the latest batch of well-wishers took their leave, Peter was alone with her for the first time since she was awake and lucid. He rounded the bed so he could keep watch on the door and took her hand that did not have a long IV needle impaled into it. Griping it tightly, he leaned in close and apologized again in earnest. He had been doing it all night, but was sure she didn't remember as she drifted in and out of consciousness.

"Peter," she said softly, silencing him. "It's not your fault."

He dropped his head to her hand and let out a long breath. "I know." He hoped the despair in his voice didn't betray that he was lying.

"Did you see the note?"

He straightened. "Yeah. Aaron found it when they went through the car at the garage. The son of a bitch thinks he's funny. Did you see how he capitalized Crown in the rhyme?"

She shook her head. "No. What's that mean?"

"He took crown meaning head, and tailored it specifically for me and my *Crown* Victoria. My car. Jesus."

"Does that mean he tampered with the car to make it do that? To match the rhyme?"

"Seems that way.

"So now he's trying to kill us, too."

"Not us. Me." He continued quickly when he saw the panic in her eyes. "Remember the pumpkin note? It was directed at me. So was the candle. He was warning me to stay away from you. Maybe he figured, since I was at home, that I was alone. He changed the end of the rhyme to read *'and Jill will tumble later.'* I don't think he counted on you being in that car."

"I don't think he counted on you being such a good driver, either," Aaron said from the hallway, back to wearing his uniform. "Hey, Jillian. Got a minute, boss?"

"You'll be okay?" Peter asked Jillian, still not comfortable leaving her alone.

She nodded. "I'll be fine. Go on."

Peter led Aaron down the hall to a waiting room with a coffeepot and vending machine. Fishing coins from his pocket, he selected a bag of potato chips while Aaron spoke.

"That mechanic guy who saw the accident told me about some race car drivers who had a similar thing happen to them, and that got me thinking. So I had the lab boys look at it and sure enough, the throttle was stuck open." He explained that the throttle is linked to the accelerator, and if damaged, the car won't return to idle, instead accelerating so fast it even overrides the brakes. "But it wasn't normal wear and tear. The throttle assembly was all scratched and bent; someone messed with it to cause it to jam up. You were lucky."

"Funny, I don't feel lucky." Peter tore open the bag of chips and stuffed a handful in his mouth.

"You should. The car's totaled. The front end's an accordion and the frame's bent to shit."

"Yes, I remember," Peter said, wanting to forget.

Aaron continued undeterred. "I remember a race a few years back when this one guy wrecked his Pontiac with that same problem. Total crash and burn. He managed to live through it, too. Dude, you should have seen it."

"I think I just did," Peter replied, tossing his empty chip bag into a garbage can. He let out a frustrated sigh. "I feel like I'm running in circles here."

Aaron nodded. "Yeah, I noticed you do that a lot lately."

"Huh?"

Aaron shrugged. "You pace when you're really thinking about something, and when you pace you walk in little circles. My brother's dog does the same thing, only she lies down and goes to sleep when she's done."

"Funny," Peter said, not meaning it. "Don't knock it. It helps me think."

"Think of anything important?"

Peter shoved his hands in his pockets. "Not yet, damn it."

"Yeah, works real good." Aaron's laughter echoed down the hall as he walked away.

*** 

Jillian leaned back on the bed and closed her eyes, intending to doze before Peter returned. She hadn't gotten much rest between nurses and visitors, despite the pain killers and sleeping pills coursing through her system. She just wanted to go home, which according to her doctor, should be soon. It just wasn't soon enough.

She finally started drifting to sleep when she heard a rustling on the table next to her. Opening her eyes, she saw the wilting daisies were gone, replaced with a dozen gorgeous long-stem red roses. Smiling, lifted her gaze to thank Peter. Her smile faded a bit when she saw Mike instead.

"I didn't mean to wake you," he said, but eagerly leaned in closer now that she was awake. "I brought you flowers. I've been so worried about you since I heard the news. My God, that deputy could have killed you!"

It took Jillian's dazed brain a minute to realize what he was talking about. "Thank you. But *Sergeant* Dack didn't do anything wrong," she said, emphasizing his rank to correct him, "and if someone else had been driving, I would have been killed."

"They said on TV your injuries weren't life-threatening," he said, making her cringe when she heard she made the news yet again. His words were rapid, almost manic, and she had a hard time following him. "I called everyone I could think of for more information, but no one could tell me anything, so I had to come and see you for myself, to make sure you were alive. Thank God you are. I can't tell you what I thought when I found out you were in that car."

"I'm fine, Mike." She shifted on the bed, moving back from him, unnerved by his excessive concern.

"I'm so glad." He sat on the edge of the bed. "Hearing what happened to you yesterday really shook me. Jillian, I know things have been tense between us since our date, but I want that to change."

"It wasn't a date," Jillian said through clenched teeth, but Mike either did not hear her or chose to ignore her. She put even odds on the latter.

"I want to see you again. Socially."

"Mike—"

"I think about you all the time, Jillian, and I really want us to work. I want to take you on another date."

"Michael—"

"I'll take you to the best restaurant, whatever you want. It will be even better than the first date. I want—"

He wasn't listening to her, wasn't letting her get a word in edgewise. The frustration and the pain and the stress and the constant invasions of her privacy over the last few days hours finally took their toll and she snapped. "Damn it, it was not a date!"

Stunned by her uncharacteristic outburst, Mike stopped talking and stared at her. She took advantage of the temporary silence to speak, before she lost her nerve or Mike started babbling again.

"We were never on a date. I would appreciate it if you would stop telling people that we were."

"But—"

"Two co-workers meeting after work to discuss work does not constitute a date."

"I'm sorry, Jillian, I'll make it up to you this time."

Jillian raised her hands to her head, wanting to pull her hair out. "Stop it! Just stop! Thank you for the flowers. They're lovely. But they won't make me agree to go out with you for dinner, or lunch, or coffee, or anything. I don't think of you that way. There is nothing between us. Not now. Not ever." It felt good for her to be so blunt and let her feelings flow unchecked.

"You're in love with *him*, aren't you." Mike sounded hurt and resentful.

"Him?" she repeated, feigning misunderstanding, but she knew he meant Peter. She blinked. Was it that obvious?

But before she could reply, his eyes narrowed into a scowl. "You never really gave me a chance. *Us* a chance. Give me one more chance, Jillian." He took her hand in his and squeezed in earnest. Unfortunately, it was the hand with the IV below her middle knuckle. Bolting upright, the sudden movement making her dizzy, she cried out in pain as the needle shifted and pressed into her, grinding against bone. "Ouch! Mike, stop! *Ow!*"

Peter rushed in, his heart in his throat and rage in his veins. Grabbing Georginidis by the back of his shirt, he pivoted and slammed him face-first against the wall, pinning him there by pressing his forearm hard against his shoulder blades, quickly patting him down for weapons with his other hand.

"Hands up, where I can see them," Peter demanded, kicking Georginidis' feet apart until he was spread-eagled. "What the hell were you doing?"

"I didn't mean to hurt her!" Georginidis blurted.

After assuring himself Georginidis was not carrying a concealed weapon and had calmed down enough to release the shorter man, Peter turned to address Jillian. She was clutching her hand to her chest and staring at them in shock. "Are you okay?" he asked, gently taking Jillian's taped hand in his. "Looks okay. Want me to call a nurse?"

She shook her head. "No, I think it's — Oh!" Her words were cut off with a cry as she saw what Peter couldn't. Georginidis attacked him from behind with such ferocity, Peter had no time to react. He sprawled across the bed in Jillian's lap when Georginidis sucker-punched him in the kidneys.

"She could have died in that crash, you son of a bitch. If she hadn't been in that car with you, she'd be fine! It's your fault!" Georginidis took another swing, this time at Peter's jaw, when Peter pushed himself off the bed.

"Peter!" Jillian shouted. But he was prepared now. He ducked the swing and fought back, jabbing Georginidis hard in the solar plexus, leaving him doubled over and gasping. He followed that with a quick uppercut, slamming his fist into Georginidis' chin and sending him flailing backwards. Georginidis fell against the wall, knocking his roses to the floor, the vase shattering and water splashing everywhere. Georginidis slumped down the wall until he sagged onto the floor, out cold.

Aaron rushed in to the room, a perky blonde nurse tagging behind him. "Jesus, what happened?"

Chest heaving, Peter turned. "Where were you?" From the guilty glance Aaron sent between Peter and the R.N., he realized his friend had been flirting with the young woman. "Took you long enough to get here."

Aaron knelt next to the prone man and automatically checked for a pulse. "Well, I'm here now. What do you want me to do?"

Peter pressed a hand against his sore back. He was getting too old for this. He certainly felt old, with all the aches and pains he had today. "Arrest the bastard for assaulting an officer. Make sure he's awake when you do it. I want him to remember it."

Aaron looked up at him, surprised. "You okay?"

With a patronizing laugh, Peter said, "I've been punched harder by girls."

Jillian leaned forward, touching his hand. "No, really," she said quietly. Her expression was imploring and full of concern. "Are you alright? There's doctors here, you know. I can call one."

Amused and warmed by her concern, Peter smiled and lifted his hand to her cheek. "I'm fine."

Aaron pulled Georginidis to his feet, draping the unconscious man's arms around his and the nurse's shoulders to drag him out of the room, when Simon Brothers appeared in the doorway. In his hands he held another vase of roses.

*Oh, hell no*, Peter thought, groaning, and wondered if he would get to punch Brothers as well. He knew he was being overly protective and possessive of Jillian, and he knew why, but he tried not to dwell on it.

"Is there a problem here?" Brothers asked, gawking as Georginidis was carried away, feet dragging behind him.

"He's allergic to flowers," Peter muttered, not bothering to hide his displeasure at seeing the township supervisor. Judging from the glare Brothers directed at Peter, the feeling was mutual. Peter would have preferred to kick him out, but he brought his son Jonathon for a visit, and Jillian's face brightened when she saw the child. He instantly felt better just seeing the delight in Jillian's eyes, something that hadn't been there in a while. She had been deprived of her students for too long, and he couldn't bring himself to stop the reunion that clearly brought her joy.

The little boy scampered across the room, grinning, and climbed onto the bed beside Jillian, proudly holding up a sloppy watercolor painting of what appeared to be a five-year-old's interpretation of Godzilla overtaking Tokyo. "I made this for you, Miss Hobart," he said, snuggling up against her side. "I'm sorry you're not at school anymore. When are you coming back?"

Jillian hugged the boy. "Soon, I hope." Peter thought she glowed as the child proceeded to tell her all the important things she'd missed: who had a birthday and brought snacks, who tripped and skinned her knees on the playground, who was sent to the office by the substitute teacher for misbehaving. By the time Brothers pulled the reluctant child away from the bed to leave, the color had returned to Jillian's face and she looked relaxed. Even Brothers addressing her seemed to do little to diminish her good mood.

"Jonathon is correct. You are indeed missed at school, Miss Hobart," he said. "The parents have realized their folly and wish you a speedy recovery. As always, you have my best wishes, and my offer to help you in any way still stands. Between the two of us, I'm sure we'll be able to come up with a solution for this mess." He leaned over her bed and patted her leg a little too high up on her thigh, either unaware of or ignoring the fact that she recoiled away from him. "I can help you, Jillian. You can make this stop if you work with me."

*That's interesting*, Peter thought, repressing the urge to clobber him, too. His eyes narrowing, Peter cleared his throat loudly. Brothers must have taken the hint because he stepped back, gathering his son to leave, but not without another irritated scowl at Peter.

Peter restlessly paced outside the door, searching for any new visitors. Seeing none, he turned back into the room. "When did the doctor say you could go home?"

Settling back into the bed, she replied, "Sometime today. I hope soon. I'd like put on some decent clothes and sleep in my own bed."

Peter didn't like that plan, at least as it regarded her own bed, but he said nothing. He simply turned and walked out of the room to the nurses' station and demanded to speak to her doctor.

# CHAPTER TWENTY-SIX

FTER SPRINGING HER FROM THE HOSPITAL, Peter made sure he was never far from her side. He wandered only as far away as the kitchen for the rest of the afternoon, when he thought she needed something to drink, a cold compress or painkillers, and a heaping bowl of her favorite butter pecan ice cream. Even while on the phone with Aaron, he kept her within eyesight. He stayed with her, sitting nearby or pacing beside her, attending to her every time she shifted or made a sound, waiting on her hand and foot until she started to feel uncomfortable with all the attention and demanded he stop.

She let out a long breath. "Peter, I'm fine. Quit acting like a mother hen." She shifted, wincing, and sat up on the couch. Peter instantly moved in and sat beside her.

"You're not fine. You have a concussion and stitches."

She laid her hand over his. "You didn't put them there."

He closed his eyes. He saw the image of Jillian bloody and unconscious and opened them again. With a heavy sigh, Peter spoke. "I thought I had killed you."

"You didn't. Stop feeling guilty. I don't blame you, so you shouldn't either."

"It scared the hell out of me," he said, continuing to speak as if he hadn't heard her. He withdrew his hand from her gentle grasp and let his fingers trace the outline of her jaw, her lips. He couldn't stop touching her, couldn't stop thinking that he came so close to not being able to touch her ever again. "I don't know what I'd have done if you died yesterday."

She raised her hand to his, pressing his palm against her cheek. "But I didn't."

"I —" Peter started, but she moved her fingers to his lips, silencing him.

"Stop worrying about it and kiss me."

"What?" He stared at her, dumbstruck. But he had little time to be surprised by her forwardness.

She leaned in and captured his mouth with hers, warm and hard. And he reacted instantly as he let the guilt and grief manifest itself in passion. She wrapped her arms around his neck, tugging on his hair to draw him closer. With a sharp breath, Peter deepened the kiss and moved his hands down, cupping her breasts through the soft, pale yellow velvet dress she had exchanged with the hospital smock.

She moaned and arched into his touch. Wanting, needing to touch all of her at once, he ran his fingers through her hair, accidentally brushing over her stitches. With a cry, she pulled away and roughly shoved his shoulders until he sprawled on his back on the couch.

Dazed, Peter looked up at her. "I'm sorry, did I hurt you?"

"Yes, but you can kiss it and make it better," she said, her voice husky. Staring at him with dark, burning eyes, she shifted her body until she brazenly straddled his lap. Capturing his face in her hands, she crushed her lips to his. Her mouth was hot and hungry. Peter fisted one hand into her hair, careful this time to avoid her wound, while the fingers of his other hand held tight to her hip. Her own busy hands moved to remove his uniform, loosening his tie and pulling impatiently at his shirt, popping buttons, tearing at the Velcro straps of his Kevlar vest, then raking her nails over his bare chest, provoking a groan from Peter. Encouraged, Jillian shifted down, focusing her lips on the hollow of his throat so her hands could reach lower. Before he knew what was happening, she unsnapped the brown slacks of his uniform and curved her greedy hands around him.

He sucked in air, then swore, trying in vain to reach her caressing hands as sheer pleasure washed over him. When he realized she wouldn't be stopped, he gave her the same courtesy: hot, hard kisses as he lifted her dress and slid his fingers under the warm silk of her panties until she moaned his name. He felt his control slipping as her hands did incredible things to him. "Slow down," he gasped, and then sat staring, breathless and disappointed, when she climbed off his lap and stood before him. "I said slow down, not stop."

Holding his gaze, she slid her hands under her dress and made a downward motion, traveling the length of her legs. He watched her movements, wide-eyed and absolutely still. When she straightened, she simply handed him her green panties. Slack-jawed, he looked down at them and then back up at her. Before he could gather his senses to speak, she straddled him again, her dress billowing around him, her knees planted on either side of his hips, and lowered herself onto him inch by tormenting inch.

"Jillian!" he gasped. Unprepared for her bold move, he sat up, eyes wide. "Wait, I—." But she was too intent on her task and quickly he was overtaken by the same unstoppable desire and gave in to her primal needs, and his own.

"I want to feel alive," she whispered into his ear, making him shudder. "Make me feel alive."

The world stopped as he felt himself sliding into her warmth, reveled in her first gasp of pleasure and her tight, wet heat. She began to rock, starting a hard, steady, tortuous rhythm, and he ratcheted up the pace when he dropped the panties he still held to grip her soft, round hips, rocking her even harder and faster as he thrust into her. Crying out, she arched over him. She didn't want gentle now and demanded more, and Peter gave her more, meeting her frantic pace. His vision grew hazy as he watched her bite her lip and close her eyes in ecstasy, then he buried his face between her breasts when she yanked on his hair and screamed and came apart in his arms. With a groan, he followed with a release so powerful, Peter thought he just might die, and he was perfectly fine with that, as long as he died in Jillian's arms.

She collapsed against him, panting, and together they lay sprawled on the couch. Jillian sighed and ran her hands through his tousled hair.

"Now that's what I call being waylaid." Peter pulled his head back to smile down at her. "So much for you being shy, huh?" he said lightly. Her hands stopped in mid-caress, and he watched the familiar bloom creep across her cheeks. "Oh, sure, now you get all modest and demure."

Giggling, Jillian pressed her face against his shoulder. "I'm not so shy once you get to know me," she said, her voice muffled.

With a chuckle, Peter kissed the top of her head, lifted her up and off his lap, then stood to fasten his pants before handing Jillian her panties. She quickly pulled them on under her dress. "See you found out green is my favorite color." Now acting every bit as shy as Peter expected, she ducked her head, letting her hair fall over her face, hiding behind it, but not before Peter her bite her lip to hide a wide grin. *God, she's beautiful.*

The passion they shared had been incredible, but a combination of worry and guilt nagged at him. "You should have waited, though, until I put on a con—"

Speaking rapidly and a little too loud in her embarrassment, Jillian spoke over him. "It's okay. I take, um, you know. We're covered." Furiously blushing, she turned away, unable to look at him.

The tension went out of Peter's shoulders and he smiled with a combination of relief, respect, and amusement at her sudden return to shyness. "Good to know." He pulled her close for a fierce hug, his arms circling tight and possessive. "I could get used to having you around," he said, nuzzling into her soft hair, inhaling her sweet scent.

He felt her body tense. "Don't get too used to me," she said, her voice flat. "You never know what might happen."

His voice became gruff. "I'm not going to let anything else happen to you." His arms tightened around her protectively as he spoke, as if to prove his point.

"I know." She pushed away from his embrace, taking a deep breath. She didn't look at him.

"What's wrong?" Peter didn't want to let go of her just yet, but he wasn't given the choice. He watched her retreat into herself again, the shyness, the unease creeping back where there had briefly been happiness. He saw how she interacted with others, especially strangers. She was different with him, until now. He wanted to hold her but stood still as she paced her way to the other side of the room.

The anxiety built inside her until she couldn't breathe. She loved him, she knew it now, but she had to be realistic. Her heart felt tight in her chest as she thought of a way to let Peter down softly. To let herself down without breaking her own heart. "You're only saying that because my kids are dying."

He went absolutely still. "What do you mean?"

Panic rose in her and she squeezed her eyes shut so she wouldn't have to look at him. If she looked into his intense, caring azure eyes, she wouldn't be able to say this. "What if this whole thing is just pure adrenaline and fear creating a sense of need and nothing else?"

"What whole thing?"

"This." Swallowing, she gestured with her index finger between the two of them. "Me and you."

"It's not." He sounded so sure.

She, on the other hand, was not so sure. "What if it is?"

"What are you afraid of?" he countered.

Her body shuddered. "More children dying."

"What else?"

"Me dying."

Crossing the room to her, his voice softened and he reached to caress a strand of her hair. "What else?"

She struggled to get the words out, her voice cracking with the emotion she tried so unsuccessfully to hide. "You dying."

"And?" There was a hint of amusement now.

"God, you're pushy. No wonder you made sergeant."

He smirked. "And?" he simply repeated.

With a deep breath, she let out all her fears – and hopes. "I'm afraid … What if it is just adrenaline and not…? I mean, what if once this is all over, and everything goes back to normal, you won't — you can't stand the sight of me anymore?"

Peter looked angry, so she automatically started to apologize. But the words stuck in her throat.

"I doubt that," he said roughly. He held her chin in his hand, forcing her to look at him. "I've been a cop for a long time. I don't make a regular habit of falling in love with all my witnesses."

With a sound that came out as a cross between a sob and a laugh, Jillian said, "I'm trying to be serious here."

He nodded. "Okay, maybe it does happen on occasion, but not regularly."

She could tell by the satisfied smirk on his face that he was joking. Maybe. Then she blinked. "What did you just say?"

Peter's cell phone rang. Irritated by the interruption, he snatched it from the coffee table, instantly reverting to the role of sergeant. He snapped brusquely into the receiver. "Talk to me, Aaron. Right. Okay. I'm at Jillian's. Let me work some things out. See you soon." He clicked off the phone. "Aaron already executed the search warrant on Georginidis."

"That was fast," Jillian said. Her legs were shaky, and she had to sit down. What was Peter trying to tell her before his phone rang? Did he feel the same way about her that she felt for him? But she couldn't ask, even if she had been brave enough to do so, because Peter was on a roll.

"The legal system works at leaps and bounds when one of the charges is assaulting an officer. I need to go in to the station. I want to be there when they question Georginidis about a few of the things they found. Who do you want me to call to stay with you?"

She stuck her bottom lip out in a pout. "I don't need anyone to stay with me."

"I disagree. What's Tina's number?" When she stubbornly refused to answer, he simply took her cell phone from her purse, found the number in its memory, and dialed it himself. Within seconds, he was making arrangements with Tina to spend part of the afternoon with Jillian, before her evening shift at the restaurant, at which point Donovan would fill in if Peter was still detained. She made it to the house in less than ten minutes. He was halfway out the door as Tina jogged up the driveway. Almost as an afterthought, he turned and took Jillian in his arms, giving her a fast, hard kiss. "I'll try not to be long," he said. "We'll finish our conversation when I get back." And then he was gone.

# CHAPTER TWENTY-SEVEN

========================================

**W**HEN PETER STRODE INTO THE WINDOWLESS, dimly lit interrogation room, Mike Georginidis sat in a metal folding chair, nervously sipping tepid water from a paper cup, while Deputy Aaron Anderson looked on with disinterest, leaning lazily against the wall, his arms crossed over his chest.

"What took you so long?" Aaron said with evident impatience.

"I had to make a phone call." Peter yanked out a chair across the bare table from Georginidis and sat, staring at him. "I know Deputy Anderson already asked, but let's just make sure all our bases are covered. Do you want an attorney present?"

He scowled. "I already told him. I don't need an attorney because I didn't do anything wrong."

Peter nodded curtly. "Assaulting an officer, with witnesses present, sounds pretty wrong to me, but if that's how you want to play it, I can work with that. So, Mr. Georginidis, you do understand why I've brought you here today?"

The teacher's scowl deepened as he set the empty cup on the table. "This isn't about punching you, which was, by the way, in self-defense. Jillian will back me up when I say you started it by grabbing me and ripping my shirt. Why don't you just say it. You think I'm the guy stalking Jillian and hurting her students."

"Don't you mean killing her students?" He kept his face impassive, his voice almost polite.

Shaking his head, Georginidis insisted, "I didn't do it. Any of it!"

Aaron sat beside Peter and opened a notebook, writing in it as he spoke. "Mr. Georginidis – can I call you Mike?" He smiled brightly and continued before he was given an answer. "Mike, we have reason to believe you had a grudge against Jillian Hobart because of a perceived job-related slight. Do you know what I am referring to?"

"A slight?" He looked confused for a moment, then laughed. "You think I'm killing her students because she wouldn't go out on another date with me?"

Peter envisioned him dating Jillian, kissing Jillian, and he clenched his jaw as he tried to keep his jealousy in check. He raised an eyebrow in what he hoped was a nonchalant response. "Well, no, that's not what we were thinking, but it is an interesting theory, now that you mention it. Why wouldn't Miss Hobart go out with you again?"

Georginidis suddenly looked uncomfortable, fidgeting in his seat. "Because you came along and took all her attention away."

*Damn straight*, Peter thought with childish pleasure. "Really. And is that why you felt the need to attack me this morning in the hospital?"

Georginidis scowled and remained silent.

Peter's terse smile displayed absolutely no friendliness. "And is that why you wrote in your diary on your computer that, and I am quoting directly here, 'Jillian will soon regret her decision to blow me off for another man'?"

Aaron leaned over to glance at the computer printout Peter was reading. "Guys keep diaries? Isn't that kind of girly?"

Georginidis exploded, rising from his chair as his voice grew louder. "It's not a diary! It's a memoir!"

Peter spoke calmly, unfazed by his outburst. "So you're admitting you wrote this, then?" Georginidis slowly sat back down, eyeing the uniformed officers warily. When he didn't answer, Peter decided to taunt him into talking. "So we have this date, or non-date I should say, as one motive, combined with our original theory that you were upset that she was awarded the teaching position you both applied for, and you've been plotting your revenge against her ever since."

Georginidis laughed and rolled his eyes. "Oh, right. I'm killing the students I wish I could be teaching."

Aaron stopped writing and cocked his head. "Hey, boss, was that a confession or just sarcasm? I couldn't tell."

Peter leaned back in his chair and tapped his chin thoughtfully, playing along with Aaron. "I don't know. Sounded like a confession to me. And you know what the Miranda Rights say: '*Anything* you say can and will be used against you in a court of law.' You did read him his rights, didn't you?"

Aaron nodded. "Yep. Twice, in fact. Once in the hospital and again when we got here, waiting for you. You know, just to be sure."

Georginidis smacked his hands on the table. "You're twisting my words."

"Huh." Aaron read from his notes. "I have it right here. You said, 'I'm killing the students I wish I could be teaching.' Isn't that right?"

Georginidis shook with anger and sputtered an incoherent answer.

Peter spoke, once again serious. "Oh, we have more than just your words. Your fingerprints, for instance. They were on the cabinet in Miss Hobart's classroom, the one knocked over during that initial robbery."

"I borrowed some pencils."

Peter steamrolled right over him. "But it's ultimately not about the children, is it. I suppose you feel bad about killing them. After all, you just want to teach them. 'Enlighten young minds,' I think is how you put it in your diary. I'm sorry, memoirs. And with Miss Hobart out of the way, the path is open for you to do just that, isn't it? Now you can take the credit for starting that pilot kindergarten program she championed." He leaned in closer to emphasize what he was about to say. "Awful convenient that Jillian's not teaching right now. I think you should know, I spoke with Principal Jones before I came here. Tell me, Mr. Georginidis, how long after her dismissal did you wait before you reapplied for the kindergarten position?"

The color rushing from his face, Georginidis spoke quietly. "I think I'd like a lawyer now."

# CHAPTER TWENTY-EIGHT

"Spiro Agnew."

"You win," Jillian conceded half-heartedly to Tina. "Again."

"I am the Trivial Pursuit Queen!" Tina stood and performed a butt-wiggling victory dance, then stopped. "Which is weird. I mean, I never win when I play you."

"Hmmm."

Tina stared at Jillian. "Why are you so quiet?"

"What? Oh. I have a headache." It was partly the truth.

Tina nodded. "With those stitches, I don't doubt it."

"Hmmm," Jillian murmured again.

Tina put her hands on her hips. "Is that all?"

"Yeah," Jillian lied outright this time. The stress from her injury and the ongoing investigation did give her the headache, but it was the unfinished conversation with Peter that she kept replaying in her head that was distracting her the most. She had almost convinced herself Peter had been trying to tell her he loved her. She longed to hear him say it, but was afraid to ask him to. She didn't want to scare the man away. She knew it would be a huge step for a long-confirmed bachelor with ingrained workaholic tendencies to say those words out loud.

Jillian's cell phone rang and Tina ran to find it, insisting Jillian not exert herself. Because Tina took the liberty of answering the phone once she found it, Jillian correctly surmised Donovan was calling. But she could not overhear the conversation because Tina spoke in hushed tones in the other room. "What are you keeping from me?" she called with a touch of humor and a lot of frustration.

Tina stepped into the living room with the phone glued to her ear. "I have to go to work soon, and Donovan was supposed to be the next shift, he *promised* he'd be the next shift—" her voice was taunting as she directed the last comment into the receiver "—but now he's stuck at the office with a *muy importante* client. Unless Peter gets back soon, you'll be alone."

"Dammit, I'm not an invalid, or a child," Jillian said, loud enough for Donovan to hear.

"She sure sounds alright," Donovan said, his voice loud and clear through the speakerphone function. "But we're worried about you. And one should always listen to and obey anything a sheriff's sergeant says."

Sighing with frustration, Jillian stood, against Tina's silent hand-waving protest, so she could be closer to the phone without shouting to be heard. "I'm not going to be responsible for either of you getting fired from your jobs."

"Unlikely, as we're both fairly high up in our respective organizations," Donovan interjected with a laugh. "Being one of the owners does have it perks."

"You know what I mean," Jillian said with exasperation. "Tina will go to work on time, and you, Donovan, will get here when you get here. I'll turn off the lights and not answer the door until you do, and I'll be *fine*." All this arguing was making her head hurt again.

"Well..." She could tell Donovan was relenting. "Your sergeant does have a suspect in custody. So I suppose that means you're safe. Until he posts bail."

"See?" Jillian demanded in an overly bright voice as she tried to sound aloof and unafraid. "Just like I said. Everything's fine. Now *stop worrying about me*."

"Oh, darling, that's just what I do best."

Tina scowled, clearly unhappy with the arrangements. "Just get here as soon as you can, Donovan." She clicked the phone shut and thrust it back into Jillian's purse, then pointed at her. "Do not tell the cop we did this, do you hear me?"

Pleased with her small victory, Jillian innocently batted her eyelashes. "He won't know a thing."

"Well, I know, and I'm not happy about it," Tina said. "Where's that Mace I gave you?"

Jillian had to think. "Last I saw it was in the kitchen. Right after Peter gave me hell for having it."

Tina rolled her eyes. "I told you not to let him see it." She went into the kitchen and returned a few minutes later holding it out triumphantly. "Found it. On the floor near the stove. Not doing you any good there." She ripped it out of the packaging and dropped it into Jillian's purse on the coffee table, within Jillian's reach from the couch. "*Now* I can leave. Promise me you won't do anything but rest."

Jillian sank back down on the couch. The pain medication was wearing off and dizziness washed over her. "I'm just going to lie here and sleep." She was suddenly very tired.

"*No!* Don't go to sleep!" Tina said.

"Why not?"

"I don't know, I just remember hearing you're not supposed to sleep with a concussion."

"We're not sleeping together, we're just friends," Jillian slurred drowsily.

Tina frowned. "Funny. I'm serious."

"Alright, fine, I won't sleep." Jillian sat up straighter and shook her head to wake up, which was a mistake because she only got dizzier.

Tina gave her another stern glare before leaving. She hadn't been gone ten minutes when there was a loud knock on the front door. Distantly, Jillian thought Tina returned or Donovan arrived earlier than expected, but then remembered they had their own keys and would just let themselves in. Suddenly she felt uneasy. As promised, Jillian did not answer it, instead lying perfectly still on the couch. She found she wished she wasn't alone after all as the silence and emptiness of the house seemed to close in around her. *Darn that Tina. She's making me paranoid now.*

She tried to relax, stretching out on the couch, determined to ignore her natural curiosity to peek outside. But soon, the pain in her head reminded her it was time for another pill. Giving in to her need to know because she had to get up anyway, she hefted herself from the couch and stumbled to open the door. She held her head as the room spun once, then settled down. Opening the door a crack, she peered out. She saw nothing except a piece of paper taped to the screen door.

"Door-to-door sales," she mused. "I hate that, unless they're selling Girl Scout Cookies." Thinking she could use a box of Tagalongs right now, she snatched the note and closed the door, locking it behind her. Unfolding the paper, she read it as she made her way back to the couch, almost tripping over her feet in shock when the intent of the words finally penetrated the fog in her brain. "Oh, God, no!"

Any thoughts of her Darvoset pain pills evaporated. Dropping the note on the floor, she grabbed her purse and with shaking hands dug out her cell phone.

# CHAPTER TWENTY-NINE

PETER WAS IN A FOUL MOOD. Questioning Georginidis hadn't been productive, and after his lawyer came, they'd had to let him go. Peter's cell phone rang and he irritably yanked it from his shirt pocket. Keeping one hand on the wheel and his eyes on the road as he drove, he snapped, "Hello?"

"Peter?"

Hearing Jillian's voice made him instantly feel better. "Hey sweetie. I'm just on my way home. How are you feeling?"

"He's back."

A chill ran down Peter's spine. If her words alone weren't enough to frighten him, her trembling voice was. "Who's back?"

"Him. Father Noose."

"What? Where?"

Jillian started babbling, her words tumbling over one another in a rush. "He was here, he left a nursery rhyme, you have to help, I have to go."

"You're not going anywhere," Peter said sharply. "Where would you go?"

Jillian's breathing was labored, coming in panicked gasps. "Old Mother Hubbard. Oh God."

"What?" He had no clue what she was talking about. Those were some drugs they gave her.

"I have to go! I'm leaving now!"

"Jillian! You have a concussion and you're not thinking straight. I'll be there in five minutes. We'll go together."

"Not enough time! Meet me there!" She clicked off the phone.

"Damn it!" Peter shouted and stomped on the accelerator. He was not sure where he was headed, but he had to get there fast. He aimed the truck toward Jillian's, hoping she had enough sense to stay put after all. But her mind was muddled, with hysteria and pain and drugs. He drove faster.

His phone rang again and hope surged. "Jillian?" he shouted into it.

"No," Donovan replied, sounded panicked. "She's not here. She's not at home. She's gone. I can't find her, but I found a note. It's from him."

"Read it to me," Peter demanded.

Donovan did, in a wavering voice.

*Old Mother Hobart went to her cupboard*
*to get her old Doug a scone.*
*But when she got there, the cupboard was bare,*
*and so the poor Doug had none.*
*She went to the baker to buy him some bread,*
*but when she came back, the poor Doug was dead.*

"What the hell does that mean?" Peter said. He tried to distract himself from the growing concern he felt for Jillian's safety by wracking his brain for his limited knowledge of nursery rhymes. "It must be about her mother, Hobart for Hubbard. But..."

"Oh dear, oh God, poor Mary." Donovan wailed into the phone, interrupting his train of thought.

"What? There's no Mary mentioned in there." Peter was growing more and more confused.

Donovan spoke quickly. "Mary's her mother. Old Mother Hobart. And Doug, the dead Doug, that's her father. Oh dear God."

Now he knew where Jillian was headed. Terror filled Peter's chest, strangling his lungs. The truck started to veer off the road and he came to his senses, yanking the wheel to put it back on course. "Do you know where they live?"

"Yes, yes of course, I—"

"Good," Peter snapped, cutting him off. "Go now. Maybe you'll get there before I do. How fast does that fancy car of yours go?"

In between cell phone calls to Aaron for backup and to local traffic patrols to alert them not to stop the speeding Porsche, Peter debated his new theory. Whoever left the note knew Jillian was alone — which meant someone had been spying on her — and further knew her well enough to realize she would not just sit and wait when someone she loved was in danger. She would act on impulse to try to fix it on her own. He admired that trait in her, but now worried it would get her killed. "It's just like her to go off running like that, without thinking first or waiting for help … damned cornfields…" His muttering trailed off as his throat constricted.

He pulled out his cell phone again and dialed her number, listening to it ring. And ring. Finally, the voice mail picked up. *Shit.* He left a terse message. "Jillian, it's Peter. Call me as soon as you get this."

He checked his wristwatch. *Ten more minutes. If this traffic lets up.*

"*Damn it.*" The sinking feeling in his stomach, and his heart, told him it wasn't going to be soon enough.

***

Jillian slammed on her brakes in front of her parents' house, the car fishtailing as it came to an abrupt stop. In her haste to check on the fate of her parents, she left the keys in the ignition and ran up the driveway as fast as the throbbing in her head allowed. Banging on the front door, she got no answer. Then she remembered that at this time of day, her father would still be at work at his law office, likely staying late after visiting her that morning in the hospital. Her mother was probably at her book club, just like every Wednesday afternoon. "You're overreacting," she told herself. "Just call them, they're probably fine."

But before she could reach for the cell phone in her purse, strong arms violently grabbed her from behind. A large, foul-smelling rag was roughly jammed over her mouth to prevent her from screaming. She started to struggle, slamming her heel into the attacker's shin and her elbows into his ribs, but he was too strong and her injury made her weak, and the smell on the rag was overpowering, gagging her and making her even weaker. Her last semi-coherent thought was *Peter is going to be mad at me*, before everything went black.

# CHAPTER THIRTY

T HE PORSCHE ROARED DOWN THE STREET and came to a smooth halt in front of the Hobart house just as Peter's truck drove up from the opposite end of the street. Peter jumped out before Donovan and ran to peer into the Grand Am parked on the curb. The door was unlocked, so he yanked it open. "She left her keys in the ignition. She must have been in a hurry." If she read that note, he didn't doubt she'd be moving fast.

A silver Mercedes glided up behind them and pulled into the driveway. Mary Hobart, dressed in an expensive cream pantsuit, slid out with a gracious smile. "Well, isn't this wonderful! A welcoming committee! Donovan, it's been so long, come and give me a kiss." She kissed the air next to his cheek, oblivious to the apprehension etched on his face. "And Peter. Good to see you as well. I see my daughter's car is here. Is she inside?"

"No, Mary, I don't think she is," Donovan replied. "I was, I mean we were hoping you had seen her or heard from her."

Mary dismissed him with a headshake, her graying blonde lacquered hair barely moving. "Not since she left a message saying the hospital released her. Oh, it's like pulling teeth to get Jillian to call me sometimes. Her own mother, too! I swear, that girl could be dead in a ditch somewhere and I'd never know it." She stopped, taken aback, when Donovan started hyperventilating.

"Oh Mary, oh no, if only you knew what you were saying! That's such a bad choice of words right now. Oh no no no." He bent over at the waist, sticking his head between his knees as he tried to catch his breath.

Peter clenched his jaw tight to keep from shouting. Standing around talking wasn't helping Jillian. "Let's go inside, make sure she's not in there," he said tersely.

Confused but nodding, Mrs. Hobart fished out her keys and followed him to the front door. She stopped when Peter flung an arm in front of her, preventing her from walking any farther. "What's that on the porch?" he asked.

"Why, it looks like a pie. One of my neighbors must have baked today and stopped by while I was out. Beverly Mickelson in particular, across the street in the white Colonial there, is fond of baking pies when apples are in season."

Peter had serious doubts Beverly made this particular pie. "She leaves them out in the open, uncovered like that?"

Mrs. Hobart cast a doubtful glance at the pie. "Well, that is strange, yes. Goodness, it must be covered with ants by now."

Donovan had followed them and now was staring, pale and wide-eyed, at the pastry, like it was a bomb about to explode. "You do realize that several nursery rhymes feature pies in prominent roles, don't you?"

"What?" Peter felt his heart fall into his shoes. He remembered the poem *Simple Simon Was a Pie Man* that Jillian had recited to him just the other day, and wondered if his previous suspicions toward Simon Brothers had been justified.

"Four and twenty blackbirds baked in a *pie* … Little Jack Horner sat in a corner, eating his Christmas *pie*." Donovan leaned weakly against the side of the house.

"Don't even think about fainting on me," Peter said. "I don't have time for that."

Mary, her fists on her hips, spoke forcefully. "Will someone explain to me what is going on?"

Peter grasped for some kind of control, however limited, before he went insane when he realized he had none at all. He thought his voice sounded surprisingly calm when he spoke. At least he hoped it was. "Mrs. Hobart, I want you to go a friend's house and stay there.

Call your husband, have him meet you there. I'm having police surveillance put on you and your house, starting immediately."

"What?" Her voice was sharp and anxious. "Why?"

"I have reason to believe this pie is some kind of threat, or at least a calling card. I'm taking it as evidence. Donovan and I are going to the station, and I want you to call me the second you hear from Jillian. Can you do that?"

Donovan, calmer now, stood upright. "Tina!" he exclaimed. "Maybe she's heard from her." He whipped out his cell phone and started dialing.

Mary sent exasperated looks between the two men. "Sergeant Dack, I demand to know what is going on."

"Mrs. Hobart..." Peter sighed. He could not think of a good way to deliver the news to Jillian's mother. "Your daughter's missing."

***

The light, dim as it was, hurt her eyes. Jillian kept them closed until a sudden wrenching pain in her wrists had her opening them wide with a cry of anguish that, in her weakened state, was more of a whimper. Her field of vision wavered in and out of focus, but she was reasonably sure it was sideways, which couldn't be right. A moment of careful concentration made her realize the point of view was skewed because she was lying on her side, in a small, hard space.

A man stood over her, roughly yanking on a scratchy rope restraining her hands behind her back. She tried to identify the nice man trying to help her, but the sun was fading, and her head was still swimming with a blinding headache. She tried to remember what happened and how she got here. Shaking her head to clear it, she recalled bits and pieces. There was a letter that wasn't very nice. Something about her parents' house. And then a really bad smell...

"Oh, God!" Jillian whimpered again, the memory of her violent abduction flooding back.

"You're awake!" The voice belonging to the shadowy figure before her said. His voice echoed in her brain, sounding like it was coming from deep inside a tunnel, but it was oddly familiar. "I thought you'd be out longer, but I guess I messed up my calculations for the strength of the trichloroethane. I'm still learning."

"Where am I? What are you doing?" Jillian's words were slurred, which she could now attribute — along with her concussion, headache, and nausea — to the trichloroethane, whatever that was. That must have been what was on that smelly rag. She wished she had taken her Darvoset.

"You're in the trunk of my car," he replied, sounding oddly pleasant. "Don't worry, it's just for effect."

*For effect?* She wasn't sure if her concussion or the drugged rag caused her confusion, or if the man was talking in riddles. She tried to sit up but found that not only were her hands still bound behind her, but her feet were tied at the ankles. She was still too woozy to be really scared, but knew it was probably the proper response she should be having. She took a deep breath to scream.

In a flash, the man leaned over and stuffed a clean, normal-smelling cotton rag in her mouth. "No, you don't," he said. "Not that anyone will hear you out here anyway." The ominous action caused her fog to suddenly clear, and fear enveloped her like a wet, heavy blanket. He stepped away from the car, out of her sight, and she panicked, thinking she was being left alone to die, then wondered if that would be a better fate than to die — or worse — at the hands of this psycho. Her heart slammed in her chest and her breath came fast and shallow. She couldn't get enough air with the rag in her mouth. But in only a few seconds, he was back, standing before her, holding her purse and muttering to himself, and she forced herself to calm down.

"I know it's in here somewhere. Yes!" He pulled her slender cell phone from her purse and flipped it open. Gathering her muddled thoughts, his features came more into focus, revealing a sinister grin across his face, but she was still having trouble concentrating enough to identify him, his name lurking somewhere in the dark recesses of her mind. When he stepped closer, leaning over her prone body, her eyes widened with alarm in anticipation of what he was about to do to her. Her shout was muffled by the gag, tasting dry and woody against her tongue.

"Perfect! That's perfect. Just the right effect. Your cell phone is pretty cool. This built-in camera takes really sharp pictures. My cell phone just takes blurry pictures. Smile now." With a sadistic smirk, he added, "Say 'cheese'!"

# CHAPTER THIRTY-ONE

ARON MET PETER AND DONOVAN AT the Sheriff's Department. Peter, grim and efficient, was determined to stay focused and professional, but it was hard when he was wracked with worry and guilt about Jillian and Donovan was weepy and inconsolable beside him. Peter gingerly set the pie he'd confiscated as evidence on a narrow table in a conference room he commandeered, then directed Donovan to a chair, ordering him to sit down before he fell over. Donovan let the backpack slung over his shoulder fall to the floor beside him with a dull thud.

Picking up the bag, Peter divvied up the contents between himself, Donovan, and Aaron. Inside were the library books Peter had insisted they pick up from his house for further study. He was determined to find every rhyme that pertained to pie, hoping it would be a clue to find Jillian before it was too late. Settling into an uncomfortable chair, Peter was about to read the index of a colorful children's book when Donovan interrupted him.

"Shouldn't you be out looking for that Mike guy you let go, which now is looking like a really stupid idea?"

The accusatory tone pissed him off, but he knew Donovan was just upset and let it slide. For now. "He can't have done it. I left before they finished the paperwork to release him and went straight to Jillian's. There's no way he would have gotten to the house before I did." But doubts nagged him.

His cell phone vibrated in his pocket. At the same time, Donovan's phone shrilled *The Ride of the Valkyries*. Abandoning his book, Donovan reached his phone first, flipping it open and reading the screen. "It's Jillian!" Donovan shouted.

"That's odd," Peter said, staring at his phone. "She's calling me, too."

"At the same time? Wait, mine says it's a multi-media message. Maybe she's texting us."

They pressed the answer buttons on their phones at the same time, but Peter's reaction to the colorful display that appeared on the two-inch-wide screen was vastly different from Donovan's.

"No!" Donovan cried. He reacted as if he had been burned, lurching back in his chair so fast that it came dangerously close to tipping over, and almost dropped the phone in his horror.

Peter went absolutely still as he glared hard at the phone, his jaw clenched, gripping the phone so tightly his hand shook. *No. It can't be. It's a joke. It's...*

The image on Peter's phone was dark and slightly out of focus, but it was obviously a full-color picture of Jillian, bound and gagged, disheveled and terrified, shoved into what looked like the messy trunk of a car. The accompanying it read, "London bridges falling down, MY fair lady. Father Noose."

He was so angry, so scared, he couldn't breathe. He wouldn't release his death grip on the phone, just stared at it with building rage, so Aaron had to take Donovan's cell phone to see the image. Donovan appeared more than happy to never see his phone again.

Donovan's head sunk into his hands. "The psycho took this picture with her own phone!"

"Who all did he send this to?" Aaron asked as he studied the picture.

Peter snapped to attention and starting hitting buttons on his phone. "It was sent like an e-mail, and there's only two numbers listed. One's mine, so I'm guessing the other is Donovan's."

Aaron's eyebrows puckered. "Alright, I can kind of guess why it was sent to you, but why him?"

"He's mocking the important men in her life, the ones who love her." He realized what he said, and that it was the truth, and spoke quickly to change the meaning of his words, hoping that would make the cold hole in his chest disappear. "The ones he feels threatened by."

Aaron lowered his voice. "Donovan is a threat? You're kidding, right?" The frail, thin man was collapsed in the chair, wracked with guilt and silent, panic-induced sobs.

"To this monster, he is. Donovan loves her, even if only in a platonic way, but to him it still represents a man standing in his way." His whole body was trembling now as the anger and fear inside him threatened to explode. He set he phone on the table before he threw it across the room. "This looks like a car trunk. Can we get anyone in here to identify the type of car? Maybe make out this license plate?"

Aaron dialed the phone hanging on the wall behind them. "The plate's mostly cut off and kind of rusty, I can barely make out the tops of the letters. They're all curved on top, could be anything. It's a Michigan plate, though, Great Lakes Splendor Mackinac Bridge edition. Jason from the fleet garage might know the car make and model."

Nodding tersely, Peter told Aaron, "Get him down here, pronto." Then he took pity on Donovan, still weeping helplessly. "Here, do something useful with yourself. Look up the *My Fair Lady* rhyme."

Sniffing loudly, Donovan straightened and reached for the book Peter handed him. "It's *London Bridges*," he corrected with indignation. "*My Fair Lady* is a musical." He flipped through several pages before stopping and reading to himself, lips moving silently. His eyes closed and he groaned in despair.

"Come on," Peter prodded, rapping his fingers on the table impatiently. There wasn't time.

"It repeats a lot, so I'll just read the main verses." Donovan's voice wavered, but he took a steadying breath and read it aloud. Peter figured he didn't realize he was singing the rhyme.

Tension already threading through Peter's shoulders tightened at the words and the madman's choice of rhymes. He vaguely remembered Jillian telling him it referred to a queen being imprisoned in the Tower of London while she awaited beheading. He didn't like the imagery that thought created.

A portly deputy in greasy overalls embroidered with the name

Jason over the left pocket came into the room. After a briefing from Aaron, he took Donovan's cell phone and studied the picture, holding it close to his face for a better angle. "Most of the shot's centered inside the trunk, but here on the left, that's the wheel well. Might be white paint. It's a small trunk, too, probably a hatchback, I'd guess, from the shape of it." After hemming and hawing over the picture, and with some impatient prodding from Peter, Jason gave his noncommittal opinion that it could, possibly, be an older model Ford Escort. But he refused to offer any opinion, however far-reaching, on the numbers on the license plate. He suggested forwarding the photo to the crime lab computers, where it could be enlarged and enhanced.

"Do it," Peter said to Aaron. "And after that call the Secretary of State, maybe they can track down something if you can get a partial plate."

Donovan and Peter continued to search through the books. The rhymes containing pies Donovan referenced earlier, *Little Jack Horner* and *Four and Twenty Blackbirds*, were scrawled on a list Peter kept as he found them. Pen poised over the paper to write again, he stopped, stunned, when he read the latest poem. "*Three Little Kittens*. Crap. They have pie."

"More accurately, they have no pie," Donovan said as he read the poem over Peter's shoulder. "Is that important?"

"It's the first rhyme he used, when the first child when missing. Maybe he's referring back to that rhyme somehow, to that little girl." He remembered that crime scene and unconsciously superimposed Jillian's face on the corpse in the creek. *No. Don't think about that. You're going to find her.* "We found Katie near a laundromat, because the kittens had to wash their mittens before they could have pie..."

"Speaking of pie, this stuff is great! Who brought it?"

Peter's swiveled in the direction of the garage mechanic's voice, standing so abruptly his chair fell to the floor with a violent clatter. Jason had helped himself to a large slice of the pie from the Hobarts' porch and was cramming the fruit-filled pastry into his mouth. Peter resisted the urge to strangle him, but gave serious consideration to ordering his stomach be pumped. "Goddamn it, you're eating evidence!"

Jason stopped, confused, his overloaded fork poised in mid-air. "I thought I was eating cherry pie?"

Clenching his teeth and fists in anger, Peter was about to unleash his frustrations on the errant deputy when Donovan's shrill voice stopped him. "*Cherry* pie?"

Peter spun to face him, saving his reprimand for later. "Does that mean something?"

Donovan reached across the table to grab another book, babbling as he flipped through the pages. "Oh God, I don't have a good feeling about this. I told her he was creepy, but she wouldn't believe me. You know how she can be. But I know things about men, and he was definitely creepy."

"Who?" Peter demanded. He was losing patience. All the carefully followed criminal investigation procedures, methodical and practiced, ingrained in him for years, were suddenly useless to him now that this investigation had become so personal. Every second that slipped by was another second without Jillian, and he could do nothing.

"Just a minute now. Let me find it. I want to make sure before I…" Donovan's voice trailed off as he read a passage. "I was right," he said in a bleak voice. "The one time I hate being right."

"For Christ's sake, tell me," Peter said, ripping the book from Donovan's hands, a cold fist squeezing tight around his heart when he heard the despair in Donovan's voice.

Donovan sang the rhyme in perfect pitch as Peter read along silently.

*Can she make a cherry pie, Billy Boy, Billy Boy, can she make a cherry pie, darling Billy?*

# CHAPTER THIRTY-TWO

"**B**ILLY?" JILLIAN'S VISION AND BRAIN CAME together into sudden, sharp focus as the face before her finally clicked with the name on the tip of her tongue. The boy's black eye had faded, the once-glaring bruise now a sickly yellow.

A smile slowly spread across the boy's face as he threw the rag he had pulled from her mouth to the ground. "Yes, sweetheart. I knew once the effects of the trichloroethane wore off, you'd be fine."

*Sweetheart?* "What's going on, Billy? What have you done? And what is trict, trick—"

"Trichloroethane. It's an engine cleaner. I found it in Auto Shop. It works kinda like chloroform. I found that out in Chemistry."

His two favorite classes. She would have to be kidnapped by the smartest kid in school.

He tucked her cell phone back in her purse and set it beside her in the trunk. "Sorry, but this is just temporary," he said, slamming the lid of the hatchback, leaving her in darkness. She heard the engine sputter then roar to life, the bed of the trunk vibrating beneath her. Claustrophobia and dread crushed her chest, making breathing difficult. Her purse was so close, but with her hands still tied tight behind her back, she was unable to reach the it, and the phone inside, to call for help. She wondered if anyone would find her alive.

\*\*\*

Peter was still pouring over the nursery rhyme with Donovan, looking for clues to who Billy Boy could be and where he had locked Jillian up, when a commotion in the hallway diverted his attention. Raised voices, both male and female, were coming in their direction. The door flung open so hard it bounced off the wall behind it, and Tina Fernandez burst in like a banshee, eyes wild, so full of guilt and rage that she was an awesome sight to behold, even at five feet one. The young deputy trailing her, trying unsuccessfully to bring her back to the waiting room, clearly had no idea how to handle her and appeared almost afraid of her.

"There you are!" she shouted, pointing first at Donovan, then Peter. "What happened? Where is she? What can I do? And will somebody tell this deputy to *shut up?*"

Aaron, closest to the door, moved to cut her off. "Ma'am, if you could just—"

Peter caught the look on Donovan's face and took a cautious step backward.

"Ma'am?" Tina glared at Aaron, her look sharp enough to cut steel. "Do I look old enough to be a *ma'am* to you?" She started to barge her way past him, but Aaron grabbed her upper arms to restrain her, saying "*Miss*, please!" just as she slapped a hand against his chest to shove him back.

Both stopped and were suddenly silent, staring at each other with surprise. Tina slowly withdrew her hand from his chest, and Aaron released his grip on her arms. They continued to stare at each other, unmoving. The silence grew lengthy and awkward. Until Donovan spoke.

"Could we do *Days of Our Lives* some other time, darlings?" His smile and his voice were strained. "You can date and marry and have babies and live happily ever after," his voice became serious again, "*after* we find Jillian."

If it had been another time, Peter would have laughed at the deer-in-the-headlights look on Aaron's face.

Aaron blinked. "Why don't you sit down?" Placing his hand on her shoulder, he led Tina to a chair.

Nodding, Tina obeyed, which Peter knew was completely against her nature. He was surprised when a single tear rolled down her cheek.

"It's my fault. I left her. I should have stayed, but she made me leave. She told me she'd be okay." Her voice was soft as she angrily swiped at the tear, then her voice rose as she deflected that anger from herself to Jillian. "Damn it, she said she'd be fine!"

Donovan shook his head. "Stop doing that to yourself. It's not your fault. It's mine. I didn't try hard enough to tell her Billy was not right. And I was tied up at work on the casino designs and wasn't there to stop her."

Peter paced in a circle around Donovan's chair. When he spoke, it was almost in a whisper, but his voice grew louder with his emotions. "No, it's my fault for not protecting her. I wasn't there for her either. I shouldn't have let her out of my sight. You're just her friends, but it's my *job* to protect her, and I didn't. I failed."

"Are you kidding me?" Donovan stood abruptly, interrupting Peter's pacing. "I am not just her 'friend,' Mr. Sergeant. She happens to be my very best friend on this whole sorry planet since the first grade. And your *job*?" He poked his finger hard into Peter's chest, and Peter's mouth dropped open in shock. "Jillian is missing, probably bleeding and crying and scared and God knows what else, and you're concerned about your freaking job? Well, I'm sorry this is such an inconvenience for you. I hope we find her soon so you can get back to your *job*. You asshole."

Peter grabbed Donovan's shirt collar with such violent rage that Donovan gasped as seams popped. Tina and Aaron both jumped up, startled but ready to intervene.

"Inconvenience?" Peter was shouting, but he couldn't control himself any longer. "Is that what you think? You think I don't care? Jillian's the best damn thing that ever happened to me. I love her, and if something happens to her, if it's my fault that she dies—" he shook Donovan to make his point — "I'll never live with myself. I'm going to find her, and when I do, I'm going to kill the son of a bitch that took her, police procedure and my job be damned. I'm not a sergeant with the sheriff's department anymore. This is personal. So fuck you."

"Peter!" Aaron said sharply.

Donovan looked upon him with such sympathy, that Peter felt stupid and released his grip on his shirt. But he was still too mad to apologize; he was shaking with it.

Donovan nodded slowly, blinking back tears. "Good. Now go find our girl."

Peter closed his eyes and took a deep, steadying breath. He had to regain control, for Jillian's sake. "I will. As soon as we figure out who Billy is, and more importantly, where he is."

Tina tugged on Aaron's sleeve to get his attention. "I think I might know where."

*** 

Peter got to the Shop'n'Fresh before Aaron, dread and rage making him drive faster. Aaron wasn't far behind, however, pulling his squad car into the parking lot as Peter stormed into the store with long, purposeful strides and demanded to speak with the manager. The store was deserted, as closing was in less than fifteen minutes.

A short, overweight man with an orange polyester Shop'n'Fresh vest stretched over his belly approached from the customer service counter, looking at the deputies with concern. "I'm Tom Flynn, the manager. Is there a problem, officers?"

Peter wanted to shout, "Yes," but tried to remain professional. "We're looking for an employee of yours, a kid who bags and collects carts. Goes by the name of Billy. Is he here tonight?"

Flynn shook his head. "Not tonight. Billy's not in trouble, is he? He's always been one of my best baggers, always on time and nice to the customers. He looks a little scary, I'll admit I was wary about hiring him with all those bodypeircings he wears, but he's a good kid."

"Let me guess," Aaron said. "Quiet, keeps to himself."

The manager blinked. "Well, yeah."

"Any idea where he is?" Peter asked.

Shaking his head, Flynn said, "He asked for a week's vacation. Said he was going on a trip."

"Did he say where?"

Again the manager shook his head.

"Can you tell me where he lives?"

The man went quiet, shifting his eyes. "Well, now, I'm not sure I should do that. Without a warrant, I mean. Billy's a good kid. If he is in trouble, I want to do everything right, legal and all," he said, spreading his hands out at his sides. "You see where I'm coming from."

Peter gritted his teeth. "Fine. Can you at least tell me the kid's last name?"

Deep in thought, he wrinkled his face until he looked like a dried apricot. "Stone. Billy Stone."

*Finally.* Peter stalked out to his car, leaving Aaron to thank the man for what little help he offered. When Aaron caught up with him, Peter barked out orders. "Get back with those friends of yours at the Secretary of State, see if a Billy or Bill or William Stone hits for our mystery hatchback." He yanked the radio from his dashboard to order the dispatcher to get him the home phone number and address of anyone named Stone in the immediate vicinity, but stopped, staring into the dark night at nothing. "Son of a bitch."

"What?" Aaron said, reaching for the mic in his own car.

"*Stone so strong will last so long, my fair lady?*" He quoted the last verse from the *London Bridges* rhyme Donovan quoted earlier. "*Where have you been Billy Boy?* His name is Billy Stone." He spun and faced Aaron with hard eyes. "That bastard was flat out telling us who he is, knowing we wouldn't figure it out. Laughing at us."

"Or maybe," Aaron said carefully, "it's a cry for help and he wants you to know who he is so you'll stop him?"

"Been reading too many psychology books," Peter muttered, and returned to his radio to demand information.

When the crackling voice of the dispatcher replied there were seven local addresses registered to people named Stone, he threw the mic back into the vehicle and girded himself for a long night.

# CHAPTER THIRTY-THREE

## THURSDAY, OCTOBER 12

ILLIAN WAS FREEZING. IN AN EFFORT to keep warm, she sat huddled on the floor in a corner of a dark, unheated room, her knees pulled tight against her chest. She wore just the dress she left the house in the day before, and the soft material wasn't enough to keep ward off the bone-chilling cold. Billy sat next to her, sound asleep, his head lolling on her shoulder in a way that would have been endearing had she not been completely repulsed. But she was freezing and he offered her shivering body the heat it so desperately needed, so she tolerated the invasion of her personal space. She didn't have much choice in the matter anyway, as Billy had securely knotted a rope to his belt and attached the other end to her hands still tied behind her back, security in case she tried to escape while he slept. She figured he was harmless as long as he continued to sleep, so remained as still as possible to ensure he stayed that way.

She had not slept much herself, between the cold and worrying whether or not Billy would take advantage of her. From the way he had been talking and leering at her, she assumed it was only a matter of time. The few moments she did manage to drift off to sleep, she would jerk awake from a nightmare or a strange sound. Judging from the pale light seeping through the closed window blinds, she figured it was just past sunrise. She gave up trying to sleep and used the new light to gain a fresh perspective on her surroundings.

When Billy brought her into the house the night before, it was dark and she couldn't see where he'd taken her. Now she could make out the room. They were below ground, as the windows were narrow and high on the walls and a set of stairs led up. It was unfurnished, explaining why they sat on the floor, decorated with cheap faux-wood paneling and green shag carpeting popular in the 1970's. The light fixtures hanging on heavy chains from the ceilings were useless. Billy had explained the home was a rental property his parents owned, and since no one was using it, utilities were shut off. No electricity, no heat, no running water. Jillian thought they might as well have stayed outside, under the trees.

Billy stirred beside her and the fear and loathing she had been able to suppress while he slept came flooding back. The boy groaned, blinked, then stretched, rubbing his chest against her arm. Lifting his head, he smiled at her. "Good morning," he said. "This is nice. I like waking up next to you." When she didn't answer, he frowned and set to work untying the rope that linked them together. When he was done, he could stand and move freely, but her hands remained behind her back, leaving her immobile and helpless.

He stood over her, glaring down at her. "I said, good morning. Maybe you're not a morning person. Well, that's just something else we'll have to get used to about each other. We'll have lots of time for that. Especially once we're married."

What did he just say? It took her a minute to find her voice. "Married?" Jillian cried out. "I can't marry you!"

"Sure you can." Billy nodded, confident in his declaration. "I looked into it. You have to be eighteen to get married. Well, I'm eighteen now. Today is my birthday."

Jillian could only stare at him. Wishing him a Happy Birthday somehow didn't seem appropriate.

"You said you'd marry me when I was old enough. I'm old enough." His grin was happy and huge. "We just have a three-day waiting period on the marriage license. I figure if we leave by nine, we can get to the courthouse in Gaylord before they close."

Jillian grasped at the only thing she could understand. "Why Gaylord?"

"My dad has a hunting cabin up there. Hunting season doesn't open for a couple more weeks, so we can have a private honeymoon."

*And so Peter will have a hard time finding me,* she added silently. Gaylord was a rural community at least five hours to the north of Detroit. She shuddered as she imagined what this child — *young man,* she corrected herself — might consider happening — doing to her — on a honeymoon. "Billy, it doesn't matter if you are eighteen. I can't marry you. I love somebody else." She stopped when she realized what she just said. It wasn't a lie told to placate a madman. It was the truth.

Billy's smile turned into a wounded scowl, betraying a hurt little boy. "You told me you'd wait for me!"

"No, I didn't! Billy, please try to understand."

"You slept with him, didn't you."

Jillian felt a hot blush rising over her cheeks. Discussing sex with a teenager made her normal embarrassment even more acute. She tried to stall. "With whom?"

"That cop. Sergeant Peter." Billy spat out his name as he stood over her, fists clenched, glaring down at her. The little boy was gone, replaced with a very angry young man. "You were mine, pure and innocent, and he ruined you. He ruined everything!"

Jillian winced. She was far from "pure and innocent", not since eleventh grade when her first boyfriend, classmate Finn Dorsey, conned his way into her pants by telling her he loved her. But she thought better of pointing that fact out right now. She forgot all about Finn when Billy crouched down next to her. "Screw the cop. It doesn't matter. I beat him. I win. We're getting married, and he can't have you."

\*\*\*

Bleary eyed and weary, Peter rubbed a hand over his face and felt the roughness of two days' worth of stubble. Donovan and Tina had long since gone home, and Aaron had wandered off in search of higher-octane coffee. Peter felt his frustration growing into despair. He knew next to nothing, but still he held out hope Jillian was alive. If Father Noose was keeping to his *modus operandi,* using nursery rhymes to detail his plans, then he could extrapolate Jillian was still alive based on the last rhyme. But *alive* didn't necessarily mean *safe.*

*…Oh where have you been darling Billy? I have been to seek a wife, she's the joy of my life…*

Despair and pure hatred at the thought of this monster wanting Jillian as his wife, and what he would be doing to her as his wife, had Peter slamming his fist onto his desk with an enraged roar.

Forcing himself to calm down, he once again went over the scant information he collected. He had finally located Billy Stone's parents after three phone calls to the wrong Stones. Stalwart William Stone, Sr., and his uptight wife, Denise, were hardly his idea of the perfect parents. Not only did they have no idea where their son was or when he was due home, they didn't seem overly concerned by that lack of information. They knew little of his social life or his friends, other than he might have been seeing "some girl." They did know, however, that he was getting straight A's in every class in school except Social Studies, in which, his father had been ashamed to report, he earned a mere B-minus. But more important, and more relevant, they confirmed that Jillian had once been Billy's teacher, and that he a drove a late-model white Ford Escort hatchback. Peter knew he had his man. Or boy. Now if he only *had* him. But he seemed to have disappeared just as mysteriously as Jillian had. An All-Points Bulletin on the car and both Billy Stone and Jillian had thus far yielded nothing. An early morning follow-up call to the Stone residence revealed the boy had not been home during the night, and a deputy visiting the high school Billy attended reported he was apparently playing hooky.

Aaron came in with a thermos and a stack of papers. "Coffee and signed search warrants. Which do you want?"

Peter stood, taking both. "I can drink in the car on the way," he said. Within half an hour, they were back at the Stone residence, heading up the stairs toward the boy's room. Technicians started dismantling his computer while Aaron went through dresser drawers. Billy's parents stood in the hallway, blustering and stalling while Peter demanded answers.

Peter's frustration at the couple's lack of cooperation reached its breaking point. "I'm sorry this situation is sullying your reputation, Mr. Stone," he said, his clipped voice filled with sarcasm. "But I have to ask: given the choice, which reputation would be worse for you? Having a son staying out all night and ditching school, or having a son convicted of kidnapping and murder?" He just spoke louder when

Stone tried to interrupt. "The sooner you start helping me, Mr. Stone, the sooner I can start helping *you* by resolving this before it becomes the second one."

Billy's father seemed unfazed, crossing his arms and meeting Peter's glare. "As a lawyer, I know my rights. I know I do not have to say anything that may be incriminating toward a member of my family or myself." His condescending attitude only made Peter angrier.

"Incriminating toward yourself? Are you knowingly withholding information? Because I'm sure you know, *as a lawyer*, that's a serious offense that comes with some serious prison time. Harboring a fugitive, impeding an investigation, providing false statements to police, which, in legal terms, I believe is called perjury."

Mrs. Stone paled and gripped her husband's arm. "William, that's enough. Sergeant, the keys to our rental property in Armada are missing."

Peter felt a warmth spread over his chest and recognized the feeling as hope. "I'm glad your wife understands the law, Mr. Stone," he said before turning to the woman. "How long have they been missing, and where is this property?"

# CHAPTER THIRTY-FOUR

THE HOUSE LOOKED DESERTED, SHADES DRAWN, lights off, grass overgrown. Peter's heart sank as he thought he had followed another false lead, losing precious time in his search to find Jillian. Weapons drawn, he and Aaron cautiously approached the front door. Peter pounded on it. "Sheriff's department! Open the door!" he shouted. The only answer was silence.

"Go round back and see if you can see anything," he ordered in a low voice, and Aaron quickly obeyed. Peter tried peering into windows, but pulled shades and closed blinds prevented any views.

Aaron returned, whispering, "White Ford Escort in the garage, boss."

Peter nodded. "He's in there, I know it." He knocked on the door again, knowing it was fruitless. He couldn't just storm in there; he didn't want the kid to freak out and hurt Jillian. He had to throw him off his guard if he was going to have any chance at all. He turned and walked back to his squad car. Aaron followed, looking confused. "We've got a warrant, we can go in," he said. "What are you doing?"

"I'm going to beat him at his own game," Peter said, reaching for a book on the front seat.

***

There had to be a way to get a message to someone. If only she could get away from Billy for only a few seconds. "Billy, I really need to go to the bathroom," Jillian said, trying to sound sweet and sincere.

"Sure." He jerked her up by the elbow into a standing position and started to lead her to the room in the corner.

"Can you untie me? I can't … you know … with my hands behind my back."

He winked at her. "I can help."

"No!" The idea repulsed her, but she thought fast. "You shouldn't see me like that until after we're married." She managed to say it without visibly gagging. She held her breath until he agreed.

"Yeah, I guess you're right." He roughly untied her hands, the scratchy rope cutting into her skin, and then she was free. She scooped her purse off the floor and tucked it under her arm.

"There ya go," Billy said, gesturing with his arm for her to enter the tiny bathroom. She was about to close the door when his eyes narrowed. "Wait a minute."

"What?" she asked as innocently as she could.

His hand shot out and grabbed a dangling purse strap. On instinct she tightened her grip. "Billy, I need that. My, uh, makeup is in it!"

"So's your cell phone," he said.

*Crap.* "Um … So?" *Yeah, that was a witty reply.*

He continued to pull with one hand while rooting around inside the purse with the other. Angry now, she gave a tremendous yank back and heard a loud rip. The strap pulled free of the purse and she stumbled backwards, the purse's contents spilling all over the bathroom floor. Billy was left holding the purse strap in one hand and her cell phone in the other. Damn.

"No wonder Kevin had such a hard time ripping off your purse. You're strong."

She stared at him. "You know the guy who attacked me?"

Billy laughed, a maniacal sound that made the tiny hairs on her arms stand on end. "Of course I know him. I paid him to steal your purse. I was going to come rescue you and get it back for you. Then you'd notice me and fall in love with me." His eyes darkened. "But that fucking sergeant showed up and ruined everything. Kevin almost got collared, and he beat the shit out of me because of it. That's how I got this." He pointed to his still-bruised eye.

Jillian felt like she was going to throw up. She remembered what Peter said about all the incidents possibly being connected and looked at Billy. She realized how he had known when she would be at her parents' house, all alone. He had left that last note on her porch. He had left all the notes. He was Father Noose. She cursed her concussion and painkillers; without them, she might have figured it out sooner. Or at least she wouldn't be here with him now, alone.

But she had to hear it from him, no matter how much it pained her, because she didn't want to believe it. "What else did you do, Billy?"

His eyes grew dark as he looked down at her. He seemed proud of himself. "I did it all. For you." His lips curled into a sickening smile as he whispered, "*Oh where have you been darling Billy? I have been to seek a wife, she's the joy of my life…*"

She interrupted his high-pitched, sing-song voice, trying to pretend she didn't hear it. "Katie? And Robynne? *You* killed them?"

He pouted like a little boy. "What, you don't think I'm strong enough to take out a little girl?"

Her stomach made another threatening roll. "But why?"

"Because you belong to me. Not to those brats. You love them too much, and you can't love anyone but me. Not those kids. And sure as hell not that dumb-ass cop." He laughed. "He never did figure it out. What a loser."

Oh God, Peter. He thought it was Mike and would never know, not until it was too late, that he was investigating the wrong person. "Why can't I have my cell phone?"

Billy was glaring at her now. "You need a cell phone to take a piss? You wanted to use the john. So use it." He slammed the door shut.

Without benefit of lights, she couldn't see her hand in front of her face. How was she supposed to do anything in here? She went to her knees, trying to pick up the scattered contents of her purse, gingerly feeling her way across the tile floor, not sure what exactly she would come across in the darkness.

She was startled by a loud pounding sound and someone shouting. The bathroom door flew open, and Billy stood there, looking flustered. "Shit," he said, pushing her roughly back against the wall. "Stay here and keep quiet," he demanded, the fear and the anger in his voice making her nod in blind obedience. He shut the door again, leaving her alone in total darkness.

***

Peter flipped through the pages of the book until he found what he was looking for. He smiled as he pulled out his cell phone.

"What's this?" Aaron asked.

"I'm betting he still has her cell phone, because the phone company was able to track the signal to this general area. If she had it, she would have called someone by now. So I'm sending him a message." He worked the keypad with his thumbs. "He's not the only clever one," he mumbled as he pressed the Send button.

"C'mon, boss, don't leave me in suspense," Aaron said softly. "What'd you say?"

Peter recited the snippet of a nursery rhyme he sent to Jillian's phone, his voice low and emotionless despite the fury he felt inside. "Hickory dickory dare, the pig flew in the air, the man in brown soon brought him down, hickory dickory dare."

Aaron grinned. "The man in brown. Good one," he said, gesturing to Peter's Sheriff's uniform.

"If he's in there, we'll know in a minute," Peter said, praying his gamble would pay off. If Billy wasn't in that run-down rental with Jillian when he received the message, his plan could backfire and Jillian could suffer as a result. But he knew he was right. He knew it.

He hoped.

***

From inside the bathroom, Jillian heard her cell phone trill, recognizing the sound as notification of an incoming text message. She heard Billy cursing as he fumbled to turn the ringer off, silencing it. She waited, crouched low on her heels, the silence suffocating, and when Billy shrieked in rage, she was so startled she jumped, almost dropping the compact case she'd picked up off the floor.

"He can't use the nursery rhymes!" Billy cried. "That's my racket! He can't know! How did he know?"

***

Peter pulled his revolver to the ready position when he heard the anguished male cry from within the house. "I'd call that probable cause," he said, and kicked in the front door.

***

Billy ripped open the bathroom door and charged in as Jillian heard the cacophony of splintering wood and shouting voices. Peter's shouting voice. Before she could call back to him, Billy wrapped an arm around her neck in a headlock. She heard a metallic click and she felt the unmistakable feel of cold steel press into the soft skin of her throat. A switchblade.

"If I can't have you, neither can he," he said softly into her ear. "I didn't want to hurt you. I love you, Miss H."

She tried to remember something, anything from the self-defense class Donovan made her take, but her mind was blank with terror. Then her hand closed around something small and cylindrical on the floor, and it all came back to her. Crossing her fingers for luck, she elbowed him in the ribs and he fell back, just far enough for her to get a good bead on her target. Holding her breath, she pressed the button on the cylinder, and a stream of pepper spray caught Billy full in the face at point blank range. With a scream, he dropped the knife with a clatter and slumped against the wall, clawing at his eyes and writhing in agony, just as Peter, gun drawn, panting, frantic, appeared in the doorway.

He grabbed Billy by the shirt collar and hauled him to his feet, shoving him out of the bathroom and into the hallway toward Aaron, who arrested him, reading Billy his rights over his cries of pain. Then he crouched beside her, gentle now. "Jillian, sweetie, are you alright?" he asked, searching her eyes intently, his anxiety evident as he repeatedly caressed her hair, her face.

She threw her arms around his neck and held on for dear life, her breath coming out in a rush when his arms folded tight around her, crushing her to him, protecting her. She could feel him trembling. "I am now."

Peter buried his face in her hair. "Oh God. I thought I lost you. I thought I'd never get to tell you." He pulled back to look into her eyes. "I love you."

Two men in one day telling her they loved her. It was so surreal she had to laugh.

"That's not the response I was expecting," Peter said, looking hurt.

She laughed again. "I know. I'm sorry. I love you, too." She leaned in and kissed him, long and hard, and when she pulled back he didn't look hurt anymore.

"Good," Peter said. "Because—." Whatever he was about to tell her was drowned out when a swarm of sheriff's deputies thundered down the stairs and filled the house to finish the arrest and start the investigation. Surrounded by investigators shouting questions, Jillian found herself being swept away from Peter by ambulance technicians.

# CHAPTER THIRTY-FIVE

WHEN THE PHONE IN HER KITCHEN rang for what seemed the millionth time, Jillian didn't want to answer it. She wanted to scream. She'd gone over the events so many times over the last forty-eight hours, with sheriff investigators, her parents, friends, the media, probably everyone on the entire planet, she was sure she'd lose her voice. She wished she would, so she wouldn't have to talk about it any more. She didn't want to even think. She wanted to sleep. *All these damn nosy phone calls, and not one from Peter.* She gave in to her emotions and let out a loud, frustrated cry, and her mother and Tina came running, concerned and frightened.

"Really, Jillian, that was not necessary," Mary said, her hand over her heart.

"Really, Mother, it was," Jillian snapped, feeling a little better as she yanked the phone from its cradle. Mary and Tina anxiously hovered, watching her every movement and expression, while Jillian listened to Antoinette Jones speak on the phone, only managing a few "yes" responses to her talkative principal. They demanded to know about the conversation when she hung up.

"I got my job back," she said, stunned but happy. "And, she said the board of education loves my ideas for all-day kindergarten. I got it! I just have to present at next month's board meeting, but she says it's a sure thing!"

The other women's exuberant celebrations — well, Tina's was

anyway, her mother was reserved as always — gave her headache an unneeded boost. She left the kitchen for the comfort and relative quiet of her couch.

More tired than she ever thought she could be, she sank into her couch, closing her eyes and laying her head back against the soft cushions, and tried to ignore the clatter her mother and Tina were making in the kitchen.

She felt the couch sag when someone sat next to her, then something cold and round dropped into her hand.

"Marry me," Peter said. His voice was earnest and hopeful.

Suddenly wide awake, Jillian opened her eyes to see a brilliant diamond ring in her hand. The gorgeous one-carat princess-cut stone was set in white gold, nestled between two smaller canary yellow diamonds. She stared at it, agape.

"Donovan helped me pick it out."

She looked up at him, too stunned to speak.

"Well?"

"I…" The ring shook in her trembling hands, sending out a paroxysm of prisms. She forced her brain to form words. "But, what about your job?" The look on his face told her that was not the answer he expected.

"Ouch. Okay, maybe I deserved that." He grinned at her. "I'm cutting back on my hours. Now that this investigation is over, nothing but forty-hour weeks for me from now on." When she looked at him doubtfully, he backtracked. "Okay, maybe fifty. If they need more help, I told them to promote Aaron to sergeant. And I told Dad once and for all that I am not running for sheriff."

Her eyebrows rose in surprise. "What did he say about that?"

"He agreed with me."

"Really? How did you convince him?"

Peter shrugged. "I told him I'm a Democrat."

She relaxed into a smile. "Poor Patrick."

"Yep. Broke his heart. Now he's got to find someone else to groom to take his place." He laughed. "Or live forever. Which I think he's leaning toward."

He wrapped his arms around her shoulders and pulled her into his chest. She curled her hand around the ring and, settling against him, closed her eyes and sighed.

"I love you," Peter whispered into her ear.

She broke into a soft smile. Eyes still closed and drifting into a comfortable sleep, she mumbled, "Me, too."

"You're going to have to marry me," he said.

She opened her eyes and looked up at him, "I have to?"

"Yes," he said emphatically. "Because I'm never letting you out of my sight again."

"That seems like a logical solution, then," she said, smiling at him.

"Oh, eminently."

"Mother will be so pleased."

"Well, I do what I can. So are you saying yes?"

She closed her eyes again so she could concentrate and memorize this moment, his words, his scent, his warm breath on her ear, his arms around her. She opened them again and there he was, strong and sure and perfect, smiling down at her, expectantly.

"I'm saying yes."

And when her mother shouted in jubilation when she discovered them sharing a kiss, Jillian didn't even care.